Snow the Vampire Slayer

Fairelle Book Two

REBEKAH R. GANIERE

FALLEN ANGEL PRESS

This book is a work of fiction. The names, characters, places and incidents are fictitious and are not to be construed as real in any way. Any resemblance to persons, living or dead, actual events, locales or organizations is entirely coincidental.

Snow the Vampire Slayer
Copyright © Rebekah R. Ganiere

ISBN: 978-1-63300-002-5
ISBN: 978-1-63300-003-2
Cover art by Rebekah R. Ganiere
Photography by Cory Stierley

Fallen Angel Press
1040 N. Las Palmas Blvd.
Bldg 24 Suite 203
Los Angeles, CA 90038
www.FallenAngelPress.com

Ordering Information:
Quantity sales. Special discounts are available on quantity purchases by corporations, associations, and others. For details, contact the publisher at the address above.

Orders by U.S. trade bookstores and wholesalers. Please visit www.FallenAngelPress.com.
Printed in the United States of America

DEDICATION
For the three Pixies who keep me on my toes,
& my one little Prince Charming who melts my heart.

FAIRELLE

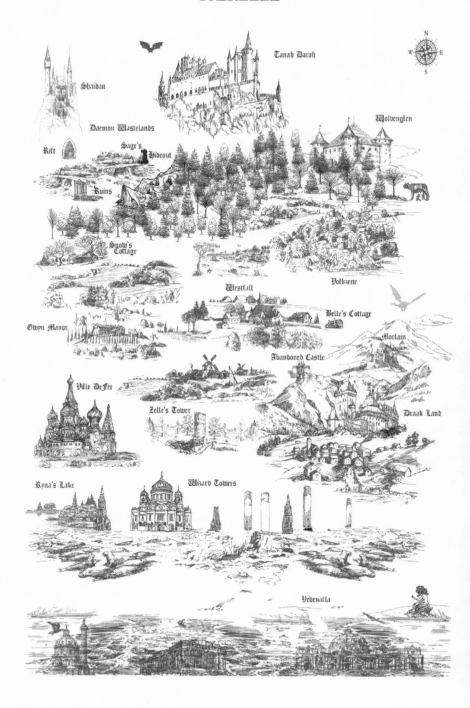

Shaidan

Tanah Darah

Wolvenglen

Daemon Wastelands

Rift

Sage's Hideout

Ruins

Snow's Cottage

Volkzene

Westfall

Belle's Cottage

Gwen Manor

Morlain

Abandoned Castle

Ville DeFee

Zelle's Tower

Draak Land

Ryna's Lake

Wizard Towers

Yedenalla

Pereum, Fairelle Year 200

Prologue

In the year 200, in the city of Pereum, the heart of Fairelle, King Isodor lay on his deathbed. With all of Fairelle united under his banner, his four rival sons vied for the crown. One-by-one, the brothers called forth a djinn named Xereus from Shaidan, the daemon realm, to grant a single wish. But Xereus tricked the brothers, twisting their wishes.

The eldest wished to forever be bloodthirsty in battle, and was thus transformed into a Vampire. The second wished for the unending loyalty of his men, and was turned into a Werewolf. The third asked for the ability to manipulate the elements of Fairelle; he became physically weak, but mighty in magick, a Fae. And the last asked to rule the sea. A Nereid.

When the king died, each brother took a piece of Fairelle for himself and waged war for control of the rest. Xereus, having been called forth so many times, tore a rift between his daemonic plane and Fairelle, allowing thousands of daemons to pour into Pereum.

Years upon years of bloody warring went by, all races fighting for control, and eventually the daemons gained dominion of the heart of Fairelle. Realizing that all lands would soon fall into the daemons' control, the High Elders of the Fae and the Mages from the south combined their magicks to seal the rift. The daemons were banished back to their own plane, but Pereum was wiped off the map in the process, leaving only charred waste behind, forever, known as The Daemon Wastelands.

Upon the day of the rift closing, a Mage soothsayer prophesied of the healing of Fairelle. Over the next thousand years, the races continued to war against each other, waiting for the day when the ancient prophesies would begin.

Nine prophesies, a thousand years old, to unite the lands and heal Fairelle. The first was fulfilled by Redlynn of the Sisterhood and Adrian, King of the Wolves when the mates returned to Wolvenglen. The second is the prophecy of the vampires of Tanah Darah.

The Border of Wolvenglen Forest and The Daemonlands, Fairelle
Year 1210 A.D. (After Daemons)

CHAPTER ONE

Sage sprinted through the dark after his prey, his vampiric sight guiding his every move. The would-be assassins rushed away from him, registering as light blue blurs in the night. Their vampiric heat signatures registering as cool as his own.

A hulking ivory bear thundered behind him.

"Keep up, Dax!" he yelled over his shoulder.

Dax bounded over a fallen tree trunk and growled a reply.

A branch whipped Sage in the face, opening a cut below his right eye. *Dammit that stings.*

He tracked the vampires over a rock less than thirty yards ahead of him before they disappeared from view. Picking up speed, he headed for it.

He rounded a tree, came to the rock and halted. An assassin waited for him several yards away. Sage recognized him as one of his own former guards.

"Your uncle, King Philos, sends his regards, usurper," the vampire yelled, lobbing something directly at him.

Sage spun to the left, but the object caught his side, slicing him open. The white knife, with a blood red-handle lodged in a tree behind him. Sage hissed. *A ceremonial Cris.*

Dark blood oozed through his fingers and hit the ground in fat drops. Rounding on the vampire he bared his fangs, but the vampire was gone. Poison blasted through him like brushfire.

Sage yanked the Cris from the tree and shoved it in his waistband. Philos would be angered by the loss of yet another Cris knife. He couldn't have more than a couple left. Too bad for him, it was Sage's now.

Dax caught up and slowed to a halt before sniffing him.

"I'll be fine." Sage scanned the area for his prey once more.

A whistling sound grew louder. Sage planted his hands in Dax's thick fur and shoved him out of the way with tremendous effort. An arrow flew through the trees where they'd just stood, and continued past them into the darkness.

"Tell Adrian they're by the northern border. If he cares to catch up, we could use some help."

Dax snorted and nodded.

Sage took off again at a slower pace. The mental connection between the Weres had come in quite handy since he'd taken to helping them patrol the borders of Wolvenglen Forest for the intruding vampires from the north. Those in Tanah Darah were loyal to his uncle, which meant they had no qualms about heading into human cities to find food. In return, Sage had no qualms about killing them.

His wound continued to seep through his fingers; his vampiric healing ability was of no use against a Cris. He hadn't told Dax the total truth. Yes, he would be fine – if he got to his den in the next two hours. If he didn't, the poison would attack his heart and he would bleed out. And if that happened…well…he'd need something stronger than squirrel blood to help him out of that situation.

4

Dax moved silently beside him. Sounds of a battle drifted from up ahead.

As Sage maneuvered through the trees, his pain intensified. Tendrils of daemon magick from the gash in his side curled their way through his body. He grimaced and braced himself on the nearest tree trunk. The burning sensation threaded up over his ribs and across the small of his back causing the muscles to tighten and cramp. Taking in a long, low breath, he tried to stave off what he knew was coming.

A series of howls rang out behind him. He glanced over his shoulder. King Adrian, Queen Redlynn, Angus, and several other wolves appear out of the tree line.

The group advanced to the edge of an outcropping at the northern border of the forest. Adrian and Dax shifted into human form next to Sage and peered down at the clearing below.

Sage's gaze moved to the dark hills of his homeland that lay beyond the valley. His gut clenched at the sight. *Tanah Darah.* The dark craggy terrain jutted straight up, surrounding the vampire lands in a giant wall. Only a narrow path connected Tanah Darah to the rest of Fairelle.

"Who's down there?" asked Adrian

Sage glanced at the naked Were King. His tall strong body was covered in sweat and clumps of shaggy dark hair clung to his neck and shoulders.

"Vampire assassins again, sent by my uncle. I'm not sure who the newcomers are," Sage said.

A dozen figures fought in the grassy basin between Tanah Darah and Wolvenglen. The remaining five vampires he and Dax had been chasing viciously attacked seven men dressed in black. He squinted and focused on the battle. His vampiric night-vision registered the vampires as light-blue, pale forms, the ones they fought glowed with a golden essence. He'd never seen anything like it.

The golden-hued newcomers took the upper hand. They fought with skill and grace pushing the vampires toward Wolvenglen and away from their escape path.

He studied the golden figures in an effort to discern who they were. Fae possibly, or— A shiver ran through him. *It can't be.*

"The black-clad figures must have ambushed the vampires." Dax scratched his broad, hairless chest with hands almost the same size of his bear paws and then brushed his blond locks from his eyes. "They had to be waiting. But who are they? And why?"

The vampires were quick by nature, but the golden-hued figures were equal in skill. The tallest among them produced a white-bladed Cris knife, and cleanly sliced the head off a vampire. The vampire fell to his knees and collapsed.

Sage swallowed hard. *One of the golden figures has a Cris knife.* A jolt of pain raced through him and he took a deep breath. He lifted his gaze to the sky. There were still several hours left before the sun came up, but he would need healing before then.

The fighting continued below. From their vantage point, the group watched the black-clad figure work together to take down their foes. Unlike the vampires who fought only for themselves.

After the last vampire fell, the strangers took a moment to regroup.

"We should go," said Dax. "We don't know who they are."

"No." Adrian shook his head. "If they fight the vampires, then we should speak with them. We could use more allies."

One of the men below looked up in Sage's direction. He grabbed an arrow from his quiver, notched it and shot, alerting his comrades. The others in his group followed suit. Adrian, Dax and the wolves moved out of the line of fire, into the trees, but Sage remained, transfixed. He swatted an arrow away from his face and caught another before it pierced his chest.

After the volley of missed shots, the figures hustled silently up the hillside. They fanned out to the quickest and easiest routes, moving with the ease and precision of a team that had fought together for years. They just couldn't be. But they were too good. There was no other explanation.

A feeling of dread ran down Sage's spine and skittered over his skin. His muscles spasmed in pain again and his knees almost buckled. The Cris poison coursed its way through him.

A breeze lifted the men's scents to him and he breathed them in. Their blood carried an aroma he'd not encountered before. His mouth pooled with saliva and for the first time in years, he craved the taste of human blood. Need pulsed through him as his fangs ached to bite into something. *This was bad.*

Adrian joined him once more. "Dax is right. We should go. This is obviously not the time for talking."

7

A figure crouched behind a shrub and shot another arrow. The arrow landed at Redlynn's feet and she yelped in surprise. Adrian howled in rage and charged toward the edge of the cliff. His skin rippled, ready to shift.

Sage caught him by the shoulder. "No, King Adrian," he said. "They're humans. They're just doing their job. They aren't after you or Redlynn, they're after me."

Adrian's gaze met Sage's. His eyes turned golden and fur burst from his skin, under Sage's hand. "Why do they want you?"

Sage was barely able to choke the words out. "They're Vampire Slayers."

CHAPTER TWO

Snow stood at the open kitchen window and peered out at the sky, scrubbing furiously at her mother's heirloom cookware. Darkness blanketed her fields, with the brightness of the full moon to cut through it. The stars twinkled and shone, mocking her with their brilliance. Stalks of malteen and oatbern grew down the hill, waving in the warm breeze of their tenants' fields.

She glanced at the cuckoo clock for the millionth time. Too long, they'd been gone too long. This was the worst part of her sisterly duties. Well, not the worst. The worst was not being allowed to go with her brothers. But the second worst was the wait.

Minutes ticked by and she continued to scrub angry circles into the bottom of the copper pot. Setting it aside, she scanned the clean pile of cookery she'd used to prepare dinner, trying to find a spot she might have missed. But she'd cleaned them, the table and the wash basin three times already, desperate to find something to occupy her mind.

Up until two years ago, she had never scrubbed a pot or cooked a meal in her life. Their manor house had employed dozens of servants. Maids and stewards, cooks and stable hands. The house had always been full of life and noise and merriment. But it was too dangerous to have others nearby, now that they had a family secret.

The great hall, covered in cloth and cobwebs, was as abandoned as the servant's quarters, chapel and other more formal parts of the manor house. Only the small solar, library and upper bedrooms were regularly used. The solar had once been upstairs, used by the family as a gathering place to spend time together. After her mother's sudden death, Snow's father closed off the room and built a new one downstairs, next to the kitchen and pantry, to use as an antechamber for intimate meetings. With their father's passing, and her brother Erik closing the house to visitors, the solar was used as their dining area and main place for relaxing.

The sound of hooves racing up the gravel road pulled Snow from the dishes. She tossed the towel into the sink and hurried through the adjoining solar to the backdoor. The riders rounded the corner of the house and headed toward the stables. She held her breath and counted them as they passed. Seven! There were seven. She blew out a sigh of relief.

Such had been her ritual for the last two years. Ever since the fae-magicked mantle of a Slayer had been placed upon her brothers.

The horses whinnied and twitched as they neared the stable. Their ordeal over, they were happy to be home.

A tall blond stopped in front of her, his horse's hooves kicking dirt and rocks her way.

"Evening, little sister."

"Look at the sky," she said. "This is nowhere close to evening, Erik. You've been gone half the night."

Erik smiled and pushed his shaggy blond hair out of his blue eyes. "What can I say? We were on the hunt."

Snow scowled. Her eldest brother was handsome, charming, and as infuriating as any man. Some men loved to fight, others hated it.

Erik was just good at it. He spurred his horse away. The rest of her brothers came to greet her, having stabled their horses. They knew the drill and lined up. She guarded the entrance. Hands on her hips, she stared at them. Dirty and stinky, most of them were blood-spattered. How could she be mad though? They'd all made it home, yet again.

She scanned the first. "Flint."

The largest at six-foot-three, and broad as the horse he rode, Flint gave her a tight smile. She reached up and turned his unshaven face. His fingers twitched, but he didn't complain. Flint didn't like being touched and he only allowed her to see him with his shirt off when he was injured. He'd told her once that the scars on his body were a constant reminder of those he'd killed. Unlike her other brothers, Flint took every death at his hand very hard. Until he had time to process the most recent battle, he'd lock himself in his bed chamber, alone.

"I'll have to stitch the cut under your eye. Food is cold on the table."

He kissed her hair and strode inside.

Her next brother approached and she sighed, "Another pair, Gerall?" The optics maker in town would be in business for life at the rate Gerall broke his lenses.

"Are there spares in the cupboard?" He ran his long fingers through his unruly strawberry brown curls that stuck up in every direction and blinked several times, almost blind without his glasses.

"I think so. Go eat and I'll check when I come in." She shook her head.

Next, twins, Hass and Ian sauntered up, grinning like cats. Grabbing her around the waist, they hoisted her into the air in a group hug.

"Hey–" said Hass

"Baby sister," Ian finished. Completing each other's sentences was something they'd done since they'd learned to talk. Her arms wrapped around their thick tanned necks. Their unkempt blond hair tickled her face.

"Put me down, you big mule heads," she protested, trying to suppress a smile at her sweet honey bear protectors. They set her down and stood in mock seriousness. However hard they tried, their boyish grins couldn't help but peek through. Her mother always said the twins had been born with smiles on their faces.

"Well, I'm sorry to say, I think you two will live," she proclaimed.

"Look," said Hass, pointing.

"We got matching cuts," Ian finished. They both pointed to their left arm.

Sure enough, they did.

"Lovely," she mused. "Go eat. I'll clean them later."

"No thank you!" said Ian.

"We need the scars," finished Hass. "Flint has us beat by about a hundred."

"But I'm sure you don't want to lose your arms to infection, so I'll clean them at the very least."

The two hugged her again and then wandered past her into the house, punching each other.

"Did you see that wolf guy?" Hass asked.

"Of course. That was horrifying," replied Ian.

Next she scanned Jamen, who was free of cuts, but sported several bruises. Like Flint, he was still pent-up from the fight. His sharp, chicory colored eyes barely even registered her. At some point this week, Erik would be pulling him out of the inn and carrying him home drunk for her to tend. It wasn't only his new calling that weighed on him.

"Hey," she said, pulling Jamen's forehead down so it pressed against her own. They stood for a minute. He smelled of sweat and blood. His gaze finally locked on hers. "I'm here. You're here. This is a good thing."

"Not today," Jamen said, before breaking eye contact.

He came home this way from every battle. Snow wrapped her arms around his solid body and held him tight. He'd broken off his engagement in an effort to save the woman he loved from pain. After fighting was when he needed her most.

"Everyday." She kissed him on the cheek and let him pass, wishing for the fun loving Jamen that he'd been.

Kellan limped to her and she wrapped him into her arms. The youngest of her brothers, Kellan was just a year older than Snow. At barely six foot, he weighed half as much as the others, even dripping wet. His body was softer as well, but not as lean as Gerall's.

"Snow," Kellan said in a soft voice, holding onto her.

She choked down a sob. Kellan wasn't meant for the fighting. Sweet and gentle, he'd had his whole life ahead of him before being called as a Slayer. He should've been a nobleman, like their father. Gerall should've been a doctor. The twins had planned on being farmers and– Oh what did it matter? Their fates were sealed.

She grabbed him tighter.

"Let the boy eat." Erik approached from behind them.

Kellan stiffened and released her. Erik motioned for him to go inside. She pressed her lips together tightly and bit her cheek.

"You shouldn't baby him, Snow."

"You shouldn't force him to kill people, *Erik*." She hugged herself, digging her nails into her upper arms.

It wasn't Erik's fault, but she needed to blame someone. It pained her to see her brothers go out night after night and come home battered and bruised, with broken bones and gashes. They'd been lucky so far that nothing worse had happened. She had basic healing skills, and Gerall had a bit more training than she did, but if something serious ever happened...

Erik took a step closer. "They aren't people, they're vampires. And you know I didn't force him. He had a choice."

Snow closed the door and lowered her voice. "What choice? You're his elder brother and the Lord of these lands. You think he wants to lose face in front of you? Any of you? He pledged himself to that stupid old witch the way the rest of you did. And for what? We still don't know who she is, and if you're even doing what you were meant to do!"

"I didn't ask to be Lord of Westfall and I didn't wish this for Kellan." Erik's voice rose.

Her temples pounded with anger over the whole situation. "No. You didn't," she said. "But don't think for a minute that he would sit home while you and the rest go out and risk your lives. All he wants is to earn your respect. I just hope you deserve his."

Without another word, she pushed open the door and stormed through the solar, past her brothers at the table. The eating ceased.

"Snow," called Kellan. "Snow?"

She kept moving toward the front of the manor house and the stairs.

"What did you say to her, Erik?" Flint demanded.

She stomped toward her bed chamber. Her shoes pounded the polished wooden floor of the grand entrance, causing the chandelier to shake. Huffing past various family portraits, she made her way up the landing and looked out into the foyer. For a moment, she swore music floated up from the great hall and the tinkle of her mother's laughter echoed through the house as her father greeted guests. But it was just her brothers' voices. The sounds of them devouring the meal followed her down the ivy colored hallway to her bed chamber.

She slammed her door, silencing them, threw herself down on her bed, and pouted like a spoiled child. The portrait of her parents above the fireplace caught her attention and she let out a long sigh.

Her mother, dark-haired and lovely, with the disposition of a dove. Her father, rugged and strong, with hair like wheat and a champion's smile. Tears welled and her chest constricted. Oh, how she wished they still lived.

She had never imagined that she'd spend her life tending to her brothers. A lady of means, she'd grown up dreaming of the day a baron, or maybe a rich nobleman, would come knocking and ask for her hand. Of the grand ball that would be thrown on her wedding day. Her white gown and veil trailing the floor behind her as she gazed into the face of the man she loved.

But that was never to be. With mother and father gone, she couldn't leave. The twins would destroy the home with their roughhousing. Jamen would drink himself to death, and Kellan—

Snow swallowed hard. She didn't even want to imagine what would become of him. Flopping onto her stomach, she screamed into her pillow until all anger and sorrow drained out.

No. Her lot was set. There would be no Prince Charming now.

Half an hour later, a soft knock sounded on her door. She covered her face with her pillow and grumbled at the second knock. The third knock got her moving. Throwing the pillow at the wall, she crossed to the door and opened it.

Erik held a plate of food.

"I know you don't eat 'til we return." His blue eyes held remorse.

"Well, you don't eat until everyone else has, either." She eyed the plate. "Is that all there is left?"

He didn't answer.

She wanted to be angry with him. To blame him for the fear that gripped her when her brothers went out to hunt. But looking at him, her chest constricted and she sighed instead.

"Come in." She stepped aside.

He gave her a weak smile and headed for the table. His shirt had a long slash down it and blood trickled from an open wound.

"Take off your shirt," she ordered. She opened her cabinet in the corner, and removed a small bottle of antiseptic and a container of salve. "Eat." She pointed at the plate.

He pushed it toward her. "I'll eat when you've eaten."

She pushed it back. "I'm not hungry. Eat."

He glanced up. Their father had looked at her the exact same way when she was being stubborn. He smiled and shook his head before turning to the plate. She opened the antiseptic and dabbed his inflamed skin. Erik hissed, arched his spine momentarily, and then settled down.

"So, what happened?" She continued to dab.

"It was strange." He tore into a piece of chicken. "We'd tracked a group of a dozen or so vampires, like many times before. They ran the border of the Wolvenglen Forest and the Daemon Wastelands. We watched them for an hour or more, but there they stayed. Waiting for something. Then, another vampire appeared with a white bear."

"A white bear?"

"I've never seen one before. It was amazing." He stared at the wall.

She dabbed him some more, pulling him out of his thoughts.

"Anyway, the original group of vampires spotted him and gave chase." Erik took a roll from his plate and broke it in half before taking a bite. "We circled around through the Daemon Wastelands and met them on the northern side of Wolvenglen. By then, it was the lone vampire who did the chasing and there were only five vampires left."

"A lone vampire was chasing other vampires?" *Why would a vampire go against its own kind?*

"Twelve vampires went into that forest and only five came out the other side, so whoever he is, he's stronger than any other we've encountered, that's for sure. Plus, in the forest somewhere, a pack of wolves joined him and the bear in the chase."

"Wolves?"

Erik looked up at her. "Weres, Snow. Wolvenglen Forest Werewolves."

"This story is getting more fanciful by the second."

She'd heard tales of the Wolvenglen wolves being Weres. Men that could turn into animals, but she'd never met someone who'd actually seen one.

"Trust me, I couldn't make up what we saw tonight. The Weres appeared to be protecting the lone vampire and white bear. I looked up and noticed a Were and the bear shift into human form. One minute they were large beasts and the next, they contorted into humans again. I can't imagine how painful that transition must be."

"Naked men?"

Erik looked at her strangely and she glanced away. "Yes, naked. Kellan shot at them, but they were on a ridge and by the time we'd made it to the top, they'd fled."

"I wonder if the females are as immodest as the men," she mused. Flame heated her cheeks and she cleared her throat. "Doesn't matter anyway, we don't hunt Weres."

Erik turned to face her, his eyebrows knit. He stared at her hard.

"What?" she demanded.

"You said, 'we.'"

"So?" She shrugged. "You know what I mean." She averted her gaze and reached for the salve.

Erik grabbed her hand. "Snow—"

"Don't." She pulled from his touch. "I can fight, Erik. Father taught me how to hold a sword before I was old enough to play with dolls. I may not have the mantle to be a big bad vampire slayer, but it should be me out there, not Kellan."

Erik's expression hardened. "No, Snow. Not you."

"But Erik—"

"I said no!" Erik rose from his chair, almost tipping it over.

Their gazes locked and she refused to turn away from the stare so much like her father's. She gripped the tin of ointment till it bit into her skin, but she kept the tears at bay. She'd had this same conversation with him a dozen times over the past year. The outcome was always the same.

Erik sighed, ran his palms over his face and then hugged her, despite her protests. "I promised Mother I would take care of you," he said. "I couldn't bear it if anything happened to you."

Snow melted. *So much like father.*

"Uh...hey!"

"What about us?"

"We care about her too." Her brothers spoke from the hallway.

Snow laughed. The twins, as well as Gerall and Kellan stood waiting to be invited in.

"Sorry to bother you, but I didn't find another pair of glasses," said Gerall.

"And we decided—"

"We prefer to keep our arms," said Hass and Ian.

"Come on." She motioned for them to enter. Gerall moved to sit. "Not on my bed with those dirty, bloody clothes."

He smiled sheepishly and sat on the trunk at the end of her bed, instead.

"Oooh! Leftovers," said Ian.

"That's for Snow," Erik growled.

"All right, all right." Ian backed up from the plate.

"We're not that hungry anyway," said Hass.

"You shouldn't be. I made enough food for an entire castle," she chided.

Snow cleaned, bandaged and stitched up her brothers. They regaled her with stories of how they'd slaughtered the vampires. While she fished around for a new pair of glasses for Gerall, Hass and Ian wrestled with Kellan, holding him down and teasing him until she made them stop.

"What? We're just playin'," Hass said.

"Don't worry about me," said Kellan from inside Ian's headlock. "I can take 'em."

Kellan was always trying to prove to his older brothers that he was just as good and tough. Being two years older than Kellan, the twins loved their little brother, and loved to taunt him, as well.

"Well come on then," said Ian. "Let's go again."

Kellan smiled a wide, boyish grin that melted her heart.

"You better not break anything of mine," she teased.

"We won't," the three replied in unison. Not a second later, they were all wrapped up in arms and legs, rolling around and laughing.

Snow handed the last pair of glasses to Gerall and then turned her attention to Flint, who'd entered and sat in the chair, staring off, refusing to speak. She sewed his cheek shut in silence.

Life had been rough on Flint. As the second-oldest, he was always second-best to Erik in his own mind. Never quite as charismatic or funny, Flint spent his time doing what he did best, training and watching out for his siblings. Inside his gruff exterior was a young boy whose only thoughts were to protect what was left of his family. It was a burden he thought was his alone to bear.

After another twenty minutes, the others said their goodnights and headed to their rooms to wash and sleep.

Only Kellan remained.

"You had a limp when you got home," she said.

"A cramp from the ride. You won't find a scratch on me." He blew out a frustrated sigh. "Erik won't let me do anything worth getting scratched over. He thinks I'm weak."

"No." She lifted Kellan's chin. "It's because he knows you don't want this."

"None of us do."

"True." She nodded. "But at least you're fortunate to have brothers who protect you, who don't want you to have to live with the guilt of killing someone up close. Look at Flint and Jamen and at the toll it's taken on them. Do you want to be like that? You deserve so much more, Kellan. That's why Erik protects you."

"I can protect myself." He assumed the same stubborn expression their mother had when she put her foot down. Snow's heart squeezed.

"You can take care of yourself. But when father died, Erik became Lord and accepted responsibility for all of us. He takes that seriously."

She stared at his boyish face. At the age of twenty-three, he still appeared no more than a teen. He held her mother's fine bone structure and soft face with dark hair. Many people thought he and Snow were twins.

Kellan's shoulders slumped and he nodded.

She wanted to confide in him how much she understood his feelings. Her desire was to be out there slaying vampires with her brothers, not cleaning dishes.

"We all have our place," she said to herself. "We have jobs to do, and if we're lucky this will end soon, and we'll get to return to the way we were."

Kellan stood. "I should wash."

"Fancy a game of chess?"

"No, thanks." His morose attitude was very unlike him.

She touched his arm. "Your time will come. There are enough vampires for all of us."

He bowed his curly, chocolate head and kissed her on the cheek. She searched his face and found nothing but sadness.

"Night, Snow."

She cleaned up the supplies, threw Gerall's latest set of broken glasses into a drawer with all the rest, and reminded herself she needed to go to town and get several new pair. Then she waited till the talking in the hall died down and her brothers closed their doors.

She slipped off her shoes, tiptoed silently to her own door, opened it a sliver and peered out. The sound of splashing water drifted down the hallway from her brothers' chambers. Closing her door again she flipped the lock, stripped off her dress, ran to her closet and rooted inside. Pulling out several items, she set a long wool traveling cloak, charcoal breeches, a shirt that she'd had tailored especially for her, a pair of boots and a sword on the trunk at the end of her bed. The manly items looked out of place next to her feminine duvet.

The clock read one thirty. She could get three hours sleep and still be up before her brothers, to have some time to herself. She braided her long walnut colored hair, then slipped into her bed in her chemise.

For minutes she watched the light peek under her bedroom door until the fuel ran out of the wall sconces.

In the darkness, she waited for sleep to overtake her. Alone under the soft sheets, her bed was too large and cold. Maybe a dog or a cat would be good company. She sighed and rolled over. A pet wasn't what she wanted. What she wanted was a husband.

One man, just one. Someone to share her dreams with, her aspirations, her joys and her pains. A strong man who'd stand up to her brothers, instead of fleeing.

She dreamed of babies, and grandchildren, and a home of her own. A man whose touch set her aflame and whose heart belonged to her alone. But she was practically a spinster at her age.

Her mind drifted to the dozens of men who'd courted her over the years. The ones who'd wanted her for her beauty or her father's money. The Lord who'd fled after meeting all seven of her brothers. The Baron Erik caught with a tavern wench and another who'd gotten drunk with Flint and confessed his gambling habit. Lastly her thoughts turned to Lord Balken. Her body tensed at the recollections. She didn't want to think of him.

Images flashed before her: Balken pushing his way into her room and trying to convince her it was natural for them to be alone since they were betrothed; the feel of his hands roaming over her thin chemise, the taste of his breath in her mouth, the fire that had burned within her as he'd pressed her onto her bed and kissed her.

And then, the door flying open. Erik and the others pouring in. The horrible crunching sound of Balken's nose breaking as Erik attacked him.

Snow breathed in deep and locked the memories away once more.

She was more fortunate than so many women. She had a family and a home and safety, but for all of her comforts, she was lonely.

Her brothers told her so little of their world. And because of that, she wasn't truly a part of their lives. They were more than happy to tell her of how they killed this vampire, or that one. But they protected her from the worst evils they saw. They never told her of the victim's bodies they found, or of their fear in facing the enemy. They never spoke of their anger over the loss of their futures, or their confusion as to why they'd been picked to be the Slayers of this generation. Those things they spoke of only with each other.

They sheltered her. Coddled her as if she were still a child. Little did they know that she craved adventure, a heart stopping romance, danger and swordplay like she read about in stories. She wanted to see all of Farielle. To travel to all the lands and meet the werewolves and the Fae. To see dragons and Nereids and the mage towers in the south. But all she got were dishes and cleaning. The only vampires she'd see were in the dusty old books in her father's library. Sketches of tall, pale monsters with fiery eyes and blood-drenched clothing.

She tossed in her bed and drew the cold sheets tighter about herself. In a house full of people, she was alone.

CHAPTER THREE

Sage sagged against a boulder and sucked in a ragged breath, his sight blurring. He needed to get the Cris poison neutralized, and he needed to feed.

"You gonna make it?" Dax asked.

The coat Sage had offered Dax barely covered Dax's large naked body. He hoped Dax didn't ruin it, it was his favorite.

"I need to get to my place. I have supplies there."

"I still don't understand why you don't carry them with you."

"Without them, I am more vigilant about not needing them. If I had them, then I would be more lax in my fighting skills." Sage gave a tight smile. He arched as another spasm wracked him.

Dax shook his head. "That makes no sense."

"Nothing like the fear of death to keep you on your toes." His smile broadened, but it was cut short by the pain that shot through his chest, causing his shoulder to twinge. He had to keep it together. "Let's move, we're almost there."

He surged forward, trying to keep his bearings. They were less than a mile from the den. The terrain of the Daemon Wastelands enveloped them. Onyx and rocky, sulfurous and cloudy, it was the perfect hiding place. Only a daemon sentry squad lived in the accursed land, stationed in the western part of the Wastelands at the rift entrance.

Sage tripped over a rock and Dax caught him by the arm.

"I could always just carry you; it would be faster."

Sage grimaced. "If you were to carry me, I would let the poison take me as payment for my humiliation. I may be a denounced prince living in exile, but I still have my pride."

Dax raised an eyebrow. "Even if that pride kills you?"

He didn't answer. The poison had caused his legs to go numb, which was why he hadn't felt the rock he'd tripped over. *Keep moving.*

"Strange that I'm now helping you, a vampire, struggle to get home. When not so long ago vampires were chasing me, much in the same condition you are, toward Wolvenglen."

Sage stopped for a moment and studied Dax. "Any more dreams about where you came from?"

He shrugged. "None, I'm afraid. It's been months since I've had one and when I do, I can never remember it anyway."

"And you weren't a bear in your dreams?" Sage took a few steps.

"I don't think so."

"So it is possible you've been a werebear since birth."

"From what I've seen since I've been in Wolvenglen, I suppose at this point anything is possible."

Sage laughed. "Very true."

After trudging onward for another ten minutes, Sage spied an enormous stone spire jutting out of the ground. He reached it and his legs gave out. He slumped to the ground, catching his breath.

Dax scanned the rock. "Is this it?"

"Home away from home."

Dax glanced around and then at the boulder again. "It's a rock."

"That's the point."

Dax again knit his brows together.

Pushing to his feet, Sage reached to the side of the obsidian stone and pulled. The rock swung out. Beyond, lanterns lit a hallway. Dax blinked several times.

"I've been here a long while." Sage dragged himself down the passage. "I had to do something with all that time. Besides, I had some help."

"From whom? A dragon?"

Sage stopped and turned to Dax.

"What?"

"Nothing." It was odd that Dax would mention dragons, having lost his memories and not knowing who he was, or where he was from. Dragons only lived in the mountains in the southeast of Fairelle. "A fairy helped me," Sage finally said with a wink. His chest constricted and he coughed violently. Dax stepped forward and clapped him on the back till Sage waved him off.

Dax shook his head. "For someone who's about to die, you sure do have a good sense of humor."

Sage stumbled forward, his legs unstable beneath him. He followed the lanterns down a steep corridor that led into the ground. After about thirty yards, the hall widened and split off in many directions.

He turned to the right and continued on, until he encountered the familiar berry colored rug. *Almost there.*

Several doors lined the hall. He used every ounce of determination to push open the largest one at the end and stepped inside.

"What the—" Dax stepped into the room.

"Nice, isn't it?" Moving to a curio in the corner, Sage bumped a wooden table with his hip. *Dammit!* The numbness had spread to his side. He needed to hurry.

"Where'd you get all this stuff?"

"From my home, Tanah Darah." Opening the glass curio, he grabbed a bottle and an obsidian bladed knife and set them on the table. Next he stripped off his bloodied tunic exposing the bluish mossy colored veins that snaked under his pale flesh toward his heart.

"That doesn't look so good." Dax stared at his torso.

"This is where you come in."

Dax held up his hands. "Sorry, I'm not donating blood."

"I don't need your blood. I need you to cut me open with that knife." He pointed to the dagger on the table.

"I think the poison's gone to your mind."

"Possibly, but that's beside the point. This," Sage said, pulling the white Cris blade out of his waistband, "is a Cris knife. A magicked, poisoned dagger. And that," he pointed to the black blade on the table, "is a Crom blade, its opposite. Also magicked, but for drawing out the poison."

Dax stared at him blankly for a moment. "Who was the dolt that came up with that?"

"A daemon. Focus, Dax. With magick, a price always has to be paid. The price for healing is blood." Sage picked up the blade. "A Crom blade can only be used effectively if the person wielding it means no harm to the one they are cutting."

"You do this often?"

"Only a couple times before and hopefully this will be the last. So, do you wish me harm? Because if you do, there are no hard feelings, but I'd rather know. I only want to do this once."

"I wish you no harm."

"Well, glad we got that settled. Take the blade." He held it out to Dax. "Cut me down my torso, hitting as many of these poisoned veins as possible."

"You'll die."

"I won't die. You have to cut my throat for that. But it's going to make me wish I were dead and bleed as if I'm dying."

"Now I get why you don't carry the antidote with you."

"Oh, and one last thing. Don't get the blood on you."

"Why?"

"It's poisoned vampire blood; do you really need to ask?" Sage took several deep breaths and grabbed the chair behind him.

"You ready?" Dax stepped forward.

"I think–"

Dax struck out with the blade, opening a wound from Sage's right shoulder to his left hip. The strike was precise, hitting every poisoned vein. He roared in pain, doubling over. Fire burst through him and blood poured onto the stone floor in a sickly bluish-green river.

His fangs burst through his gums, his vision sharpened and he took in every particle of the room. Concentrating on the intricate pattern of silk on his bed, he breathed through the pain. Every individual strand wove and twisted together. He followed them, trying to distract himself from what he wanted most. Blood. Human blood.

How many years had it been since he had feasted? How many decades since he'd felt warm human skin beneath his fangs? It was a good thing Dax wasn't completely human.

The burning reduced to throbbing, and his breathing evened.

"That's a lot of blood." Dax stared at the widening pool on the floor.

Little by little, Sage's wounds closed until all that was left were two bright red scars. One across his chest and another across his hip.

He grabbed the Cris from the table and bowed over it, chanting an ancient prayer. The blade glowed white hot and he touched it to the puddle on the floor. The blood quivered and then, like his chest, inky veins ran up the blade and disappeared. The Cris drank until not a drop was left. When the blood was gone, the blade's light faded.

Sage staggered to his feet, placed the blades into the curio, picked up the bottle of spirits, and took a long swig. Every muscle in his body ached. His arm quavered from the strain of lifting the bottle. Dax stared at him, his mouth slightly ajar.

Sage wiped his mouth with the back of his hand. "I need to rest."

"How can you bleed? I thought vampires were dead."

"No." He breathed deep. "That's a lie told to non-vampires to scare them off."

"Vampires have enough about them to scare people, without everyone thinking you're dead, as well."

He shuffled across the room. "Our ancestor asked the djinn to be bloodthirsty in battle; therefore, he made us thirst for blood. But we're still very much alive. We have some enhancements, such as rapid healing, akin to you and the Weres. We also have influence over weaker beings, but we live."

"You can't go out in the sunlight, though?"

"We cannot. A limitation put on our hunger. Even the djinn who cursed us knew that the curse would consume Fairelle if not curbed. Forcing vampires to only go out at night gave the other races a fighting chance at survival."

Sage handed the bottle of spirits to Dax as he passed by.

"There's a bedroom next door, and there should be clothes that will fit," Sage said. "You're welcome to make everything in it your own, if you care to stay. If you wish to return to Adrian's, I understand." Sage waved Dax away and collapsed onto his bed.

"Nah. I've had enough of wolves for a while. As much as I love them, I feel a need to move on, to stop hiding and find out who I am."

"Well, you're welcome to stay until you decide to move further," Sage said, his voice muffled by his pillow.

"Thank you."

Picking up his head, he added, "I ask that you not wander about. It can get very confusing down here."

"Don't worry," said Dax, "I'm not big on snooping."

Sage nodded and Dax left, taking the bottle of spirits with him. His mind wandered to Dax's comment about dragons. Somehow he got the feeling that the past Dax searched for, was not going to make him happy.

Sage awoke several hours later, his tongue thick in his coated mouth. His dry, gravely throat burned and his gums ached. If he didn't feed soon, nothing would keep him from draining the nearest village of humans, and he couldn't afford to fall into old addictions.

Standing, he dragged himself to the bureau and removed a clean tunic. He barely noticed a twinge in his chest as he put it over his wounds. Grabbing his long leather coat, he threw it on and strapped his sword to his back. In the hallway, he paused outside Dax's room. He didn't have to be a vampire to hear the snores that emanated from the other side. He smiled and continued up to the rock entrance. As he stepped out on the ashy ground, footsteps came up behind him.

"Going out? You just returned," said Sonya.

He glanced over his shoulder at the diminutive vampire. "I need to feed."

Greeg sauntered up beside them and put his long arm around Sonya's slender waist. "We need to have a meeting, Prince. The others are getting restless."

"There've been developments I need to look into before a final decision is made. We've been here for fifty years and the others have had nothing to worry about but their library of books and how much blood I put in their goblets. A few more days should make no difference."

Sonya sniffed the air. "Do I smell Were?"

"His name is Dax. He's a werebear and my guest. I have told him not to leave his room. But the others need to be told that he is here."

"A werebear? How did that happen?" asked Greeg.

"He can't remember. Make sure he is undisturbed while I am gone."

"Yes, Highness." Sonya bowed.

"I'll return before sun up." Sage slid out the rock face. He knew the others were anxious to regain their homelands. Siding with him had not been the exciting resistance his father's few remaining friends had expected. Hiding in an underground cave, barely feeding, was not the luxury they were used to, even with everything he'd stolen from the castle. The timing wasn't right though, and there weren't enough of them to live through a battle should they attack Tanah Darah. Not yet. But with Slayers on his side, it might turn the odds in his favor.

*****

Snow dropped a rope outside her window and descended to the grass below. She waited, listening to the sounds of the predawn world. Sunlight had yet to peek above the horizon. Looking to the windows of her house above, she held her breath and let a minute tick by. No lights flicked on.

She ran behind the stable and down the hill to the rear field. Reaching the bottom, she crossed the fields and passed the tenant

34

houses, heading for the glade behind the property. The farms her brothers rented out were still dark at that early hour.

Winding around a silo, she sprinted through a field of beans toward the trees. She loved these moments more than any others in the day. Everything felt alive and new, just before the world consumed nature and people made everything their own. In the dim moonlight, she spotted the familiar shadow of her favorite calan tree. Rushing up to it, she skimmed her fingertips over her parent's initials carved into the trunk before continuing on.

Once inside the tree line, she hopped over a brook and landed softly on the other bank. The tall, thin trees in her woods were draped with moss and ivy. Pine needles and eldarn bushes blanketed the ground.

Moving swiftly, Snow made her way to the clearing she used for practice. She'd been to it so many times that she could have run blindfolded. On the edge of the clearing stood her own, secret cabin. Dusted, cleaned and furnished modestly, it was the place she came to be alone. She wondered, as she did every night, what Erik would do if he ever discovered she snuck out. She'd found the cabin after her mother's death, while walking to clear her mind.

Striking a match from a tin on the table, she used it to light a lantern. The small structure was same as ever. She laid her bag on the table and opened the closet. Several practice dummies she'd made from wood and hay rested there, awaiting her return. The dummy weighted her down as she hefted the first and dragged it to the clearing behind the cabin. By the time she had moved all four dummies, she paused to catch her breath. Then she retrieved her sword, unsheathed it, and began her routine.

She attacked the dummies for over an hour, going over the things her father had begun teaching her at the age of three.

"Snow, do you know what this is?" he'd asked.

"Swowd," she'd giggled.

"That's right, Snow. And what's a sword is for?"

"Kiwl," she said.

"No, Snow. A sword is not to kill. A sword is to protect."

She lunged at a dummy. Unfocused, she tripped over a root and fell to the ground. The memory faded. Pain shot up her arm as a gash opened on her palm where she had landed on her sword.

Great! How are you going to explain this?

Blood flowed from her palm and dripped onto the grass. Getting to her feet, she wiped the blood on her pants and clutched her fist tight, pulling the wound against her shoulder to slow the bleeding.

She trudged to her cabin, chastising herself for her dumb mistake. Inside her bag, she found antiseptic and gauze. She cleaned the wound and wrapped it tightly. Her gaze drifted out the window and she groaned. Darkness clouded everything in a deep cocoon. She had less than an hour before the bright rays of dawn crept over the trees.

She sighed. Might as well clean up for the day and start again tomorrow. It infuriated her that her time was being cut short by her own clumsiness, but she could at least spend a few minutes of peace in her cabin before heading home.

Snow stepped outside and the hairs rose on her neck. A feeling of being watched overcame her. She wasn't alone. In the two years she'd been coming to the cabin, she hadn't seen so much as a squirrel at night. The grasslands of her home were relatively sheltered from the wildness of Fairelle.

Her gaze swept the wooded area for predators. She dashed for the glade and retrieved her sword, her palm burning where she grasped the hilt.

"Who's there?" she called.

No answer.

A chill ran down her spine and she swung in the other direction. She should've brought her bow. Had Father taught her nothing?

"I know you're out there. Show yourself." Adrenaline coursed through her at the prospect of an imminent fight. Her heartbeat quickened and her skin flushed with heat. Her fingers twitched and she scanned her surroundings.

A rustle in the trees by her cabin caught her attention and a tall, well-built man stepped out of the shadows.

"Who are you?" She pointed her sword at him. "What are you doing in my glade?"

"Your glade? I was under the impression that this glade belonged to no one."

She swallowed hard. Legally this was not her land, but by rights of her having claimed the abandoned cabin, this was practically her own backyard.

"Why are you out at such an hour, girl? Should you not be at home in bed, instead of playing swords?"

"I am no girl. And I have trained with swords since I was young. Besides, what matter is it to you what I do?" Who did this man think he was talking to her the way her brothers would?

The man shrugged and moved closer still. "True. It is not my business what you do. But what kind of man would I be were I not concerned for the well-being of a lovely maiden, alone, in a glade near dawn?" He brushed his long, blond hair from his face.

He'd called her lovely. Her cheeks heated and her heart thundered in her chest as he circled her. It had been a long time since a man had called her lovely. His tall, broad-shouldered frame moved with the precision of a cat.

He stopped and examined a dummy. "What are you doing out at this hour?" he asked again.

Thoughts of secret rendezvous and kisses in the moonlight flitted into her mind. She shook her head. She retreated a step. What was she thinking? She was far from home and her brothers were unaware she was gone. Her loneliness must run deeper than even she knew to be thinking such things.

He glanced at her, his bright aquamarine eyes flashing in the moonlight. "Did you make these?"

She squared her shoulders. "What if I did?"

"Impressive. For a lady." He poked the dummy in the face. "Personally, I enjoy strolling at night, when everyone still sleeps. It's like seeing the world as it was meant to be."

Her sword drooped a fraction. *He felt the same way?*

"You should go." She raised her sword again.

He watched her with an intensity that made her shiver. She backed up a pace. Midnight rendezvous were fanciful in storybooks, but in real life they rarely ended well. Trusting a stranger was not only reckless, it was stupid, and she wasn't stupid.

"I'm not going to hurt you, love." He put up his hands and smiled. His pearly teeth shone.

"Don't' call me 'love.'"

"I'm Sage. And you are?" He held his hand out to her.

His manner was fine, as was his speech, and yet there was something so predatory about him that scared her.

"Snow." She swallowed hard and waited to see if he recognized her name as the youngest of Lord Gwyn's children.

It appeared he did not.

"Where are you from? I don't recognize you."

He continued to smile. "You've been introduced to everyone in the area?"

Embarrassment heated her cheeks. "Most people, yes. And a man of your speech and manner is someone I'm sure I would have been introduced to, or at least heard of before."

Sage stretched and rubbed his chest. "'I'm not from here."

His voracious stare made her stomach flutter and her heartbeat quickened. "Are you from Wolvenglen?"

He laughed lightly. "I'm no werewolf, if that's what you're wondering."

She scanned for a means of escape, but from where he stood, the only direction to go was opposite where she needed to be.

A peace fell over the grove and her skin grew warm and comfortable. Her feet sank into the ground as if she had suddenly sprouted roots.

He moved closer. In the burgeoning dawn, his face came into full view for a split second before he stepped into the shadow once more. He was handsome, with high cheekbones and a regal nose that gave way to crimson lips.

He stopped a foot from her and pushed down on the tip of her sword, causing it to hit the grass with a soft thud. His gaze locked on hers and she shuddered.

"I'm from far away," he said. "A place you've never been."

"How would you know where I've been?" Though she couldn't seem to get her body to move, she refused to give over her mind.

"Because I would have remembered if *you'd* ever visited."

"And you know every person that visits your lands?"

His face grew serious. "Yes."

She inhaled the scent of his leather jacket. It mixed with the musky scent of his skin and she was overcome with a sudden longing deep inside that had her pulse quickening. She cleared her throat and tried to calm the rush of heat in her veins.

An aura of danger surrounded him and the risk of the encounter thrilled her. But the graceful way he moved, the way he tracked her, stirred a note of warning inside her.

She tried to grab her sword, but his gaze fell upon her heavily and she found she couldn't.

"What are you doing to me?"

He inched even closer, bent his neck and breathed her in. Her stomach clenched. She'd never craved a man's touch so badly. She didn't like it. "You're using magick on me. I command you to stop."

"You command me?" He gave her a wry smile that she wanted to smack off his face.

"Are you fae? A mage? What are you?"

"You're bleeding," he said.

"I fell. You didn't answer my question."

"No, I didn't. Let me see it."

Snow's arm lifted though she willed it to stay down. "You're infuriating."

He took her palm gently in his cool grasp and unwrapped it. "Thank you."

"Why are you doing that?"

"To make sure it heals," he whispered. He lifted her palm, examining it, and let out a shuddered breath.

"Don't touch it. I've already disinfected it." Snow's mind felt cloudy and thick, like she'd taken too much medicine. She wanted to pull her hand away, but she couldn't. His touch was gentle and cool on her skin.

Something nagged at the edge of her mind. She should be afraid, but she couldn't concentrate long enough to figure out why.

Sage reached down and sniffed her palm. Snow's instincts screamed for her to run. When he licked her wound, she sucked in a breath. Somehow the feel of his skin touching hers made her knees almost buckle.

"What are you?" she asked again.

He lifted his mouth from her skin, his eyes glowing brightly in the moonlight.

Her brain finally caught up with her. *No!* It wasn't possible. Her brothers had said that vampires were vile and evil. They were dead, blood-sucking killers. How could this handsome, sensual man possibly be the monster they hunted at night?

*****

Sage's mind screamed for him to stop, but her scent overpowered him and drew him to her like a starving man to food. For that's what he was, a starving man.

He'd been drinking from a deer when he'd smelled it.

Blood.

Human blood.

It was so intoxicating that it guided Sage from his kill straight to this glade. And there she'd stood, dripping right onto the unworthy ground.

What a waste.

He used his magnetism to draw her in and make her hold still. But it was for her own good. If she ran, he wouldn't be able to keep from hunting her, and he didn't want to kill her. Not someone as lovely as Snow. With creamy skin and hair the color of, oak she was a vision of beauty, even in the shadow-filled night. Her lush, cherry lips tempted him, and her large, deep eyes, round as saucers and slightly turned upward at their outer corners, mesmerized him. Her will and air of royalty were apparent. As was her strength of spirit. He'd always been drawn to spirited women. There was no place for weak females in Tanah Danah.

"Tell me the truth. Are you the monster that we've been taught to fear? The killer of women. The slaughterer of children."

He couldn't answer. How could he tell her? Her gaze flicked sideways. She fought him. To be able to even recognize he was doing something to her was more than most. But to actually try and fight his influence showed true spirit. *Fascinating.*

She smelled of fruit, and springtime, and life. So much life. Sage savored the lingering taste of her blood.

Lifting his finger, he traced the line of her elegant throat. His fangs begged for her taste. He could take her. Drop her to the ground and drink her dry. She wouldn't be willing, but what did it matter? How many women had he terrorized by feeding off them?

Too many. He came to his senses and withdrew his fingers from her throat.

"You're— You're a vampire, aren't you?" Her voice was barely audible.

Her eyes sucked him in and refused to let go. His brain fogged at her scent. She reached up and placed her fingers on his cheek. His chest squeezed and his eyes closed at the sensation. Happiness washed over him and his vision flooded with images of them in his bed, her body intertwined with his.

"You can't be. Your skin is cool, but not icy." She dropped her hand to his chest. "And your heart beats. But much slower than it should."

Sage retreated. "You need to leave. Run home. It isn't safe for you out here."

"No danger has ever found its way to my glade. Not even bears live here."

She had no idea how many hundreds of women he'd killed when they thought they were safe. "Well, danger has found you now, so you need to go." Sage retreated further. He should leave. Return to his underground hovel and forget he'd ever seen her.

"Are you a—"

"Go!" Sage shouted, moving to her so quickly she blinked twice, startled.

Bloodlust slammed his body. He turned from her as his fangs burst into his mouth. A strange sensation overcame him. He didn't want her to see him, not like this. He shouldn't have played with her, toyed with her. He should have run from her scent instead of showing himself.

"My dummies —"

"I'll put them away." He tried to gain control of the bloodlust that spread inside him. He hadn't had a female in too long. Human or vampire. And this female, though he was the one using his influence, had a peculiar power over him that was greater still. What the hell was happening to him? His stomach clenched and his gums burned as he forced his fangs to retract.

She watched him unflinchingly. This couldn't all be his influence. The way she gazed at him, the lack of fear. Part of that had to be her.

In the past, all the others had said they weren't afraid when inwardly they were cowering rabbits. But why not her? Why was she not afraid? The sweet scent wafting from her skin was her own, not born of fear. The scent was a siren's song.

The moon had retreated for the end of night. Panic scratched over his skin. In mere minutes, the sun would be up. He needed to get somewhere safe.

"Why won't you run?" he yelled, barely able to think straight. He needed to go.

She straightened her spine. "Because I'm not afraid of you." Her voice was a soft caress.

Run away. Run now. He wanted to scream. But he couldn't. *Drink her dry. Make her your own and you'll never be alone again.* He pounded on his skull. His gaze met hers and he suddenly lost all reserve.

One moment he was inches away, the next he grabbed her braid and forced her body against his, crushing her lips with his own. His tongue plunged deep into her mouth. She stiffened at his touch initially, but then relaxed against him. He needed this.

Her supple body pressed against his, her curves sparking every inch of his skin to wake up and pay attention. Out of sheer will, he forced his fangs at bay. He wanted her all to himself at that moment.

Just her. The feel of her lips on his lips. Her tongue danced and licked his with a palpable need. Her apparent lack of experience made Sage savor her all the more.

He was dangerously close to losing control. She pushed against him roughly and he let go. Her eyes widened before hardening. Quick as light, she swung to slap him, but he caught her wrist.

"You don't want to do that, love. You'll split your palm open again."

"You had no right to kiss me."

Need pounded through him, making his body quake. He let go of her wrist. "I didn't see you protesting too much."

"I...I..." Her mouth opened and closed several times, but no words formed.

His gaze trained on her throat. The pulsing vein and the thundering of her heartbeat called to him. He licked his lips.

He stepped forward, gripped her arms and locked his eyes with hers. Her pupils contracted and then flooded open.

"You will go straight to the cabin. You will get your things and you will run. Run 'til you get safe in your bed. And when you wake up in the morning, you will remember nothing."

Her eyes glazed over and he eased his grasp on her. She picked up her sword and ran. A minute later, the light in the cabin flickered out and the door slammed. Sage didn't dare let himself even breathe until he knew she'd gone, for fear that he would chase her down and ravish her.

When he no longer heard her footsteps, he fell to his knees and clutched the bloodied gauze she'd left behind. So long he had been in exile, underground. So long he'd denied himself the companionship of a woman. And here, in the middle of a glade, he'd found her. His heart's desire was a human. What the hell was he going to do now?

CHAPTER FOUR

Queen Terona glanced at her husband out of the corner of her eye. Philos gripped the arms of his throne, awaiting the return of his Private Guard. They'd been gone too long. His gaze swept over the feedings taking place at the edges of the great hall, but even the sight of his subjects drinking and sexing in his honor did nothing to calm his agitation. For a moment, she contemplated doing something to calm him herself, but she thought better of it.

For fifty years, she'd sat at his side, lain in his bed, and put up with him in order to be ruler of Tanah Darah. She'd lied, schemed and murdered to get where she was. But for all of that, the vampires were worse off under Philos' rule than they had been under his brother Lothar's. A pang of guilt swept over Terona for having helped kill Lothar. If she'd been less greedy and more patient like her brother had believed her to be, she'd have seen that in the long run Lothar was the right vampire to rule, not inadequate Philos.

Her gaze raked over the scribe that stood at Philos' feet, a large ancient tome in his hands, awaiting Philos' command. Killing Lothar had brought many perks, but also a world of problems. With the death of Philos' son, Garot, and Sage dropping the body off at the castle gates, Philos had become more anxious than ever for his demise. That combined with the rumors that the first prophecy had been fulfilled had the entire castle buzzing about what would be coming their way.

"Read it again," Philos said, motioning to the scribe.

"Philos, we've heard it twice already," she said.

He ground his teeth together. "I need to hear it again."

She rolled her eyes and continued petting the beast at her side. Philos' knuckles whitened as he gripped his throne tighter. The presence of Terona's pets, Jale and Juda, in the court constantly reminded him of his failure to bring down King Adrian. Which was precisely why she kept them. She had designed inhibitor collars that were shackled at their throats to prohibit the wolves from changing into human form.

The scribe cleared his throat. "Uh…" He scanned the book again and then began.

"The blood shall cease to flow and the land will grow dry,
until the ones, once thought extinct, join the fight.
Then will the change come like a wave
and ever again the lands will be fruitful,
as old alliances are reforged."

Their lands had become dry in the last hundred years because of fewer slavers to trade with. Which meant fewer humans to bring into Tanah Danah. The wolves had all but blocked off their route through Wolvenglen forest. And someone else kept the Daemon Wasteland route covered. Philos' nephew, *Sage.*

The door to the throne room burst inward and Remus stalked in, his stride quick and heavy.

"Your Majesty, the Guard is dead," Remus said with a bow.

"All of them?" Philos sat forward. His Private Guard were the best fighters they had.

"All, King Philos. I am sorry."

Remus' gaze flickered in her direction and then to Philos. His blond hair clung to his scalp and neck. The scent of woods and blood wafted off him.

"And the Cris knife?" Philos sighed. Sitting back, he rubbed his temples.

"Gone." Remus locked gazes with her again and a flutter of desire lodged in her belly. His handsome face and sinewy body held great pleasure for her.

Philos cursed.

Terona stopped petting her beast. How had Sage been able to take down the entire guard? One thing was for sure: he was no longer the swaggering youth, that she'd watched while in the court of his father, whose only thought was the arrival of his next female. She smiled at the memory of his handsome face. "Are you telling me that Sage took out my entire guard single-handedly?"

Remus looked at her. "No, your majesty, he had help. I awaited my brethren's return on the edge of the ridge when I saw the Guard flushed out of the woods by Sage and the Weres. They ran straight into an awaiting group below."

A knot formed in the pit of her stomach. Not only had the Cris knife been lost and Guard killed, but Sage seemed to be gaining more allies in exile than he had when he'd been prince.

Philos jumped from his throne, startling her. Remus backed out of the way of Philos' wrath.

Reaching the nearest candelabra, Philos flung it across the hall. It hit the wall with a crash, and wax spilled onto the floor. Their subjects stopped what they were doing and fled the hall. He scanned for something else to focus his rage on. His gaze lit on the Were at her side. He was on it in a stride. Terona barely had time to react when he grabbed it by the neck and twisted.

She let out a cry as the beast hit the floor, motionless. The dead Were's brother was up on his feet in an instant, teeth bared, pulling at his collar and chain to get at Philos. She rushed in front of the second Were before Philos could reach it. She glared at him, daring him to advance on her. Though she held no love for the beasts, they were hers, and she didn't like others to destroy things that belonged to her.

Remus and the cowering scribe, cleared the hall. Only Philos, Terona and her pet remained. For a tense moment, they stared at each other. She readied herself for a fight, instead he took a deep breath and turned away.

"How will I rid myself of Sageren? The last rock in my shoe. Until his life is ended, I will never truly be king."

She'd heard this speech before. It was always about Sage lately. Ever since he'd befriended the Weres, Philos had become increasingly obsessed with killing him.

"There are those in my kingdom whose loyalties are still divided. I'm not oblivious to the whispers of my subjects. Their complaints of the lack of flowing blood fill every chamber of this castle."

Terona stroked the ear of her remaining Were. "You need to let me handle it."

Philos' face hardened again and she saw his tantrum coming.

"Sage prospers in exile while we wither!" Philos yelled.

She shrugged. "What does it matter? He cannot return here. Even with a thousand friends he couldn't get in. Why won't you let me take care of him?"

"Because I am king! Taking care of him is my job!"

He'd ignored the first part of her question. Her gaze met his. "He can't get in, can he Philos?"

"No."

Terona could entice men to tell her the truth if they gazed into her eyes, even if they didn't want to. Philos hated her for it, but he loved when she used it on others for his benefit. She knew that with the face of an angel and the body of a succubus, Philos could never resist her. She'd ensured she was the most beautiful of all vampires. Hair the color of gold and lips like ripe berries. Though she stood barely to his shoulder, her long, sleek legs were only outdone by her ample, soft breasts. She prided herself on her form.

She stopped petting her Were and let her gaze fall upon him like a vise grip, twisting the truth from him. He had her off the floor by her throat in an instant.

"Stop that," he boomed.

She made no effort to squirm or retreat from his crushing grip, she simply leveled her icy gaze at him. Philos backhanded her, sending her plummeting to the ground. Blood trickled from her lip as she caught her breath. He was so weak. He couldn't even withstand her gaze. Instead he had to resort to violence to get her to stop.

Weak. So weak.

She got to her feet and strode to where he stood. Wiping the blood from her lip with her finger, she studied it for a moment before she stuck her bloodied finger into his mouth.

Philos tried not to give in, but her taste was something he'd never been able to resist. He closed his eyes and moaned. She moved her hips closer, brushed up against him and felt his need build. He hadn't been aroused in days.

He pinned her to the stone floor in half a second, rummaged under her skirt with his hands, and felt his way up her naked legs. She smiled. This was the only part of Philos she actually enjoyed and only because her pleasure always came before his. Raising his body from hers, Philos rolled her onto her stomach. He dropped his weight onto her, grinding onto her rear. He dipped his mouth to drink from her, but before he struck, Terona grabbed him by the neck, flipping him over. Philos bared his teeth as she positioned herself above him.

"Don't. Ever. Try. To. Lie. To. Me. Philos." She raked a long nail down his chest, slicing his shirt open and drawing blood.

Philos swallowed a grunt. She bent down and bit his lip. Kissing and sucking his mouth, she licked the blood from his chin, plunging her tongue into his mouth with force. Philos matched her fury. His hands roamed under her skirt again but she slapped them away. He broke the kiss and glared at her.

"You, husband, need to remember that I will not be toyed with. You may be king, but I put you on that throne."

Lifting her skirt she ground her hips into his, making him moan. She struck before Philos could react. He gasped as she bit into his throat. She ripped his shirt apart and dug her nails deep into his stomach. She always got what she wanted first.

*****

Terona slipped out of her bed, tied on a satiny robe, and headed for the hall. As husbands went, Philos was one of the better ones she'd had, especially in bed. His appetites matched her own and he didn't mind when things occasionally escalated from rough to brutal.

Stepping into the darkened hallway, she glanced over her shoulder. Philos didn't move. She walked swiftly down the hall to the west wing. Turning the corner, she ducked behind a tapestry as someone passed. She didn't care that people saw her out in her robe, she just didn't need rumors circulating as to where she crept off to at the break of day. When the footsteps faded, she darted out again and across the landing to the other side.

Coming to the first door on the left, she didn't bother knocking before she entered. Remus stood bare-chested and ready for bed. The sight of his hard body made her temperature rise. Beautiful Remus, tall and lean, his muscular body built for pleasuring a woman, he stared at her with desire, his long blond hair tied with a leather strap at the nape of his neck. She enjoyed the appreciation he showed her, his cerulean eyes skimming over her body.

"My Queen," Remus said with a slight bow.

She moved into his arms in a second. Planting her lips firmly on his, he grabbed her buttocks and hefted her off the floor. She wrapped her legs around his waist, her hands sliding down his sinewy arms. She planted playful kisses on his neck, descending to his chest. Remus let out a moan and his fangs grazed her skin. She stopped short. Anger flashed in Remus' eyes, but Terona leaned in, flicked out her tongue and ran it the length of his throat.

"Not today," she whispered. "We have much to discuss."

Remus let out a groan and set her on the floor. "Why do you tempt me so?"

She slid a long finger down his muscular chest and over his quivering stomach to his waistband. "You know why, darling."

He pushed away from her and fell onto his bed. Terona admired him as he lay splayed before her. She imagined that's what Sage looked like bare-chested. His rebuffs of her affection, when she'd first come to Tanah Darah, galled her still.

"We need to kill Sage."

"Do you not think that is what your husband has been trying to do? Kill Sage?" Remus threw his hands over his face.

"Philos is useless," she said. "Merely killing a werewolf king proved to be too much for him. No Remus, it needs to be you. You heard the prophecy. '...when ones thought extinct join the fight the tides will turn...'"

"You think that's me?"

"Who else?" Terona paced the floor, tapping her lips with her fingernail. She needed to find out where Sage hid. They knew he stayed in the Daemon Wastelands, but in his fifty years of exile, they had yet to find out where. Someone had used a sizeable amount of magick to hide him, and hide him well, but there was one...one who could find Sage. She didn't want him to discover her failure, but she could wait no longer.

The prophecies had begun.

"I will go to Dragos," she said.

"As you wish, my Queen."

The tone of Remus' voice had changed, making her stop. He eyed her with a lustful gaze. Terona licked her lips, the taste of him still in her mouth. Remus rose from his bed. His broad shoulders and youthful form called to her. Planting his hands on her waist, he trailed light kisses down her throat. She knew he wouldn't give up until he had her. No male had ever been satisfied with having her only once, and with Remus, it had been many times this week alone.

"I'd do anything for you," Remus whispered into her ear. He caressed her body through her thin gown. He drew the satin tie at her waist and her robe hit the floor.

He admired her form for several moments before trailing kissing down her flesh until he knelt before her. It was her turn to quake with need. Remus gripped her hipbones.

"Tell me I'm beautiful," she said.

His gaze locked on hers. "You are the fairest of them all, my queen."

She smiled with pleasure. She entwined her fingers in his hair.

"I would give you the world, Aunt. You only need ask," he said.

Terona moaned, anticipating the pleasures she would experience over the next hour at Remus' expert hands.

CHAPTER FIVE

Snow roused drowsily at the sounds of her brothers moving about the house. The sun shone through her curtains. Why was the sun so bright this morning?

It wasn't until a loud knock sounded on her door that she fully awoke.

"Snow? Snow, are you all right?" Kellan asked.

She pulled her skull off her pillow to see her door knob twist.

"Why's your door locked?" Erik demanded.

She groaned as her brothers gathered outside her room.

"Snow, are you sick?" asked Gerall.

"I'm tired," she grumbled, sitting up.

The clock read nine. *What?* She was always up by seven.

"Snow," said Flint. "Open the door."

My troth! I oversleep once and it's the end of the world. "I'm coming!" she yelled.

Sliding out of bed, she glanced down. She still wore her practice outfit. Suddenly she was wide awake. She scoured her brain, trying to remember what had happened the night before. Had she even gone to the cabin or had she simply fallen asleep?

Odd.

"Snow!"

"I said, I'm coming!" She stripped off her outfit and yanked on a nightgown.

She got out of the way just as her bedroom door burst inward and her brothers piled in.

Erik inspected every surface and then strode to her window and peered out.

She held her breath. Had she removed the rope?

After a minute Erik turned. "Why did you lock your door?"

Narrowing her gaze, she crossed her arms over her chest. "Because I wanted it locked."

Erik eyed her up and down.

"You have something to accuse me of, Erik?" Snow gritted her teeth, knowing what he was thinking. The memory of Lord Balken coming into her room in the middle of the night made her chin quake. The image of Erik and Flint dragging him out with Hass, Ian and Jamen following behind was burned into her memory, something she would never forget. It had been a good thing their mother and father were still alive then, or her brothers would have killed him.

"Erik, it's not a big deal," said Kellan. "So she wanted her door locked? We lock our doors."

Erik shot Kellan a scathing look.

"Leave him alone," said Jamen. "Kellan's right. Snow isn't a child. If she wants to lock her door, it's her right."

"Honestly, Erik." She flopped on her bed. "I wouldn't wish the seven of you on anyone." With that, she tugged up her covers and rolled on her side. Erik's implications infuriated he, but if he found out the truth about her sneaking out, the door would be removed altogether.

"So, no food then?" asked Hass.

Snow screamed, and threw a pillow at the group. "Get out!"

Her brothers made a run for the stairs. Erik walked out into the hall. When the others were gone, Flint closed the door and Snow turned away from him. She didn't need another lecture. His heavy footsteps thumped across her floor and the weight of his large frame made her bed creak. He sat silently, patiently, on the edge. Finally, she rolled over and looked over at him.

"Are you feeling well?"

"Yes," she said. "I'm just a bit groggy."

"Possibly because of your late night adventure?" He raised an eyebrow.

Snow stiffened.

"I know you've been doing it since mother–"

She stared at the ceiling. What could she say? Her mind traveled to the night before, she still wasn't sure what had happened.

"I followed you once," Flint said. "When I first saw you go out into the fields to think and stare up at the stars." He sat silently for a minute. "I understand your need to get out by yourself for a few hours."

"Flint, I'm sorry I didn't tell you or Erik, but—"

He turned his gaze toward her. "You don't need to apologize. I understand. That's why sometimes I—"

He didn't need to complete the sentence. She wasn't naïve to the things her brothers did to deal with their pain. All of them had their own vice. Flint's was women, the kind that did what they were paid to do, and wanting nothing else in return. Jamen took to drinking and occasionally cards. Even the twins had their vices. She'd seen them limp home, supporting each other after participating in an underhanded fight ring. She didn't judge, especially Flint. His life was full of more pain than most. He may have been born into money, but money couldn't buy peace in the soul.

"You need to be careful. We're relatively sheltered here in the grasslands, which is why Father chose this area to lord over, *and* why I'm not going to say anything to Erik. But danger can penetrate even the most formidable places. Promise me that you won't leave our property." His eyes softened toward her.

He thought she still went to the fields to think. He had no idea where she really went. After Erik, Flint was the brother that would be most angry about her midnight fighting sessions.

The cabin was her property though. Sort of. "I promise."

"Do me a favor. When you return in the mornings, come to my room and knock once. It doesn't have to be loud. Just so I'll hear it and know you are safe."

"Thank you, Flint." She took his hand in hers and squeezed it. A slight twinge shot up her arm and she jerked.

Flint frowned. "What's wrong?"

Snow studied her palm. It looked normal, but the muscles ached. "Nothing," she said. "Probably just a sprain."

"You work too hard for us," he said. "I'm sorry for what you have to put up with."

She laughed. "You aren't that bad."

"No." He shook his head. "But it isn't the life you deserve. Having to live here and cook and clean for us."

"Well you're welcome to help out a bit. Maybe cook a meal once and again. Scrub the floors, dust the—"

"Uh…I meant maybe we should get another woman to help you."

Snow raised an eyebrow. "Oh really? So taking care of the house is strictly a woman's job?"

He gave her a strange look. "Of course."

Her mouth dropped open and she laughed, smacking him with a pillow. "Thank you very much, Lord Gwyn."

He laughed and hit her back with the pillow. "You're welcome, Lady Gwyn."

"You seven would be lost without me."

The smile fell from Flint's face and he grew serious again. "Yes. We would."

She laughed again lightly, but the moment was over and Flint got up to leave.

"Flint," she said. "You know I'm here for you, don't you? If you ever need something, someone..."

He smiled. "I know." It had been so long since she had seen him smile. And though his eyes still held sadness, it was nice to see.

Snow lay on her pillows and tried to remember what had happened the night before. She remembered getting her things out, getting up, going to her cabin and setting up her dummies. But after that her memory became hazy. Like trying to see through a dense fog.

Looking down at her palm she rubbed at it absently. It twinged again and she was sure she'd injured herself. An image flashed into her mind of a handsome man with aquamarine eyes. Warmth spread through her body, and a single word came to her mind. *Sage.*

By noon, each of Snow's brothers had come to visit. She'd stayed in bed late enjoying the pampering she received, for once.

The twins had arrived bearing a tray of random foods, piled so high that she knew they'd raided the entire pantry to assemble the meal. Gerall brought a vase of flowers from the yard and then proceeded to explain to her what each stood for, and their scientific names. Kellan had stopped by to play a game of chess. He'd beat her as usual and apologized again for all of them bursting in on her.

"They shouldn't have overreacted," said Kellan.

"Well, thank you for standing up for me."

Kellan smiled. "That's what big brothers are for, isn't it? To stand up to the bigger brothers?"

Snow laughed. Always her protector.

Erik stopped by last. Already dressed in his fighting outfit, his bow slung over his shoulder and his sword at his side, he stuck his head in.

"You need anything before I go?"

"No, thanks." She stared at the wall.

He didn't move. Snow waited.

"Sorry about this morning," he said.

She knew it pained him to say the words, but she wasn't cutting him any slack.

She gazed over at him. "How could you think I would sneak someone in?"

"You wouldn't, I just–" He stopped and ran his fingers through his hair. "I hope you feel better soon. You know where we'll be if you need us."

Snow listened to his footsteps go down the stairs and outside. She lay for a moment longer before deciding, finally, to rise.

She threw her covers aside and walked to her great grandmother's full-length mirror in the corner. Pulling out a hairbrush, she untangled her braid and brushed her dark hair. Lifting her arm, her sleeve fell away and she gasped. A long trail of dried blood ran from her forearm to her elbow. Snow's heartbeat quickened. Where had that come from? Was it hers? She glanced at her palm again and pushed on it. The vision of the handsome man filled her mind once more. The same tingling sensation she had gotten earlier spread through her. Why couldn't she remember?

She had to get it together. She had responsibilities. She couldn't go through life in a fantasy world.

Snow shook herself to clear her dreamy head. She couldn't let the face of an attractive stranger from her dreams distract her. She put down the brush, got her things and headed for a bath. After filling the tub with the tepid water her brothers had left her, Snow stripped down and stepped in.

An hour later, she saddled her horse and rode to town. The brisk ride took no more than twenty minutes, but the fresh air was just what she needed to wake her from her foggy state. When she reached the gate of Westfall, she slowed her horse and trotted onto the main street.

She maneuvered toward the stable, stopped out front and waited. People bustled to and fro on the busy street. It was afternoon and the busiest time of day. After several minutes, she called out to Armie, the stable hand, to retrieve her horse, but he didn't come to meet her. Jumping down, she wrapped the reins to a post and headed for the stable door. The sounds of arguing drifted out to meet her. Swallowing, Snow pushed open the stable doors to find four men inside. Two men held Armie by the arms, while a third man held a knife in his face. Armie's eyes were wide with fear.

"Hey!" Snow shouted, rushing forward. "What do you think you're doing?"

The man with the knife swung to face her and her heart sank. *Klaus.*

Recognition dawned on Klaus's face and he lowered the knife and smiled. "Snow, my dear. How are you?"

Ugh! Snow marched to Armie's side, and Klaus's two men let go of him. "I asked what you're doing to Armie, Klaus."

"Just having a friendly conversation. He and I have a business arrangement and we're just ironing out the details." Klaus stepped away.

Friendly my foot. As a small-time ruffian and gambler, she sincerely doubted anything Klaus did was friendly.

Snow eyed the three men. If it came to a fight she could handle herself pretty well, but she wouldn't be able to take them all. However,

64

she had a major advantage which would keep the men from getting violent with her. Her brothers. Especially Jamen. Though Klaus had been a friend of Jamen's in their younger days, and lately they'd been spotted playing cards at the inn, Jamen would lay Klaus out flat if he so much as looked at Snow sideways.

"I think you should leave," she said.

"Well, we'll just finish our business here and be on our way, Lady Gwyn," said Klaus.

Armie shuffled his feet and refused to meet her eye. If there was a fight, it was obvious he would be no help.

She thought fast. "Are Belle and Chloe in town today?"

Klaus had a weak spot; Belle, his fiancée and Snow's oldest friend, as well as their two-year-old daughter Chloe.

Klaus's eyes narrowed and his smile faltered. "Belle is at home today. I'm picking up what she needs."

"Well, why don't you tell me and I'll get it and take it to her while you finish up your... 'business'." She flashed a smile. "I haven't seen her in too long anyway, and I'm sure my brothers would love a chance to visit with little Chloe."

"Come to think of it, I do need to get home." He motioned to his men and the three moved toward the exit. "I'll see you soon, Armie, and we can finish our talk. Lady Gwyn, a pleasure as always. Tell Jamen I'll see him at the tavern soon. He owes me a round."

Klaus walked out of the stable and disappeared.

"You shouldn't have done that," Armie said.

Snow's eyebrows shot up. "I shouldn't have stopped them from hurting you?"

"It's better than the alternative way they deal with people who owe them money."

She'd heard rumors about Klaus' unsavory dealings, but she couldn't believe Belle would be engaged to such a man.

"What's the alternative?"

Armie bent and picked up his hat, dusting it off. "You should go home, Lady Gwyn."

"I'm not scared of Klaus." She laughed.

"You should be." Armie glanced at the stable exit again.

Armie plodded to the front of the stable and brought her horse in. His shaken demeanor gave Snow the feeling that Klaus was much worse than she knew.

*****

Night was falling when Sage walked into the corridor. The door to Dax's room stood open, and Dax lay on his bed, staring at the ceiling.

"Evening."

Dax glanced over, a look of concern on his face.

"Something wrong?"

"You went out last night?"

"I needed more blood to heal. Is that a problem?"

"Not as long as no one got hurt."

"I told you before, I don't drink human," Sage said, thinking of how he'd broken that vow by licking Snow's hand. Memories of her

66

made Sage antsy. He'd barely returned that morning before the sun had come up. He disliked that Snow held sway over him so tightly that he'd almost gotten himself killed. He'd fallen asleep with her bloodied gauze in his grip. Now awake, and thinking of her, all he wanted was to see her again.

Dax nodded. "Lots of talking down here. You aren't alone?"

"Want to see?" Sage changed the subject. He motioned for Dax to follow him and he walked down the hallway. "The night my uncle, Philos, murdered my father and younger brother was chaos. I had no clue what was happening." His memories turned to his younger brother for the first time in months. The pain of losing his best friend still stung after fifty years. The death of his father had been a terrible blow, but it had been his brother's death that hurt the most. Sage coughed and tried to clear the lump that formed in his throat whenever he thought of how he'd let Sasha and Greeg whisk him to safety that night, instead of returning to see if he could save them.

"What about your mother?"

"Her name was Helena. She died a few years prior." They passed the corridor leading to the entrance and continued further down into the earth. The area smelled of coal and fire.

"Two of my father's closest advisors got me out of the castle. We ran to the Daemon Wastelands, not knowing what else to do. Once here, we realized we needed help in order to stay hidden from my uncle's assassins. Years before, my father had introduced me to an old friend of his; Lord Rondell was an advisor to the Fae King. I went to Rondell for help. As fae and vampires don't mix, he could do little, but he did build me this." Sage gestured around. "So we'd have shelter and protection."

"How long ago?"

They reached the end of the hall and turned left.

"A long time," Sage said quietly. *Too long.*

They followed the passage, past several corridors that branched off the main hall, to an open den. The large space had all the things that Sage loved from his castle; volume upon volume of leather-bound books, alchemy supplies and knick-knacks. The dozen or so chairs in the den were filled with vampires. They looked up and acknowledged Sage in turn.

"This is Dax," said Sage. "He is my guest and will be staying with us for a while."

"He isn't one of us," said an older vampire, wrinkling his nose.

"He isn't one of any, Omni. He's one of a kind. A werebear."

The vampires exchanged looks.

"How did that happen?" asked Greeg.

Dax shrugged. "All I remember is running through a forest, being chased and almost killed by vampires."

"Are you saying vampires did this?" asked another vampire.

"Don't be so dramatic, Vill," said Sage. "All he's saying is he doesn't know how it happened, and he doesn't trust us. Which is just fine. I don't even trust us."

"Sage!" Sonya rose from her seat. "How can you say that?"

"Don't take offense, Sonya. I have good reason, as you are well aware." Sage waved his hand. "But I wanted to tell you that our wait is almost over, my friends. I have a few more pieces to put into place, but soon we will be going home."

Minutes later as Sage and Dax walked toward his room. "Do you want to go out and get some supplies?"

"I have no money," Dax said.

"What kind of host would I be, if I let you pay for your own food?" Sage grabbed his sword, long coat, and a bag of coins.

"Do you go into town much?"

"Only when absolutely necessary and only at night. But I'm not going to go into town with you. I have an errand a few miles north. Will you be able to make your way back, if I show you to Westfall?"

"Sure. Anything you need help with?"

Sage pushed opened the rock façade. "No, thank you."

"Is it the female?"

Sage stopped moving.

"I smelled her on you. I just hope you've thought this through and that neither of you gets hurt."

Sage hoped so too.

CHAPTER SIX

Sage waited on a tree branch near the cabin, scanning the area. He shouldn't be there. It was dangerous for them both. But thoughts of her scent, the beauty of her face, and the taste of her lips all haunted him. She had affected him so intensely and drawn him in. He needed to find out why, but this was the last time. He refused to allow her to have a hold over him. He'd see her, figure out her secret, and forget her forever.

After showing Dax the way to Westfall, Sage made his way to the cabin, being sure to stop for a meal before his arrival. The last thing he needed was to be tempted by her blood again.

He needed to be careful. He looked human enough in the dark, but he needed to be sure his instincts didn't get the better of him again. His lust for her blood had caused her to figure out what he was last time.

He waited for more than an hour, replaying their encounter from the previous night.

What the hell was he doing? He'd commanded her to return home and not even remember him. What did he think was going to happen if she saw him again?

Images from long ago, of the last human he had fed from, flashed through his mind. The decades had done nothing to diminish the tormenting memories of what he used to be. He remembered his calming influence as he told her she would be fine. Recalled the terror in her eyes as he struck, her silent pleas for him to stop. Her lifeless body in his arms when he'd drunk too much.

Like so many before her. Slaves purchased and ferried to his castle for the mere pleasure of vampires.

His father hadn't been a great humanitarian, but he'd done what he needed to, to take care of his dying people. However, Sage's uncle, Philos, cared for nothing more than his own pleasures. Even now, Philos sat upon the throne and let his people wither.

In his fifty years of exile, Sage had seen all of Fairelle. The humans, the Fae, the Weres, the dragons, even the Mages and Nereids. He'd seen how the lands failed. The races were divided, even amongst themselves, and it had become apparent that the only way they would survive was to work together, as the prophecy told them. The arrival of Queen Redlynn of Wolvenglen had boosted Sage's hope that soon his own prophecy would be fulfilled, and he'd return home.

A soft set of footsteps a hundred yards away wrenched Sage from his thoughts. Snow emerged from a group of dense trees, dressed in the same shirt, tunic and boots as the night before. The sight of her made him smile. His insides burned, remembering the taste of her blood on his tongue. Springtime and life. Honey and tangerines.

In the bright moonlight, she walked to her cabin, opened the door and rummaged around inside. A dim light emanated from within. When she stepped out, she scanned the area, standing still for several minutes before hauling her dummy into the glade.

For an hour, Sage watched her practice with her sword. Her movements fluid, her ability sound. She'd obviously had training.

If she were a vampire, she'd be amazing. With increased speed and senses, she would be unstoppable. The perfect consort.

The overwhelming desire to turn her raced through him. To take her to his den and taste and love her every waking evening. His breeches became tight and uncomfortable, making Sage shift his position in the tree. His movement caused a broken branch to tumble from where it hung and crash to the ground. Snow stopped. Sword raised, she peered into the darkness.

Damn!

"Who's there?" she called.

Good job, Sage. Stealthy.

"Show yourself," she demanded, swaying from foot-to-foot.

He had no choice but to jump from the tree and emerge into the glade. He wanted to be near her. Even if she didn't remember him, he longed to hear her say his name, to take in her lovely scent once more.

"Who are you?" She stepped back. Her sword raised, she stared at him in wary confusion.

"Hello."

*****

Snow's throat went dry. The tall man with aquamarine eyes drew ever closer.

It couldn't be.

He had the same eyes she'd been dreaming of all day. A memory waited for her on the other side of the wall in her mind, but she couldn't quite pull it to the surface.

They circled each other and though she wasn't foolish enough to lower her sword, being near him was comforting, yet frightening at the same time.

Images flashed through the block surrounding her mind. *Together in the glade. His lips on hers, his tongue on her hand, the desire in his gaze as he looked at her.* Her fear deepened.

"I remember you," she murmured, "but I don't."

He stopped moving for a moment, his brows knit together. He stepped closer again.

"Don't do that." She spun out of reach. "Stop where you are."

"Oh, come now, don't act that way." He smiled.

What a great smile.

"I mean it," she said, "Don't come near me. I don't want to have to hurt you." Her body trembled, but her voice held steady. Snow's inner alarm sounded. Something about him set her on edge. What was it she couldn't remember?

"Oh, you wouldn't hurt me." His gaze locked on hers. "You don't want to hurt me."

She broke eye contact and shook her head. "You're right. I don't, but I will." She thrust the sword in warning. He took a cautious step back and smirked.

His sensuality drew her in. He spoke with such familiarity, like a joke she wasn't in on.

His broad shoulders cut straight down to his trim waist beneath a long leather coat. Snow wondered what his hands would feel like on her skin. He sucked in a long, deep breath; a look of complete peace crossing his face.

"What are you doing?"

He opened his eyes and she could swear they shone a bit brighter in the moonlight.

"Smelling you."

Smelling her? Why would he do that?

"What? That's just–" She fumbled for something to say. "You're trespassing. You should go." The nagging feeling of unease increased.

"Make me, love." A smile played across his lips.

Why did men always think they could treat her as a lesser? Lunging, she swung her sword, but he wasn't there.

"Over here, love," he said.

He stood behind her. She swung around, huffed and lunged again. He stepped out of her way and she missed. Running at him, she thrust at his stomach, but he swatted the sword away and spun behind her. Grabbing her about the waist, he tugged her into his chest, bent over her neck and kissed it playfully.

"I love this side of you." His cool breath raised goose bumps on her skin.

Slamming her head back, Snow caught him by surprise. He let go and stumbled to his knee, his nose dripping blood into the grass.

"Don't ever touch me without my permission, you rake." Memories of Lord Balken made her pulse race and a bead of sweat trickle down her spine.

His eyes flashed dangerously, but then softened. He gritted his teeth, wiped his nose on his sleeve and spat on the ground.

"Who are you?" More images broke through. Though she only caught bits and pieces, she'd met this dazzling stranger before. But she would be damned if she would let him play her for a bar wench.

In a blink, he had her in his arms again. Her breath caught as he bent down, his lips inches from hers. She took in his musky scent. He was so handsome with his long blond hair hanging loosely around his shoulders. Her stomach fluttered at his nearness. His gaze locked on hers, piercing into her very soul. His intense stare skimmed over her face. Beyond his jovial façade lay loneliness and longing.

"Why are you so sad?" The words came out before she had time to think.

His brows furrowed, but then he laughed. "Who said I'm sad?"

The smile on his lips didn't reach his eyes. He was lying.

"You do. It's written all over you."

"I—I—" Sage stared at her. He dropped the smile and anger clouded his features. "Everything I loved was stolen from me."

"Take it back."

His gaze hardened. "It's not that easy."

"Everything worth loving is worth fighting for." Snow softened toward him. Despair oozed off him. His hard exterior and playful wit only covered a loneliness she knew all too well.

His face was so close. The feel of his strong arms encasing her sent chills down her spine. She licked her lower lip. She shouldn't be here, in the dark, letting a stranger hold her. But the contact felt so good.

His gaze drifted down to her mouth. "Someday soon, you'll beg me to kiss you, love."

His toying ways made her blood boil. She wrenched free of him, rolled across the grass and retrieved her sword.

"You will see death before that happens." She lunged at him and this time instead of moving out of her way, he retrieved a sword and the two pieces of steel clashed. "Ah." She chuckled. "You've finally done something worth getting my attention, sir."

Sage's smile faltered as she attacked and he parried. She spun and attacked again. Again he parried. Her smile broadened "Come on then, give us a go. I've been dying for a real fight for months."

He laughed. "If you insist, love."

"Stop calling me that!"

She rushed him, swinging wildly. He parried, stepped out of the way, and swatted her on the backside with his sword. *Ouch!* She leapt out of his way.

"Why? Does it bother you?"

Snow attacked again, but when she swung, he parried too high and she ripped his pant leg. He inspected the slice momentarily. "Good. You can be taught."

This time he attacked first, wielding his sword with precision, putting Snow on the defense. She dodged, jumped back, and even rolled on the ground to get away from him. The speed with which he moved was frightening. His training had to be extensive.

Repeatedly he came at her, talking to her, taunting her, or telling her how to improve. At first it made Snow even angrier, but soon she found herself enjoying their session. Her brothers hadn't sparred with her in ages. She learned quickly, and soon took the offensive again. Several times he even lost ground against her.

When she was all but spent, she made a last attack. Moving to her left, she spun and ended up behind him. He turned just in time for his throat to come in contact with the tip of her blade. She wasn't sure how she had gotten the advantage. But she smiled at the outcome.

"I am at your mercy," he said sheathing his sword. "What would you have me do?"

She took a moment to catch her breath. "Tell me your name."

"You know my name." His intense blue eyes caused her cheeks to heat.

"I don't."

His pupils contracted and then widened. "You know my name, love," he said again, in a lower tone.

The words bounced inside her mind in an echo.

"Sage," she whispered. *How did she know that?*

"Put the sword down, love." He stepped closer. "Ask me to kiss you."

"No." Snow gripped her sword hilt to keep from grabbing onto him. "I am a lady, not a common wench. And you sir, are no gentleman to treat me as such."

He laughed. "If you were a common wench, you'd have done what you were told by now." He took a step away. "You want me to kiss you. I can smell it. The sweet scent of vanilla. That's how you smell. You smell like vanilla when you want me to kiss you."

77

Her mouth dried like the Wastelands. Part of her did want him to kiss her. To feel something other than loneliness and boredom. But it wasn't right. She didn't even know him.

"Say it. Tell me to kiss you, and I will."

"No." In an effort to avoid his gaze, she swung her sword lightly around in a circle, practicing the moves her father had taught her. Her clammy, slick palms slid down the pommel of her sword slightly.

"You're stronger than any female I have met before," he said. "Resistant. I appreciate that about you."

"Will you meet me tomorrow?" She swung, lunged and continued moving away from him. Her heart pounded in her chest.

"What?"

She glanced at him over her shoulder and wiped her damp hair from her forehead. "Tomorrow. To spar. Will you return?" She shouldn't ask. But for all of the impropriety and the annoying way he treated her, he was someone to talk to. *What could it hurt?* He didn't know who she was, or her brothers. In this situation, that was a good thing. Besides, he wasn't bad to look at. Well, for having only seen him the dark.

He stared at her for a minute. "Yes."

She couldn't help but smile. "Good. Then I'll get to beat you again."

CHAPTER SEVEN

Terona looked both directions before continuing down the old abandoned corridor, a heavy gold key clutched in her fist. Her long gown clung to her skin as she moved. It still amazed her how accustomed to wearing beautiful clothing she'd become. Stopping by a dust-covered door, she pushed the key into the lock and turned it with a creak. A spider climbed higher on the web that had glued the wood shut.

Once inside, she moved directly to an object in the corner. She yanked the drape off, and coughed as a blanket of dust rained down from the surface. Underneath waited a tall, thin gilded mirror set with a currant colored red stone on each of the four corners. She pushed the four stones in turn, causing them to light from within. The mirror's surface quaked and shimmered, like a pool of water. A light grew from the middle and shone out. After a minute, a long, dark corridor with countless mirrors appeared.

"Dragos," she called. The mirror rippled again.

The corridor image moved and shifted, racing past mirror after mirror until finally coming to a stop. Reaching through the mirror, she pushed a button on the other side. There was a flash of light and she saw into the room through the adjoining mirror. A medium-built man with soot colored hair and stern slate eyes stared at her.

His dark cloak shook with his hearty laugh. "Ah, sister! How long it's been since I've heard from you. How fair thee in Tanah Darah?"

"Well enough, brother. And how fair thee?"

"Very well. I have all I could ever ask for here in the lands of Fairelle. From a fair daughter to all the alchemy this world can provide." He studied her, appraising her form. When he spoke, his voice held disdain. "But it has been years since we've heard from you. I assume this is not just a visit because you missed me."

"I need your help," Terona said. "You may have heard that the first prophecy has been fulfilled. It has begun."

"Rumor had reached me of such. So our little helper has failed. The wolves and their mates have reunited? Morgana is most displeased."

Terona crossed her arms over her chest. Morgana's displeasure was not her concern at the moment. "My kingdom is next."

Dragos's eyebrows lifted. "But you have nothing to fear. You did, after all, put a new man on the throne, did you not?"

"Yes, but–" It had not gone entirely to plan. She did not dare tell Dragos that she couldn't get rid of a puny vampire prince. "I need you to locate someone for me. To make sure that my position is secure."

"Ah. Someone has slipped through your fingers, perhaps?" Dragos scratched his chin and turned away from her. "A prince, maybe?"

He already knew, and if he knew, Morgana knew. It was time to stop playing coy. "Yes," she said. "Sageren is still out there. I have spent years hunting him, but I believe he is being shielded by magick."

Dragos flipped through the pages of a book. His lack of attention made her want to scream. She dug her lengthening nails deep into her palms to keep from reaching through the mirror and strangling him.

"And what will you give me in return for this favor?"

Terona swallowed. Of course Dragos wanted payment for his assistance. "What do you desire?"

He stopped thumbing through the book and pierced her with his gaze again. "Nothing," he said. "I want nothing, but for you to assure me that this will end. That you yourself will take care of stopping the prophecies, for good."

"Of course, brother." She smiled.

Dragos waved his hand in dismissal of her. Terona balled her fists even tighter. Tiny droplets of blood hit the floor from her palms. "Return on the morrow and I will tell you where Sageren, heir to the throne, has been keeping himself."

"Thank you, Dragos," she said in a tight voice. Dragos pushed a stone and the mirror dulled to its normal sheen. When the surface of the mirror normalized, she stared at her reflection and admired the form she had chosen. Not as lovely as her natural form, but for a humanoid, it was definitely one of the better ones.

Terona covered the mirror, and left as quickly as she had come. She had much to do and only a day to get organized. She must gather a group.

A group that could not fail.

CHAPTER EIGHT

Sage took Dax out to hunt the following evening, and left him in Wolvenglen Forest with the wolves before racing to Snow's cabin. The thrill of seeing her made him run faster than normal. Even the fear of bloodlust overtaking him couldn't keep him away. In a lot of ways, she reminded him of a vampire. Her strong will and noble air were both refreshing and comforting.

He reached the cabin just as she did and they walked to the grove together. The moon was shadowed by clouds tonight, which played to his advantage. He'd moved too quickly with her before. He'd teased her and it was obvious that wasn't the way to win her trust. He needed to slow down.

In his years being away from the vampire courts, he'd forgotten what the highborn females were like. Living in a cave, even a Fae-made cave underground, with only decaying vampires to talk to, had caused his conduct to become lax. In exile, he'd forgotten the manners his mother had taught him. The thought of his mother made his chest tighten.

"Is something wrong?" Snow asked.

Her voice pulled him from his thoughts. "I was just thinking."

"Regretting that you came? I'll go easy on you, if it helps you feel better."

A sly smile crept across her face and it made him smile in return. "Thank you. I appreciate your concern for my ego, but I'll manage."

"I didn't think you'd come," she said.

"Why wouldn't I?"

She gave him a sly smile. "I figured you wouldn't want to be beaten by a mere girl again, Rake."

He smiled to himself. *Spirit. Such great spirit.*

They reached the grove and she stretched her arms, warming up. He followed suit, though he didn't need it.

"I'm surprised *you* came." He smiled.

"Why? It's my land, my cottage, and I've been coming here for years."

There it was, that backbone of hers that he liked so much. It was going to get her in trouble someday.

"Because you're a female, alone, in the dark with an unknown man. I could be anyone or anything."

"Like what? A Werewolf? A vampire?" She paused. "A dragon?" She laughed, hefted her sword and squared off. Then she nodded.

He circled her. "Suppose I am?"

"Then you would've killed me yesterday."

She advanced and he parried.

"Maybe I'm just a patient monster." He spun and jabbed, but she jumped out of the way.

"Then you'd have to be a really controlled monster, and that's something in Fairelle I *haven't* heard of. Besides, you're not menacing, or evil, or dripping in blood. You're just…"

He stopped moving. "Just what?"

She shrugged. "Plain."

"Plain? How positively insulting."

She laughed.

They sparred for several minutes. He taught her a new move and soon they were nose-to-nose with only swords between them.

She smiled. "Yup, even close up, I can see you're not a monster. You're just a rake." She pushed him away.

"A rake, love. Really? First I'm merely plain and now I'm a rake?" He clutched his heart. "You wound me to the core."

She chuckled. "Liar."

"A plain, lying, rake? I'm getting worse by the second."

"All right then. Tell me a truth."

He stared at her. He'd not played this game before with a female. He'd always just gotten what he wanted from them because of who he was without all the hassle of opening up and getting close. With her though, he wanted to be honest. To let her in. The mystery of why he wanted to gave him an uneasy sensation.

"What do you want to know?" he asked.

They continued their dance. Circling each other thrusting and parrying. He took a wild swing at her and she batted it away. Her sword play was improving.

"Tell me what you were thinking about when you arrived tonight," she said.

The questions stabbed him to the core. He didn't speak of his family to anyone.

"I was thinking..." He wanted to lie. "About my mother." He swallowed again at the thought.

She stopped circling and her expression grew serious. "My mother died a few years ago."

"Mine died—" he paused. "*Quite* a few years ago."

"You were young then?"

"Young enough."

They took a step away from each other and nodded for a break. She rubbed her sword arm and breathed heavily. He pretended to be winded.

"Let me get that for you." He took a step toward her, but she backed away.

"I'm capable of rubbing my own arm, thank you."

Too fast. He held back the disappointment at not being able to touch her and nodded. Why did she affect him so?

"So your mother? She was a good woman?" he asked.

Her smile was so genuine that her eyes sparkled with delight. "The best. She was kind and gentle. She had a wonderful sense of humor and loved everyone. She was quite generous."

"So she was like you then?"

Snow laughed and shook her head. "Oh no. I, unfortunately, am nothing like my mother."

"You could have surprised me."

"Oh, really? Because you know me so well?" She shook out her wrists. "What about your mother? What was she like?"

"Kind, but firm. She was gracious and lovely. I only ever heard her raise her voice a few times in my life. When she lived, everyone was welcome at our table."

Snow lifted her sword and nodded to begin. "And after she died?"

His gut clenched. "Let's just say things changed. I changed. As did my father. Not my brother, though. He stayed eager and fun as ever." *Until they were murdered by my uncle.*

"So you have other family?" She advanced and he backed up.

He didn't want to talk about it. "What about you? Do you have family?"

She attacked suddenly. The swiftness of her movement told him that the subject was closed to discussion.

"Let's get down to it, shall we?" he asked.

For an hour they sparred, until her moves became erratic. It had been a long time since he'd had a real practice session. With Sonya and Greeg, he ever only fought with his body. The vampiric art of fighting with hands and teeth was their chosen way. But fighting with a sword was his favorite.

After, Snow sprawled on the ground, catching her breath, and he sat near her, watching. Her chest rose and fell with rhythmical ease. The clouds parted and the moon shone down on her. In the dim light, her cheeks had taken on a beautiful pink hue. His gaze slid down her cheek to her neck. The vein pulsed with life at her throat. Beat after beat, he watched the vein throb. His fangs descended into his mouth, and he hopped to his feet and turned away.

"What's wrong?"

"I should go." *Yes, you should.* Things had gone well tonight. He had been able to control his hunger until that very moment. Hadn't even thought once of taking her blood. It was an improvement. Maybe

86

it was possible to be near her after all. But not right now. He grabbed his sword, sheathed it on his back, and walked to the edge of the glade.

"Will you come back tomorrow?" she called.

He paused. *No!* "Yes."

*****

Over the next two weeks, Snow spent her daylight hours in the house taking care of her brothers, and her nights in the glade with Sage. She found herself looking forward to the sessions more and more as the days passed.

For the first hour or so, they would spar, with him teaching her new moves and her questioning him about his life. His predatory stance, the way he tracked her when she moved, all told her that he was a formidable warrior, and if he really wanted to, he could be deadly. Yet he never did anything to make her feel in danger. Uncomfortable was a different story.

The smooth way he called her 'love' and the intimate way he looked at her should have sent her running home with blushing shame. Instead, she enjoyed the attention.

She'd determined that he had to be of noble blood. His extensive training was something only a nobleman could afford. And both his demeanor and manners were fine, though he tried to hide it. She'd asked him if he hailed from the south, but it had become obvious, that like hers, his answers were veiled. Never saying anything that would divulge who he really was.

She'd heard about his wonderful mother and his strong father. He told her about his travels around Fairelle. His fondness for wine and his abhorrence for scratchy clothing and bedding. They both talked about how they'd come to learn swordplay and where he'd gotten his favorite leather coat that he never seemed to be without. Through it all, though she knew there was something he hid, she'd begun to trust him.

It'd been a long time since she'd had someone to talk to besides her brothers. She hadn't seen Belle in almost a year, and with the servants gone... It was nice to have a conversation with someone without having to pretend to be something she wasn't.

Some nights after they sparred, they would sit for hours and just talk. Sometimes they talked about what they wanted from life, sometimes he would tell her stories and sometimes he would listen to her ramble about chores and housework or her birds in her aviary. He never pried, never scoffed, just listened.

Tonight as she rounded the bend and headed for her cabin, her heart fluttered at the thought of seeing him. She stopped abruptly. The feelings left her conflicted. She'd only meant to find a friend. How had she come to... care for Sage?

A shiver ran through her. She'd gotten close to a man once before and it had ended badly. Yes, she wanted to find a man, a husband, someone of her own, but faced with the possibility of having feelings for someone frightened her.

It had started out as a friend to spar with, someone to talk to. Yes, he was handsome, but he was also infuriating, and arrogant, kind and gentle. *No, no, no!* She covered her face with her hands. What had she been thinking sparring with him?

Her heart pounded in her chest and she turned for home. She couldn't let this happen. It wasn't supposed to be this way. She couldn't get close, couldn't let him in. She couldn't let *anyone* in. It was too dangerous for her brothers. If she left now and went home, would he look for her? Would he know where to find her? Panic caused her skin to itch.

"Evening."

She spun around and there he stood, leaning on the outside of her cabin, in his familiar long leather coat, his hair tied behind him. His handsome face hidden in shadow.

"Leaving so soon?"

"I..." She cleared her throat. Her stomach tightened and her heartbeat hammered in her chest. "Yes. I was thinking that maybe tonight isn't such a good night."

"Not feeling well?"

What could she say? Whatever she said would be a lie and he'd see right through it. "Something like that."

"Why don't we forgo the training tonight?" He pulled a satchel from his shoulder that she hadn't noticed. "How about a picnic instead?"

It was a bad idea. Her mind and her heart battled. Just the day before, everything had been fine. Why was today any different? Because she was suddenly seeing him and wondering how it would feel to be in his arms? She swallowed hard.

"Come on. I promise not to bite." He smiled and offered his hand.

She nodded, hugging herself instead. He dropped his hand and she followed him past the cabin and into the glade. He went to sit and she stopped him. "Not here."

They strolled north of the glade until they reached a large pond in the middle of a cluster of trees about a mile away. She moved to the edge of the pond and sat on the cool grass. He sat beside her and began pulling things out of his satchel. He set the food on the ground between them. There was cheese and fruit and bread and a skin of something to drink.

He stared at her for a minute before stretching out and looking at the pond. "So tell me something about yourself. Something that you've told no one else," he said.

"Why would I tell you that?" She picked a handful of berries and popped them into her mouth.

He shrugged. "Why not?"

"Because if I tell you, then maybe someday you'd hold it over me."

He plucked a blade of grass and twirled it between his fingers. "Do you think so little of me, love?"

"I don't think anything of you," she lied.

He cocked an eyebrow. "Truly? You don't think of me at all during the day?"

She shoved several berries in her mouth. "So where do you live?"

"North of here and to the west." He dropped the grass and tossed a rock into the pond. It skipped across the surface, making ripples as it went.

North and to the west? "But, that's the Daemonlands."

"Is it?"

He couldn't possibly live there. No one lived there. "So if you live in the Daemonlands, what do you do all day?"

"Sleep mostly. Sometimes I read, or talk to my companions. But mostly I sleep."

What kind of man slept all day? She sucked on a berry and he looked at her out of the corner of his eye. She threw a berry at him and hit him in the cheek.

"Hey!"

"You're lying," she said. "You don't live in the Daemonlands and sleep all day. You just don't want to tell me the truth." She shook her head and muttered, "Rake."

A slight smile turned up the corners of his mouth. "All right, you tell me what you do all day then. You've told me about cooking and cleaning and your birds, but surely you do more than that. Needlepoint and dancing lessons I suppose."

She snorted and then covered her mouth. "The season my mother forced me to take dancing lessons, I broke the instructor's foot by tripping him. And my needlepoint was so atrocious that my *father* begged her to let me stop."

He laughed so hard that he snorted in turn. Suddenly, they were both laughing. She grabbed her side as a cramp set in.

"Stop, stop," she cried, wiping the tears from her face. She took several deep breaths and tried to focus. When the laughing died down, she noticed him staring at her again. The same stare he'd given her before. Butterflies formed in her stomach and she looked away.

"My brother, Flint, tried to teach me to dance for a while. Problem was, he was no better than I. So together, we were horrible." She sighed and shrugged. "I don't dance nor do needlepoint. I can cook well enough, and I've learned how to clean in more ways than I care to, but reading is what I enjoy most. Besides fighting."

"So you like books then? What kind? History books?"

Her jaw dropped. "Do you really think that I'm the kind of old spinster that would sit around all day reading history books?"

He shrugged. "Why not?"

She dropped her jaw in mock offense. "Was that an insult, sir? See, I told you. You are a rake."

"Touché."

"So you admit it, then?"

He paused. "I admit that in the past I have been a scoundrel and selfish and self-serving. But now, I try to be better."

She watched his serious expression and her cheeks heated at his unspoken innuendo. The truth in his eyes and in his words touched her. He'd let her in.

She flopped onto her stomach, propping herself up on her elbows. "To tell the truth, yes, I do enjoy history books. I find learning about Fairelle and how it came to be fascinating."

He rolled on his side and faced her. "What do you like the most?"

"Just the fact that we used to be all one kingdom. We became divided because of hatred and greed. I can't imagine that happening in a family. Brothers fighting for power. What kind of person would value power and possessions more than family?"

Sage looked out over the pond. His face held the same sorrow that she'd seen before. She watched him for several minutes as he became lost in thought.

"Is that what happened to you? You said you lost everything."

He turned his gaze to her, but didn't speak.

"I'm sorry," she said. "I didn't mean to upset you."

"It's not you that's upset me."

She wanted to make it better, to retract the words that made him think of his sorrows. She picked up a grape and threw it at him. The grape hit him in the eye and a smile crept across his face.

"So that's how you want to play, is it?"

He moved to sit up, but before he could, she took off running. She laughed as she went and ran straight into the trees.

CHAPTER NINE

Sage tracked her movements, his instincts kicking into overdrive while watching her race away. He was up on his feet in an instant. He caught sight of her dark braid swinging as she ran, and then it disappeared.

He raced to the other side of the pond and took a deep breath. Her scent traveled north. The sounds of her feet crunching over leaves and rocks echoed around him. He sprinted forward.

"You can't find me," she called.

He smiled. He hadn't had a good chase in a long while. He tore into the moonlit woods, his fangs aching to be let free. Arousal overtook him. He wanted her. He'd never held out so long for a female before, and though he'd enjoyed the past weeks with her more than any other in his long life, he wanted her for his own.

"I'm over here," she called.

He swung to his right. The game had him wanting her more than ever. She was his perfect blend of sass and heart. And the scent of her blood was something he couldn't ignore.

A snap sounded to his left. He whirled in that direction and inhaled. *Vampires.*

All thoughts of the game left him and panic lodged in his chest. He needed to get her to safety. Racing, he bounded over logs and rocks trying to find her. He scanned the area, but couldn't locate her.

"Snow," he whispered. "Snow!"

A tinkle of laughter floated toward him and he continued north. The scent of the vampires grew stronger. He picked up speed. He needed to get to her. A flash of blue glowed to the left. Sage looked over in time to see a male and female vampire heading in the same direction.

He dodged a tree and leapt to the left. Sprinting toward the vampires, he came upon them from behind. He pulled the Cris knife from the back of his belt and threw it. The blade hit the female between the shoulders. She cried out, and stumbled to her knees. Her comrade stopped. His gaze locked on Sage and bared his fangs. Sage's fangs descended into his mouth.

"Well, well, well," said the male. "This should be fun." He ran at Sage. The two collided next to the female, who was trying to remove the protruding knife.

Sage slashed at the male with his nails, opening a wound on his chest. The male swung at Sage, but missed.

He had to act fast. Snow had to have heard the female's cry.

Wasting no time, Sage yanked the Cris knife from the downed vampire and stabbed the second one in the heart. The male gasped and sputtered.

"No!" cried the female.

Sage took the vampire's head off. The body fell to the ground in a heap.

"Sage?" Snow called.

His head whipped up. *Damn.* She was coming back.

He jumped on the second vampire, knocking her on her back and slashing her throat with the Cris. The female's eyes widened, then dimmed.

Sage got to his feet quickly and wiped the blade on his pants. The sounds of Snow moving toward him had him rushing north to meet her. He didn't want her seeing the mess he'd made. He shoved the Cris knife into his belt.

"Sage, where are you?" she called.

He was less than twenty feet away. She turned in a circle, her braid swinging behind her. He ran up to her and threw his hands over her eyes.

She screamed and elbowed him in the stomach. The air whooshed out of him and he doubled over.

"It's me," he groaned. "It's just me."

She spun around and slapped him on the shoulder. "My toth! Where have you been? You startled me."

"Sorry." He laughed. "I was hiding. I thought that was the game."

Her eyebrows knit together. "The game is where the first person to run off is the person who hides. *You* were supposed to find *me*."

"Oh, sorry. It's been a while since I've played." He scanned the area and took a deep breath. All he could smell was her. "Come here, love." He opened his arms.

"Why?"

"So I can hug you." *So I can rub my scent all over you so no one else can smell you. And so I can make sure you're really all right.* He shook with fear. What if he hadn't been fast enough? What if they'd gotten to her before he could? What if she'd seen what he really was? The fear of what might have happened to her awoke his protective instincts.

96

She lifted an eyebrow. "I said you startled me, not that you scared me. I'm not a child."

"Well, maybe I'm scared and I need a hug."

She rolled her eyes. "Come on, it's late. I should get going." She walked past him and he reached out and grabbed her hand.

She stopped and looked down at it and then up into his face. He wanted to pull her close and feel her body press against his. At that moment, there was nothing more important in the world than making sure she was really safe.

He pushed a stray hair behind her ear.

She slipped her hand from his and gave him a small smile. "Rake," she teased.

"Come on, love," he said. "Let's get you to bed."

On the walk to the pond, all of his senses were alight for danger. Her cabin was only a few short miles from where the vampires had been. If he hadn't been here... He didn't even want to think about it. Her skills had improved, but she was still no match for a vampire who really wanted to kill her. Especially if there was more than one.

*****

Snow glanced sideways at Sage. His mood was tense. She wasn't sure what had happened, but sometime between the pond and now, something had occurred that upset him.

They reached the abandoned picnic and began gathering their things.

"I think maybe we should take a few days off," Sage said. "I have some things to attend to."

97

"Oh." She tried to keep the disappointment from her voice.

He put the last of the bread and cheese into his satchel and stood.

They stared at each other for several minutes and again she got a flutter in her belly. It was probably a good thing to take a break, at least from each other anyway. She was getting too close.

"So I'll be here, practicing, if you find your way back this direction in the near future," she said.

He was in front of her so fast she barely saw him move. "No. You need to take a break from practicing."

"What? Why?"

He grabbed her by the arm. "Trust me, you need a break. The area isn't safe out here."

She shook her head. "What do you mean? What happened out there? You're not telling me something."

"Nothing." He let go.

She grabbed the sleeve of his coat. "Tell me," she said. "You can tell me anything."

He scooped her into his arms without a word and pulled her close. The butterflies in her stomach soared at the feel of his hard body. His skin was surprisingly cool beneath his shirt.

"Promise me you'll take a break," he whispered into her hair. "Just for a few days. You've worked hard. Get some rest. And I'll meet you at the cabin in a week or so."

A week? It'd feel like a year.

He pushed her to arm's length and leveled his aquamarine gaze with hers. "Promise me," he demanded.

98

She swallowed hard. He'd never asked her for anything before. "I promise."

He tugged her into another hug and kissed her hair. She wrapped her arms around him and closed her eyes. His body felt so good pressed against her. He let go and walked off into the trees without a word.

She stared at the spot he'd disappeared into, wanting to follow him. Instead, she grabbed her sword and headed for home. As she walked, an image flashed into her mind of Sage in the glade, with her. His aquamarine eyes staring at her hard. His voice drifted into her mind. *"You won't remember."*

Sage waited just inside the trees and hid from view. She had such a strong spirit, every minute he spent with her was one more minute he risked falling for her. Who was he kidding? He'd already fallen. The need to protect her grew at an alarming pace.

Vampires didn't venture into the meadowlands and farmlands often, but he couldn't take a chance. The male and female that he'd killed would've made their way down there if he hadn't found them first. How they'd gotten past Dax and the wolves was anyone's guess. Most likely they'd come through the Daemonlands, which was his fault. Instead of patrolling the border, he'd been spending time with her. He needed help. He needed to tell Sonya and the others.

Snow turned from the pond and headed south. He followed at a comfortable distance and she never once glanced back.

He followed her past the cabin and through the trees that separated the farmlands from the glade. The smell of humans made his skin itch. He hadn't been this far south in decades.

After walking for several miles, she trudged up the hill of an enormous, two-story manor house. He hid by the corner of an aviary and watched her climb a rope to a second floor window and slide inside.

Sage surveyed the property. So, she was a woman of means. From the look of the lands, her family was the ruling family, or close there to.

A series of whinnies came from a large stable to his right. He turned, catching a scent that made the hairs on his neck prickle.

A sinking feeling churned in the pit of his stomach as he moved toward the stable. He pulled the door open with a creak. His vampiric sight registered eight stalls, holding eight pitch-black steeds inside. He walked from stall to stall, his anxiety building. The horses pawed the ground with fear as he passed. They knew what he was.

At the end of the row, a lone door waited. Dreading what he would find, Sage opened it. He blew out a long, low groan. Seven black cloaks hung on hooks. Seven sets of black clothing and black boots lay by the cloaks on a bench. He stared for several minutes, unable to move. Snow lived with the Vampire Slayers. How could it get any worse?

CHAPTER TEN

The following day had been almost normal for Snow, except for the loneliness she already felt, knowing she wouldn't be seeing Sage. She spent time in her aviary, feeding her finches and canaries. After lunch, the Westfall Magistrate, as well as the family landlord, stopped by to meet with Erik and deliver the monthly rent payments from their tenant farmers. When she brought in tea and cakes, she overheard the landlord mention that several townspeople had gone missing. A phenomenon that had apparently become more frequent in Westfall.

Later, a tenant stopped by with a dispute and Flint went to mediate the problem.

It was close to seven in the evening when a sharp knock on the front door pulled Snow's attention from her stew pot.

"Erik! Door," she called, peeling potatoes and putting them into a pot of boiling water.

Another knock.

"Jamen! Door," she yelled, cutting another potato.

A third knock sounded.

"Hass, Ian, Kellan, Gerall!"

Still no reply. *Grrr.* Did she have to do everything?

Snow hastily dried her hands on a towel and then stomped to the entrance. She threw the door wide and for a second she was taken aback. A huge, tan man with piercing hazel eyes and shoulder length blond hair stood on her front steps. His scruffy face was ruggedly handsome. He gave her a tight smile as she stared, completely forgetting her manners.

"Hello?" he finally said, eyebrows raised.

She cleared her throat and smiled, remembering herself. "Sorry. May I help you?"

"Yes, I am looking for the man of the house."

"Of course. May I tell him who's asking?"

"My name is Dax."

"Do you want to come in, Dax?" She stepped aside, gesturing for him to enter.

"No thank you, my lady. I'll just wait here."

"Just a moment," Snow said, a bit flustered.

He nodded. For all of his enormous height and girth, she got the impression he was more of a gentle giant.

She looked at him once more before heading up the stairs. Ascending the staircase, her brothers' raucous laughter floated down to greet her. She marched down to the end of the landing and threw the door to her parents' old room wide. The noise stopped immediately. Her brothers sat at a large table playing cards, in various states of undress. Several bottles of ale stood open on the table. Kellan was telling one of his usual stories.

"And so the baker says—"

"I'm trying to make your dinner while you're all up here, playing. Did you not hear me yelling?" Snow huffed.

Kellan's face fell and he set down his cards, his story forgotten. "Sorry."

One by one, her brothers got up from their game and threw on their shirts.

"Gerall, Kellan, set the table," Erik ordered. "Jamen, go help in the kitchen. Hass and Ian, clean this up."

"You'll have to finish telling us later," Hass whispered, as Ian clapped Kellan on the shoulder.

Snow turned and headed for the stairs. "There's someone at the door."

Sometimes she felt like her mother, having to take care of all of them. Difference was, she was the youngest.

Erik met her at the staircase and followed her down. "Who's here?"

"Someone named Dax."

"Do we know him?"

"I don't believe so." She reached the bottom step and turned to go to the kitchen when Erik grabbed her hand.

"Sorry," he whispered in her ear. "I know you didn't ask for this job."

She gave him a half-hearted smile. Erik pulled her into a hug and then let her go. She moved into the solar and Erik greeted their visitor, who still shadowed their doorway. Kellan and Gerall were busy setting the table. Flint had returned from the village and sliced potatoes in the kitchen, while Jamen peeled them.

She walked over to check on the meat.

"I already checked it, little sister. Looks great," said Flint.

"Tastes great, too." Jamen smiled at her.

"Really, Jamen? You couldn't wait?" she asked in mock irritation.

"Not with how you cook." When he smiled, a boyish dimple that she hadn't seen in months appeared on his right cheek.

She couldn't stay mad at them.

Erik strode in with a letter in his hand and the smile vanished from her face.

"What is it?" she asked.

"We need to have a meeting." Erik looked from Flint to Jamen.

Snow didn't like the tone of his voice.

*****

Dax walked across the front lawn and through the gate to the road where Sage waited.

"How did it go?"

"I don't think he was very happy, but he said they would be there," Dax said.

"Good." Now more than ever, he needed the Slayers on his side. If there were any hope–

"I saw her." Dax broke into his thoughts. "The one you spoke of. She answered the door. She's quite beautiful. I think she might be married to the head of the household."

A surge of jealousy raced through Sage. *Married?* The very thought that she might belong to another had never occurred to him. Probably because before now, it'd never mattered when it came to women. He had taken any female without discrimination. But at the prospect of finding someone he wanted, it was different. Because he was different.

"Did you hear me?"

"I heard. Come on, let's get moving." Sage headed north.

"Tell me again why you couldn't have just walked up there to talk to them." Dax kept pace.

"Because I'm a vampire and they're Slayers. Their job is to kill me, and if they find out I've seen her, I won't even have time to explain."

Sage took off at a run, with Dax at his heels. He planned to meet the Slayers near the southern border of the Were King Adrian's woods.

"So what's the plan?"

"Meet with them and try and convince them not to kill me?"

"Sounds challenging."

"The enemy of my enemy is my friend." Sage grinned.

"Under the circumstances, I doubt they will agree with that philosophy."

"Then I'll have to make them agree."

Dax might be right. But Sage knew that if he succeeded, it would turn the tide in the war and possibly, his life. And he'd finally avenge his father, his brother, and take back what was rightfully his. *Tanah Darah.*

It was time. Sage cracked his neck and rolled his shoulders, trying to loosen the tension that had been mounting the last hours.

"Are you sure I shouldn't get Adrian?" Dax asked for the third time.

"I don't want the Slayers to think I've come prepared for a fight. I just want to talk."

105

Dax shook his head uneasily. "I still think this is a bad idea."

Sage laughed. "Is there a good way to convince people hell-bent on killing you not to?"

Dax chuckled. "Probably not."

It was the first time Sage had seen Dax laugh. "You've told me you have dreams of where you were from. Maybe I can help piece it together. What do you remember of your dreams?" Sage asked.

"Nothing much," replied Dax. "Flashes. Images. A woman with dark hair. A silken bed. Pain..." Dax looked off for a moment before speaking again. "But every once in a while, I have a memory of girl. Maybe fourteen or so. Beautiful and kind. Those are always followed by an image of a giant shadow and then... there's nothing."

"And you want to find her? This girl?"

Dax stared off for a minute. "Yes. I get the feeling I need to, but my gut tells me that if I do, I'll bring danger to her."

The sound of approaching hoof beats reached Sage's ears. They slowed at the edge of the woods, and then stopped. He couldn't see the Slayers yet, but he smelled them. He hadn't told Dax, but the aroma of their blood had been another reason he hadn't wanted to meet in their home. Though it was purely masculine, and he had never been attracted to the scent of male blood, its purpose was to entice and distract vampires, which it did well.

The animal blood isn't holding off the cravings as long as it should, Sage realized.

Several sets of heavy footsteps entered the wood. He watched the dark shapes fan out. The youngest looking took position high in a tree, his bow at the ready. The shortest stopped on top of a rock. Twin forms, with shaggy blond hair, hung back. The remaining three, a tall blond, an even taller and broader brown-haired man and a thin male with glasses walked underneath the tree where Sage and Dax waited.

"You got us here, vampire," said a blond one.

Sage continued to watch the men whisper among themselves. They appeared so normal. Ordinary. But he couldn't underestimate them. These men were not mere humans; they were lethal, as he'd witnessed first-hand.

"If this is a trick, it won't end well for you," the taller, dark-haired, scruffy slayer said, spitting on the ground.

Sage's eyes narrowed in anger at the disrespect. The spitting signified the wishing of a person's crops to drown. It was a bad omen.

The blond Slayer grabbed the dark-haired one by the arm. "That's not very helpful, Flint."

The spitter, Flint, shrugged.

In a fluid movement, Sage jumped to the ground and leaned casually against the tree. The three men in the front drew their swords. The blond, who appeared to be the leader, was a head shorter than the spitter.

"You called us here." The leader gestured toward Sage. "Why?"

"An allegiance." Sage, wiped at his nose, trying to rid himself of their scent.

"With a vampire? Never," said Flint.

"I can handle this," the leader said, his eyes never leaving Sage. "You're the vampire we saw with the wolves."

"My name is Sageren. Prince Sage to my friends."

"A prince?" said Flint. "We should kill him, Erik, and be a step closer to our goal."

"And what is your goal, *Erik*?" asked Sage.

"We are bound to eradicate all vampires."

"By whom?"

Erik exchanged a look with Flint and the man with glasses. "We don't know."

"So, someone came to you and magicked you with the abilities of Slayers, yet you never asked why?"

"She didn't really give us the chance." The man pushed his glasses up his nose.

"What exactly did she say?" Sage folded his arms. The legend of whomever had started the Slayers was a mystery. They had to be very old as Slayers hadn't been seen in ages.

"That we were being given a gift to help rid Fairelle of the root of evil in Tanah Darah."

"So the person didn't specifically say vampires, then?"

The three men exchanged a look. "She said we should begin with the vampires."

Interesting. "Well then, we have a common goal." Sage smiled.

"How do you figure?" Flint crossed his arms over his broad chest.

"I was forced into exile by my uncle, Philos, the new vampire king, after he murdered my family. I'm interested in avenging that wrong."

"And why should we help you?" asked Erik.

"Because until my uncle took the throne, Slayers hadn't been needed in a thousand years. My father was a good man. Not a great man, but a good man, and fair to his people. Hunting in the farmlands wasn't allowed. There were no wars with the wolves."

"And now?"

"And now, *I* alone have a truce with the wolves."

"So if you have the wolves, I ask again, why should we help you?" asked Flint.

"You've heard of the prophecies. The first has been fulfilled. The Sisterhood of Red has returned to their mates in Wolvenglen. Next is the prophecy concerning my kind. The prophecies being fulfilled will reunite all of Fairelle and bring peace. For humans, Vampires, Fae, Mages, dragon, Nereids, everyone."

"But what's the fun in that?" called a new voice.

Sage's blood chilled. Spinning around, he faced a group of newcomers as they strode into the clearing from behind. He blinked twice, trying to believe what he saw. Seven vampires appeared from the dark.

"Remus," Sage whispered. His emotions ran the gamut. He wanted to hug Remus, punch him in the face and fall to the ground and thank the gods. All at the same moment. His brother was alive! All these years, alive and living in Tanah Darah as a prisoner to their Uncle Philos.

"Hello, brother," answered Remus.

Sage's knees threatened to buckle as happiness and confusion swept over him. "But–You're dead. They said you were dead. That Philos killed you, alongside father."

"Oh no, brother. I assure you, I'm not." Remus smiled a broad, toothy grin, making Sage shiver. "I'm alive and well, and reaping the rewards of being faithful to our uncle's cause."

Sage tried to comprehend the words. Remus had been faithful to Philos? A familiar lump clogged Sage's throat and his cousin Garot's last words – before Sage had beheaded him – replayed in his mind, *"You have no idea how many traitors were in your father's house."*

Sage's chest tightened. How was it possible? What had Remus done? "You betrayed our father," his voice hardened. "You betrayed me." He could barely contain his rage. For decades, he had mourned the loss of his father and brother, only to find Remus had been alive, under the protection of Philos, the murderer. He'd watched as Philos had slaughtered their family and friends. Preyed upon the Sisterhood of Red, and fed on any human they found.

"Yes. And I've come to finish it. Thank you for inviting the Slayers, by the way. We can get this over with in one fell swoop. And don't they smell delicious? How on Earth can you resist them, Sage?" Remus' fangs gleamed.

Remus had half a dozen vampires with him whom that Sage didn't recognize. Their eyes glowed like embers in the night. Something was wrong with them. *Different.*

"What have you done, Remus?" Sage asked.

Remus smiled. "Sold my soul to a daemon."

"You tricked us," a Slayer yelled from behind Sage. Before he could respond, an arrow flew from a tree, hitting one of Remus' vampires in the throat. The vampire didn't dissolve; he simple yanked the arrow out and attacked.

Remus laughed and jumped on Sage, taking him to the ground. Dax roared from somewhere above and the ground shook as he crashed to the forest floor.

"The werebear," said Remus, momentarily distracted. "I've heard about him."

Sage kicked Remus off and flipped to his feet. He jerked the Cris knife from his waistband.

Remus' eyes widened. "Uncle will be most pleased when I return that to him."

The two circled each other as all around them vampires and Slayers fought. Sage's gaze drifted over to the battle; it wasn't going well for the Slayers. The vampires weren't dying.

"What have you done?" Sage asked again.

"Me? Nothing. However, I do believe a bit of magick was employed to enhance our brethren."

"They are not my brothers," Sage said.

Remus attacked with a ferocity Sage had never known his younger brother to possess. The two fought, equally matched, for the first time. Remus' skills had improved. Using the ancient art of vampiric fighting, they fought with his fists and feet, nails and teeth. Remus kept Sage at bay through stealth and agility, rather than force.

"Did Philos make you do this?" He punched Remus in the gut.

"No," Remus laughed. "I volunteered." Remus lunged at Sage, swiping with sharp nails at his chest, but Sage spun out of the way.

Dax cried out, trying to dislodge a vampire from his neck.

In the distraction, Remus grabbed Sage from behind, climbed onto his back and raked a long nail across Sage's throat. Blood poured from the wound. Sage sucked in a bubbly breath as white hot pain scorched his skin. He threw his head back and his skull smashed into Remus' nose. Grabbing Remus by the neck, Sage wrenched free and hurled Remus into the nearest tree. Remus landed with a crash. Sage took the advantage, jumping on top of him, holding a Cris to his brother's throat.

"Why, Remus?" Sage's body shook. "Why?"

"Because I am the one prophesied to change the fate of our people. I will be the one to make the blood flow free. I will be hailed the conquering hero, not you. For once, not you, and not father. And when Philos is dead," Remus replied. "I'll bathe in virgin's blood. I'll get everything."

"What are you talking about? You aren't the one from the prophecy."

"*The blood shall cease to flow and the land will grow dry, until the ones, once thought extinct, join the fight. Then will the change come like a wave and ever again the lands will be fruitful, as old alliances are reforged.* I am the one once thought extinct."

Someone had been filling Remus' head with lies.

Remus kneed Sage in the groin. Pain shot through his body and he crumpled to his knees, dropping the Cris. He gasped for air and his stomach lurched from the burn between his legs. Remus crawled out from beneath him as Sage tried to suck air into his lungs. Remus grabbed the Cris and Sage got to his feet.

The two circled each other, stumbling and panting.

"It doesn't have to be this way. You can still join me." Sage sucked in large gulps of air but the burn of being kick suffocated him still.

"Join you for what? To be your puppet again? To always lurk in your shadow and to always feel second best? Why would I want that when I can be king!"

"I would share, Remus."

"You say that now, brother. Now that you've spent years in exile without the comforts of your home, but we both know the truth."

Sage hesitated. How had Remus fallen so far? What had he done to be so hated his brother? "Remus, you aren't the one in the prophesy. Whoever told you that is lying. Listen to me. I'm so–"

"Don't!" Remus ran straight into Sage, and stabbed him in the stomach. "Don't you dare feel sorry for me. I don't need your pity."

Sage's vision blurred, and pain shot through his gut. Shoving him backward, Remus pounced on top of him. Images flashed before him. Images of himself and Remus playing as children. Happy with their father and mother. Sharing their first drink together.

Remus poised above him, ready to strike. "You are the weak one, Sage. Not me. Not anymore. I will be hailed the hero for having finally killed you."

Sage lay motionless on the ground. His heart sunk into his stomach. At that moment, he wished he were dead like his father. Like his mother. So as not to have to witness what his brother had become.

An ivory blur of movement flashed from the trees and knocked Remus aside. A cold wind whipped across Sage's body. He stared up into the night sky. Clouds floated above, and stars twinkled without a care, unaware of the heartbreak and pain that took place below them.

A tree-rattling roar reverberated through the trees, and then the sound of crunching bones and tearing. Sage lay, unable to move, listening to Remus' screams as Dax tore at him. Finally the screams stopped and he sucked in a ragged breath.

His neck wound slowly sealed shut. Bloody tears dripped from his eyes as he continued to stare upward. He had loved his brother, and for over fifty years had mourned and held the guilt of not saving Remus. And all those years his brother had hated him. Had cursed Sage, and had awaited the day when he could kill him.

An arrow whizzed by Sage and lodged in the ground next to him. He rolled over, surveying the scene: Several vampires lay beheaded on the ground. The Slayers fought with all they had, and so far their numbers remained strong. They cut down the remaining vampires two at a time. Dax lumbered to his side and stood over Sage protectively. One after another, the vampires fell to the earth, but not without cost. The largest Slayer, Flint, wielded the Cris without mercy. As if possessed, he attacked with a fury Sage had never before seen. The Cris knife seemed to be the only way to kill these enhanced vampires. It took magick to fight magick.

When the battle ended, the slayers surveyed the damage before spotting Dax and Sage.

"You did this," Flint bellowed.

"No." Sage tried to get to his feet, but slipped back to the ground. "They weren't here for you."

Flint ran at Sage.

Dax stepped between them and roared.

"Flint! Stop!" Erik grabbed him around the waist.

"We should kill him. Maybe then they'll stick to their own lands."

"You could kill me, and leave me on their doorstep, and they will still come," gasped Sage.

"Flint, don't," came a young voice from the rear of the group. The archer in the tree dropped to the ground below. "He didn't–"

A vampire sprung from the ground and grabbed the young slayer from behind. Four arrows stuck out of the vampire's chest and his throat sported a gash from ear-to-ear, but still he lived. The young Slayer's eyes widened in surprise. His brother's looked on, frozen. The vampire sunk his teeth into the Slayer's throat and drew from him twice before tearing it out.

The men shouted in horror and rushed as a group toward their brother. With a swift twist, the vampire broke the Slayer's neck and vanished into the trees. The body slumped to the ground. The twin Slayers and Flint tore into the trees after the vampire. Erik and the tall one with glasses, rushed to their fallen comrade. Their peals of anguish pierced Sage.

"Kellan! Kellan," Erik roared, gathering up the young man.

"Let me look," said the other.

"Kellan," Erik cried again. His howls of torment were a horror to hear.

The second brother felt for a pulse, but Sage knew it was no use. The boy's lifeless gaze stared up at the canopy of branches above them. He was dead.

So young. Sage's thoughts turned immediately to Snow. He wished he could go to her, hold her, and comfort her.

The other men crashed through the trees, fell to their knees and cried over the body. Sage pushed Dax's stomach to get the bear to move. Weakly, he clutched at Dax's side, trying to keep on his feet. His dark blood seeped into Dax's white fur, staining it. The bleeding on Sage's throat had slowed, as had his stomach wound, but he'd lost a lot of blood.

"I'm sorry for your loss," said Sage.

The Slayers looked up at him and got to their feet.

Dax growled and lumbered from foot to foot. Sage knew he wanted to leave. "I, too, have lost family at the hands of my uncle, Philos."

"Your family just killed our brother," said Erik.

"No." Sage shook his head. "Those were not my family. Not anymore."

"It doesn't matter. You're mine, bloodsucker!" Flint ran at Sage.

A series of howls sounded close by. In a flash, a dozen wolves entered the fray and formed a protective circle around Sage and Dax. Two giant reds stood at the front. Redlynn shifted into human form, her flame colored hair covering her down to her thighs. Angus shifted and stood beside her. The Slayers retreated from the sight.

"I am queen Redlynn of Wolvenglen, and this is my father, Angus."

"Step away, and let us avenge our brother," said Erik.

"Sage did not kill your brother." Redlynn stood her ground.

"He is a bloodsucker, in league with the others," said Flint.

"No. He isn't. I know that first-hand." Redlynn's voice gentled. "Take your beloved brother and depart from my lands. Give him a warrior's burial and mourn his unfortunate passing. I respect your calling, but this is my land and I make the rules here. Those who come in peace are welcome, but those who mean harm are not."

"We trespass anywhere that vampires lurk," said Flint, taking a step closer, his knuckles white on the hilt of his Cris.

Angus slid in front of Redlynn and the wolves behind her snapped and growled. Redlynn placed a hand on Angus' shoulder.

"I understand the pain you feel; I have been there," she said. "But do not take my compassion for weakness. Take your brother, honor his life and when you're clearer headed, you are welcome to seek us out and council with us for an alliance, just as Prince Sage has. But know this: if you harm Prince Sage or the werebear Dax, you will have made enemies of the wolves. And calling or no calling, that is a war you will not win."

The Slayers stood for several minutes. Finally, the one with glasses said, "Come on, we need to get Kellan home to Snow."

Sage's gut clenched at the mention of her name.

117

The Slayers gathered their things. As they carried their brother from the woods, Flint turned and pointed the Cris at Sage.

"This isn't over between us, Bloodsucker."

The men disappeared, and Sage was in a worse position than before he had called them out. Bodies of the fallen vampires lay strewn on the ground. Sage, Dax and the wolves waited for the Slayers' horses to leave before they relaxed.

"Sage." Redlynn shook her head and looked over him. "What are we going to do with you? You're a mess."

"Nice to see you too, Red," Sage replied with a weak smile.

She walked closer and touched his face. Her golden eyes met his. "You need to feed."

"I'll be all right. I'll get a rabbit or something." He smiled again, his defense against the pain. *Just smile.*

"I think you are going to require something bigger than that." She looked at two wolves. "Paulo, Christos, find a buck and bring it for Prince Sage." They nodded and took off into the woods. "Sit," Redlynn said, putting his arm over her shoulder and helping him to a rock. "It's a good thing we went out for a run tonight and heard Dax's call."

"Thank you," Sage said to Dax.

Dax shifted into human form and sat next to him. "I'm gonna need some new clothes."

Sage nodded.

"I'll take care of the bodies." Sage gazed at the dead vampires and wondered how they'd become so strong. He tried not to look for

Remus. His heart couldn't bear the thought of seeing his brother's dead body, mangled on the ground.

So much death because of his uncle, and once again, he'd lost his brother. Though Remus hated him, he just couldn't bring himself to hate Remus in return. Unable to hold off any longer, Sage glanced over to the spot where Remus' body lay. His eyes widened in surprise.

"What is it?" Redlynn turned to look.

"My brother," Sage said. "He's gone."

CHAPTER ELEVEN

Snow tried to relax on the couch in her father's library and read a book, but she found herself glancing up at the clock every few minutes. The fact that she wouldn't be able to practice or even see Sage had her irritated. But with her brothers' sudden disappearance, she was more antsy than before.

Why had she promised Sage she wouldn't go to her cabin? He was not her husband. She grumbled and looked down at her book once more, not seeing the words on the page.

After Dax appeared, her brothers had spoken in private. Then they'd left, saying they would return soon. She was accustomed to her brothers going out for meetings with the magistrate or other officials of Westfall, but they always told her where they would be. Tonight they hadn't.

For the first time, the silence of the manor house made Snow uneasy. She'd gone to her room to nap, and when she awoke, it was ten pm and they still had not returned. She'd picked up a book in an effort to occupy both her mind and her nerves.

The sound of her brothers' horses galloping toward the house broke into her thoughts and the clock chimed midnight. Several pairs of boots crunched on the gravel. The door swung inward and she looked up.

"It's about time. I–" Snow stopped short at the sight of Flint, Hass and Ian. They were torn, battered and bruised. Dropping her book, she rushed toward them. "What happened? Why are you in your fighting clothes?"

The three brothers moved to her in unison, crushing her between them.

She laughed lightly. "Come on, there's no reason to be squeezing me to death. What's going on?" Their bodies quaked, and fear skittered up her spine. "Flint," she choked. "What's going on?"

She grabbed onto her brothers, tears beginning to fall. Something bad had happened. Hass, Ian and Flint released her. Gerall and Jamen waited somberly. Jamen held his cradled his arm and Gerall had a slash across his face and neck.

Snow looked from brother to brother. "Where's Erik?" she whispered. "Where's Kellan?"

"I'm here." Erik's voice floated in from behind Gerall and Jamen. The two brothers parted and Snow's heart went cold. Erik held Kellan in his arms. Her mind glazed and she swayed on her feet. Hass threw out a protective arm so she didn't fall. Kellan wasn't moving. His legs dangled with Erik's movements and hit the doorjamb with a thud. His head hung at an odd angle and lolled as Erik entered the room.

"No," she said. "No, it's not possible." She wrenched out of Hass's grip, tripping over her own feet. Strong arms caught her as she crumpled to the floor. Her ears buzzed and her temples pounded. Her mind caught up with the reality of what was before her; it slammed into her with the force of hitting a wall. "NO!" she screamed. "Kellan!"

Tears streamed down her cheeks and she tried to claw her way free from the arms that bound her. She tried to propel her body from the floor, but she couldn't get up, her legs wouldn't hold her. Her soul

121

ripped apart. No longer conscious of her screams, she stared at Erik whose own tears flowed like rain.

Her brothers surrounded her in a cocoon of bodies. All of them pressed into her, holding her, shedding tears of their own as they tried to soothe her. Erik joined the group, laying Kellan on the floor. She leaned over him and placed her forehead on his bloodied chest. *So young. Kellan was so young.* Her sweet, tender brother, who'd desired nothing more than to please and bring happiness, was dead.

Her brothers kept a vigil with her as she wept and watched over Kellan's body waiting, hoping he would breathe again. Finally, when she had no more tears, Flint picked her up and carried her upstairs.

He put her on the bed, slipped off her shoes and pulled up the sheets. After covering her with a blanket, Flint turned to leave.

"Flint," she said, finally meeting his eye. "Don't go."

His haggard expression held even more pain than usual. "Of course, little sister."

He sat next to her on top of the covers. She placed her cheek on his arm. There was a soft knock and she looked over to see Gerall. No words were spoken, but she pressed closer to Flint. Gerall came around the bed and lay on the other side of her. Soon all of her brothers gathered. They sat on the floor, her chair, her trunk, and stared off at nothing. Out the window. At the floor, the walls. No one spoke. Every once in a while, she heard a sniffle or shuddered breath, but no words. Hours passed and she drifted in and out of a fitful sleep. Her mind played and replayed special moments that she and Kellan had shared.

Playing as kids near the creek. Him teaching her to play chess, and her trying to teach him needlepoint.

She awoke at to find her brothers sleeping. Erik leaned on her bedroom door, a knife clutched in his fist. Her other brothers lay everywhere, covered with blankets, obviously something Erik had done. Gerall snored softly next to her. Flint, wide awake, watched her with a strange expression.

"What?" she whispered.

He shook his head.

She took a deep breath and her nostrils filled with the scents of her brothers. She smelled the sweat, blood and forest on them. She rubbed her nose at the strength of it.

"You guys reek," she mouthed.

Flint continued to stare at her. "I know."

Erik stirred at the sound of Flint's voice and got to his feet. Flint stood from the bed and Snow slid out. She walked to Erik and embraced him tightly. He held her close and kissed the top of her head.

"He was brave tonight, Snow," he said into her hair. "So brave."

Erik's shoulders heaved. Sobs wracked him. She hugged him tighter and spoke words of comfort. Soon all of her brothers were up. They gathered again in a group hug.

*****

The buck's blood helped Sage enough to close the wounds, but he knew it would be days before he fully healed. He needed a place to hole up and wait until he was better before returning to the den. The others would question him to no end if they saw him this way. And if he told them the truth, they would be out before sunrise trying to avenge him. They wanted to return home to Tanah Darah more than anything, and any little provocation would send them running for the gates.

"You can come with us," said Angus.

"Thank you, but no. I'll find another place." He leaned on Dax for support.

"Don't be foolish," said Redlynn. "We have a healer. We can take care of you."

"Is she human?" Sage flashed his fangs.

The wolves growled in reply.

"That's what I thought. No, it is better that I stay away from humans for a few days, I think, but thank you for the offer." The last thing he wanted was to lose himself and eat a wolf mate. Let alone forfeiting their treaty, that was a fatal indiscretion for anyone.

"When you've found a place, send Dax so we know you're all right. We'll bring any supplies you might need," said Redlynn.

"Again, I thank you." Sage bowed.

Redlynn and Angus shifted and the wolves bounded into the trees.

"Come on," Sage said to Dax. "There's a place we can stay for a bit. There's a pool nearby. We can clean up there."

Dax stared at the small cabin. "This is it?"

"Yeah." Sage's body ached in exhaustion. His injuries and the days of fighting had taken their toll. If he drank human, he would already have healed. *Don't think that way!*

"It's about to fall down."

"Trust me, it's better on the inside." Thank the gods he'd told Snow to stay away. Not that she'd be back anytime soon due to the death of her loved one. He stepped into the cabin and fell into an overstuffed chair by a small window.

The weight of Remus fell upon him once more. Was he alive or dead? The others had been difficult to kill making Sage doubt his brother's demise.

Dax stooped to enter. "Not much better in here."

"Well, it's better than hanging out in the trees," Sage snapped, and then sighed. He shouldn't be short with Dax. He'd done nothing but help.

Dax eyed him for a minute before answering. "True."

"There's a closet." Sage pointed. "See if there's anything in there you can wear."

He dragged himself to his feet, slung his coat and weapons onto the floor, and then removed his bloodied and ruined tunic.

"There's a bunch of dummies in here, but not much else," Dax said. "Oh, wait." He held out a dress. "Wear this often?"

"Funny. The cabin isn't mine. It belongs to– a friend."

"The girl. I can smell her. It's the same scent you've come back with every night for weeks. This is dangerous Sage. We should go." Dax threw the dress in the closet.

"Nowhere else for me to go, my friend. The sun will be up before I can make it to my hideout."

Dax shook his head.

Sage grabbed a towel by the large wash basin. "Come on, let's get cleaned up."

Sage dragged himself north through the glade to the small pond that Snow had shown him. They drew closer and his gut clenched. They reached the spot where he'd held Snow in his arms. He sniffed the air and halted at the edge. Something was wrong.

Dax bent down to inspect the water.

Sage threw an arm out to stop him. "Wait! Don't touch it."

"What?"

Sage took a step closer to the edge and peered into the middle. A soft ruby red glow emanated from the bottom. A chill ran up his spine and he turned to see a caravan come through the trees to the east. He and Dax ran to the trees, hiding themselves from view.

A lanky man with dirt colored, shaggy hair rode out front. A group of six to eight humans huddled together in a wagon driven by two more men. The humans ranged from young to old, male and female. Behind them rode three more burly men, also on horses.

The lead man swung off his horse and scanned the area. He stood in silence for several minutes, as if waiting for something before walking to the edge of the pool and looking in.

The men on horses helped the humans from the wagon and moved them toward the edge of the pond.

The lead man addressed the group. "Friends, this is the hour of your repayment. Each of you came to me in time of need. You asked a favor, and I granted you that favor. Now it's time for you to repay your loan."

"What do we have to do, Klaus?" asked a man from the rear of the group.

"Simple. You jump into the water, and your debt is repaid," Klaus said, gesturing to the pool.

The group looked suspiciously at the pond. "That's it? Jump in?" asked an old woman.

"That's all." Klaus smiled.

From his vantage point inside the tree line, Sage had an uneasy feeling, but he couldn't put his finger on what was happening. He peered around the large oak, trying to see, but his sight was strained due to fatigue.

"What's in there?" A man walked to the edge of the pond.

Klaus shrugged. "Water. Well, come on, who wants to be first to repay their debt? Here, I'll even help you." He stepped up and gave the old lady a push. The woman held on to Klaus for a moment, then let out a cry and fell in. She splashed and bobbed to the surface, sputtering for breath.

"See," said Klaus. "Nothing to it. When all of you have jumped in, it will be over. But we can't leave, until everyone is in the water."

"I can't do this forever!" the old woman shouted. Her arms flailed in the water.

The group watched her apprehensively for a moment before a young man stepped forward. "Let's help her." He jumped into the pool and waded out to the old woman.

"Wonderful, Armie," said Klaus, clapping his hands. "Yes, we wouldn't want her to drown." Klaus motioned to the others. "Well?"

The group glanced at each other and whispered. After a minute, the others got in the pool and waded out to the middle.

"There is one more small thing I forgot to mention. John, if you would be so kind as to go to the bottom of the pond and retrieve the red stone you see down there. Then we'll be all through."

John took a deep breath and headed for the bottom. He'd only been gone a few seconds when there was an enormous flash of light.

Sage looked on in horror and his gut clenched. "No!" he yelled, moving out of the trees toward the pool. "Get out! Get out!"

But he was too late. The people screamed. Wrenched from the surface, they were propelled downward, under the water. The light grew brighter and brighter, until finally there was a blinding ruby red flash. Sage blinked rapidly, clearing the flashburn from his sight. Howling in anger, his fangs descended into his mouth. He rushed at Klaus and his men.

Klaus took a step backward and brandished a dark object from his waistband. Sage was almost on him when Klaus leveled the object and there was a loud boom and a flash of fire. Something small ripped through Sage. Agony burned through him like the small projectile.

Dax shifted and roared.

Sage stumbled. *I really should start trying to win some of these battles.*

Dax continued to chase the men as Sage's vision slowly returned. Breathing heavily, he slumped to his knees. *This is getting embarrassing*. For fifty years he had been refusing to drink from humans. It was bound to take its toll sometime.

Klaus jumped on his horse and took off, with his companions at his heels. They disappeared into the trees. To drink the blood of those men, he'd be willing to break his vow.

Dax returned and shifted. "What the hell was that?" he demanded.

"A slave exchange," Sage groaned.

"An exchange? With whom?"

"Vampires."

"In the water?"

Sage's mind grew fuzzy and he could barely keep his eyes open. "No, through the portal at the bottom."

Dax crouched over Sage and looked at his shoulder. "What was that thing he had? It put a hole right through you."

"A gun." Sage fell over and everything went black.

CHAPTER TWELVE

Snow's brothers each awaited their turn for her to look them over. Gerall had two broken ribs and a couple of gashes. Jamen had dislocated his shoulder for the dozenth time. Erik and Flint popped it into place. Erik had to be stitched up in five places and Flint had a broken, dislocated finger, and a large, ugly bruise to his lower spine. Hass and Ian remained relatively unharmed.

When she finished, they filed downstairs and headed into the great hall where Erik had laid Kellan. She hadn't been in the great hall in over a year. Muslin sheets covered the tables and chairs, except for the main table where Kellan's body lay. Someone had removed the sheet, revealing the beautiful carved wood. The smell of oranges permeated the surface from where one of her brothers had rubbed it down.

Snow sat in her father's seat and stroked Kellan's soft hair. Four of her brothers went to collect lumber to make a coffin.

"We'll bury him next to Mother and Father," Jamen said, his arm in a sling.

"I'll get the hole ready," Flint said, standing.

Snow looked up to see the far away look in his eye. "No," she said. "Your bruise is worrisome. Let the twins do it when they've finished with the casket."

"I'm capable." Flint's eyes flashed.

"That's not what I meant. I just…stay with me, Flint." She held out her hand to him.

He glanced down at it and softened. Uncovering a chair, he sat next to her.

"I remember when he was born," Flint said. "He was so small and fragile, I was terrified to touch him."

"Mother used to force you to hold him," Jamen said. "She'd tell you that the only way to make him strong was to surround him with your strength."

Flint reached out and put his hand on Kellan's shoulder. "I think she was trying to teach me gentleness more than to teach him strength."

"Remember when he put frogs in your bed, Snow?" Jamen laughed. "He wanted to scare you so badly. But you played with those frogs all day."

"I remember when he stole your flask, Jamen. He wanted to prove that he was just as manly as you were so he drank the whole thing." Flint smiled and squeezed Jamen's shoulder. "Thing was, it wasn't your flask it was mine."

"I thought father was going to whip his hide for sure, but mother stepped in and just gave father that look of hers and he softened immediately."

"He was as strong as all of you, and just as manly too," said Snow. "If only he'd believed it himself." The three sat in silence for several minutes with Snow stroking Kellan's hair. "We need to wash and clothe him."

"We'll wash him, Snow," said Jamen. "You go pick out something for him to wear."

She nodded and wandered from the great hall. She crossed the front hall and took the stairs slowly, venturing toward Kellan's room. When she opened his door, her tears flowed again.

An hour later, she brushed Kellan's hair. Erik, Ian, Hass and Gerall entered.

"Coffin's done," said Hass.

"Hole's dug," finished Ian.

She nodded.

It was close to dawn. The sun would break over the horizon soon. Farmers would be in their fields.

A soft knock sounded on the front door and voices echoed through the entryway. Jamen returned, followed closely by Father Ohana.

"What's he doing here?" The very sight of the preacher of false gods made her gut clench.

"Morning, Daughter Snow," said the priest.

"I asked him to come," said Erik.

Flint rose to stand by her. "We don't need him."

"We do if we don't want anyone whispering about how Kellan died," said Jamen.

"No," she said. "I won't have a man from that made up religion burying our Kellan."

"It wasn't so many years ago, Daughter, that you sat in my pews and worshiped alongside us." The short priest gave a friendly, toothy grin that he reserved for collecting money.

"I sat many years ago at the bequest of my mother, but I never worshiped. And do not call me 'Daughter.' My father was no priest." Snow spat at his feet. The professed preacher took money from poor villagers promising them favor with unseen gods, all in an effort to keep his nice home and fat wife happy.

Father Ohana took a step toward the hall. "Maybe it's better if I go."

"No," said Jamen, blocking the exit. "I won't lie and say we believe in your ways, but we've paid you handsomely to bury our brother and keep any gossip at bay. A deal was struck. Besides—" He looked at Snow. "It's what our mother would have wanted."

Snow glanced away from Jamen's stare. Her heart clenched. It was what her mother would have wanted.

"All right," he consented. "But if we're going to do this without too many prying eyes, it must be now."

Erik moved to her side and put his hand atop of hers. "He's ready, Snow."

She stared down at Kellan. "His hair," she said through her tears. "It's the only part of him that's right."

"No." Erik hugged her. "You did a great job. He looks peaceful."

Her gaze traveled over Kellan's neck. Her brothers hadn't told her what had caused the horrible gashes at his throat, but she knew what had killed her beloved Kellan. The red-eyed monsters from her books. *Vampires.*

The high collared tunic covered most of the wound. She ran her fingers over the soft sutures that Gerall had made to close the wound.

Erik motioned to Hass and Ian. The three of them picked up Kellan and carried him outside. She waited inside, listening to the hammering of nails into the coffin lid. Every strike flooded her with memories of her mother's death, her father's and now Kellan's.

When silent emptiness filled the air, Gerall helped her across the porch and over near the stables. On the side stood a small gate. A section of earth next to her mother's grave had been dug. Erik, Hass and Ian set the coffin inside. Father Ohana spoke words that no one listened to as each of her brothers took turns throwing dirt in the grave.

Jamen handed her the shovel. Bleary-eyed, she pushed it away. He wrapped his good arm around her, pressed the shovel into her palm and helped her dig into the dirt, tossing it onto the coffin.

"He loved you the most," he whispered.

It was all too much. The pain ripped through her and her stomach twisted like she needed to vomit. Casting down the shovel, she raced across the green. Her brothers called after her, but she didn't stop. She didn't turn. She just ran and ran.

Snow burst into her cabin. The curtains were partially drawn, and the imminent dawn peeked through, casting shadows across the room. Tears streamed as she sniffled and snorted in her pain. She felt for a match on the table to light the lantern, but the container lay empty. Giving up, she closed the door, leaned heavily against it, and wailed. She slumped to the floor, allowing the pain of her loss to pour over her.

A creaking noise from her chair caught her attention. She stiffened and peered around the gloomy cabin.

"Who's there?" She wiped her face on her sleeve. Standing, she fumbled in the dark for a weapon, but couldn't find one. "This is my cabin. What are you doing in here?"

A floorboard creaked. As her sight adjusted to the dark, she made out a figure standing near.

"Get out!" she shouted, pulling open the door behind her. "I am Lady Snow Gwyn, and if you know anything about that name, you know I am not to be trifled with."

"Snow," said the voice.

She recognized it. *Sage*! Relief flooded her.

"I'm so sorry for your loss," he said. "I know how it hurts to lose someone dear."

Snow peered into the dim light to see him. A dark, long coat hung from his shoulders. The scent of it comforted her, like the smell of her father's old riding saddle.

"How did you hear about my brother?" She wiped at her face, trying to dry the wetness.

He moved closer and a tingle skittered over her skin at his nearness. The floor board groaned. He was just a foot from her. With the quickly growing light at his back, she could barely make out his face.

"I lost my brother too. I know how it hurts," he whispered in her ear.

Snow sucked in a breath and held very still and swallowed. It was wrong, but she liked the feeling of his body near hers. The sensations it sent through her were a welcomed break from the pain. The mere thought of her dead brother caused a sob to escape.

"Oh, Snow." He gathered her into his strong arms. His leather coat fell from his shoulders to the floor. She pressed against his cool, bare chest.

She clung to his familiar frame, shutting out anything and everything but him. Sobs wracked her body once more. "What are you doing here? You told me you'd be gone."

"I was supposed to, but…" He stroked her hair. "Snow, I know your pain. You feel as if you will never heal. That your loss is too great and that you will forever feel the sting of it. In a way, you will—"

"Stop talking." She placed her fingers on his lips. She didn't want more words. She didn't want to think about the pain. She swept her fingers over his cheek. "Your skin is cold."

"There's no fire to warm me."

She swore his words meant something else altogether and a sudden rush of heat ran down her belly to her thighs.

"What do you need?" he asked.

"You." She brought her lips up to meet his.

He froze, but then his hand wrapped in her hair and he pressed her into the door. She sucked in his cool breath. Kissing him was wrong. It wasn't proper for a lady to be kissing a man to whom she wasn't

136

engaged. But her brother was dead. Her beloved Kellan, and she needed to feel something other than pain and loss.

Gripping Sage's shoulders, she yanked him to her and let her body melt into his. He kept his kisses soft as she plunged her tongue deep into his mouth, begging him to give her more.

He withdrew his lips from hers. "Easy, love." He brushed a finger down her cheek and kissed her nose. "Don't do anything you will regret later."

"I won't regret it." She kissed him again.

A chuckle rumbled in his chest and he stepped away once more. "You're hurting and you think you need this to make you feel better. And it would, for both of us. But as soon as you leave, you would despise me."

"I want to feel something else."

"Oh, Snow. Snow, Snow, Snow." He trailed light kisses over her forehead, eyelids and lips. "Come, let me hold you instead." He guided her toward the chair.

She yanked free of his grasp. "No, if you hold me, I'll think again."

Sage grasped her wrist, but she tugged from him again. A tear leaked from her eye and he caught it with his fingertips. Gently, he reached out to her again. She stared at his hand for a moment before giving in and allowing him to pull her toward the chair and onto his lap. He cradled her in his arms, running his fingers down the length of her. She stiffened at his touch but then relaxed into him. They sat for a long while with him holding her close, speaking words she didn't understand.

"Gi, ussta Ssinssrigg. Hush, Ssinssrigg. Gre'as'anto, Ssinssrigg. Nindol ichl orn k'lararl lu'dos orn knan garethur wun draeval."

The language was neither common, nor Latin. But there were so many other languages in Fairelle that had grown over the centuries that she couldn't be sure which it was. His chest was cool and firm against her cheek.

"I told you I had a brother," he said, trailing his fingers down her arm. "A younger brother. It was my responsibility to look after him and keep him safe."

His deep voice resonated in his chest where her cheek lay. "I thought I did what I was supposed to, but now—" He paused. "Now I know that I did nothing for him. I was selfish and at times unkind. I hadn't meant to be, but when you grow up having every luxury at your feet..."

Her heart went out to him. She traced her fingers over his bare chest, feeling the sinewy muscles beneath her fingertips. Though over the past weeks they had become closer than she'd wanted, it felt so right being held in Sage's arms.

"He was a good kid. He was eager, trusting..."

"What happened to him?" Snow looked into his face.

A familiar sadness crept over his features again.

"I thought he'd been killed by my enemy. My uncle. But I was wrong. He hadn't been killed, he'd been recruited. Looking back I can see how it happened. I remember noticing little changes in him.

Feeling his affections for me slipping away. Seeing him spending more time with our uncle, but how could I have ever known..."

"It isn't your fault," Snow said. "Everyone makes their own choices in life. We cannot blame ourselves for the decisions that others make. At the end of the day, the choice was his."

"Just as I am sure your brother made choices that, through no fault of his own, brought his death as well," he replied.

Anger surge within her. "No." She shook her head. "My brother was sweet. He was kind. He didn't deserve what happened to him. Vampires did this. Vampires killed my brother. I'm going to kill the monster responsible and I'm going to avenge my family."

"You shouldn't go searching for trouble. Please don't—"

She pushed away from him. "Look me in the eyes and tell me that's not what you're planning. Tell me you aren't going to exact revenge on your uncle who you say took everything from you."

He stared at her for a long time. He ran his fingers down her cheek. "I can't."

"Then why should I not get my revenge? Because I'm a woman? Because you think I can't take care of myself?"

"No. Not because you're a woman. Because I don't want anything to happen to you."

Her heart pounded in her chest. He cared for her.

A stream of light peeked between the curtains and crept across the floor. She stared at where her palm sat on his pale chest. Several scars crossed his torso. His neck sported a wound that looked to be several days old and his abdomen held a four inch gash. She ran her fingers over every scar.

"How did you get all these?"

He swallowed. "My uncle has been very persistent in wanting to see me dead."

"Why? Why are you such a threat?"

"Because he killed my family. My father. He killed him for land and money and power."

"Like the sons of King Isodor."

"Yes."

"I'm sorry," she said. "I've lost my mother, my father and now my brother, but I haven't been turned on and hunted by my own family. I can't imagine the pain of that."

"No," he said softly. "You can't. And I'm glad for that. I would hate to see you suffer so."

The butterflies returned to her stomach. He reached out and drew her close. Their lips met in a gentle embrace. Her skin flushed as her mouth opened and she swirled her tongue with his.

He ran his hand up her waist and over the outside of her breast. She sucked in a sharp breath. His hand traveled upward until his fingers entwined with her hair. The sensation sent shockwaves through her soul. His soft lips moved down her chin to her throat. She wrapped her fingers in his thick blond hair and arched her body toward him. He continued down and down till he reached the hollow of her throat. His tongue flicked out and licked swirls into her skin.

She grabbed his hair tighter. Her head swam and she moaned. His teeth grazed her skin and an image of him licking her palm flashed in her mind. She jumped to her feet.

He stood equally as fast. "What's the matter?"

"I don't know." She shook her head and then looked down at her palm. "I had the strangest image of you licking my hand. Like a memory or something."

"Does that happen often?" His voice sounded strangled and thick.

She looked up into his face. For the first time, she noticed how pale it was.

Bright sunlight rolled almost to the door now. Flint and Erik would be a mess of worry if she didn't return. They'd come looking for her.

"I have to go," she said. "My brother's will be vexed, but I'll return tonight."

He rose from the chair and stepped toward her. "No. I told you. You need a break."

She picked up his leather coat from the floor, smelled it and handed it to him. "I will anyway."

"I won't be here."

A shiver ran through her. She needed him more than she wanted to admit. "Be here."

She stepped out into the morning and turned to see the perfection of his chiseled chest and broad shoulders. Their eyes met and then he stepped into the darkness of the cabin.

Snow waited for him to say something. But he didn't, so she closed the door and headed for home.

Making her way through the forest toward the farmlands, she reveled in the feel of his touch. He'd been so gentle. Suddenly a sharp pain traversed her side. Snow stopped and clutched at it in agony. Looking down, she took in deep breaths. There was no reason for her to have a cramp, she hadn't been moving that fast. She continued on, up the hillside behind the manor until she rounded the house to the front. Another pain hit her leg. She rubbed at it, annoyed. The muscles relaxed a bit, but they ached. Something wasn't right.

CHAPTER THIRTEEN

The day wore on and the ache in her hips and sides increased to include her legs and shoulders. By dinner that evening with her brothers, Snow's body hurt worse than ever. Besides being emotionally drained, the little sleep she'd gotten did nothing for her physical pain. Her skin flushed with heat and she wondered if she were becoming sick.

They ate in silence, the mood in the house still somber. It had been quiet all day. Everyone had kept to their own rooms, mourning. Except for Jamen, who hadn't been seen since the burial. Erik and Flint planned on heading to the tavern to drag him home after dinner. Her thoughts turned momentarily to Klaus and the upsetting scene she had witnessed between him and Armie days earlier.

Shoving a piece of overcooked meat into her mouth. Reaching for her glass of water, she knocked it off the table. Before it hit the floor, she caught it, midair, right-side up. She stared in disbelief at the glass; not a drop had spilled. A smile spread across her face.

"Did you see that?" Hass stared at her, eyebrows raised.

"Impressive, Snow," finished Ian.

Flint eyed her warily.

"Lucky catch." She took a sip and set the glass on the table.

"That was more than lucky," said Hass.

"That was almost as amazing as me," said Ian.

Snow, Hass and Ian laughed lightly at the joke. Flint and Erik exchanged an odd look.

"What?" Her smile faded. "I can't have a moment of great agility like you do all the time?"

Her brothers stopped laughing and glanced at each other.

"What?" Her skin prickled from the heat of the room and her heartbeat quickened.

"Stop looking at me!" she snapped. She felt like a bug under the inspection of a fat toddler. "Why are you all staring at me? It was just a glass of water."

No one spoke for several minutes before Ian said, "Uh…Snow…Is it…I mean…Are you…uh…Your womanly thing…is that why you're so–"

Ian didn't even get to finish his sentence before she picked up her plate and threw it at him. He ducked and the plate hit the wall behind him. It clattered to the floor, splattering food everywhere.

"No!" she screamed. "No, Ian, I am not on my monthly. I'm upset that my brother died, and you're all looking at me as if I've grown horns." She rose from her chair so quickly that it tipped backward. Gerall, Ian and Hass jumped from the table and out of her way. Only Erik and Flint remained in their seats, watching her wordlessly. Her anger rose to a fevered pitch and blood pounded in her ears. She wanted to claw their eyes out.

"Stop looking at me like that!" She fled to her bedroom, slammed the door and locked it. Why were they staring at her? All she had done was catch a glass before it hit the floor, but her brothers acted as if she'd made it disappear completely.

She was hot, so very hot. She stripped off her dress and flung it to the floor and touched her brow. It was warm and the way her body ached she was sure she'd caught the flu. She grabbed a tincture from her cabinet, gulped down the bitter liquid, and then opened her window. Cool air skimmed over her limbs. Closing her eyes, she breathed in the smell of the oatbern growing in the nearby farm, hay that had been cut recently, and the dampness of the dirt in the fields.

Her eyelids flew open. How could she smell all that? *What was happening?*

Her thoughts traveled to Kellan's body laying in a grave by the barn. Her brothers were all she had. As annoying as they could be, they were her family. Her thoughts darkened at the sight of her family graveyard. What if her other brothers– Snow squeezed her eyes shut and pulled her pillow over her head. *No!* She wouldn't think of that. She refused to give in to thoughts of what she would do if she lost them all. The pain would be too much to bear. She moved to her bed and plopped down, unable to cry, but the wound in her heart opened wide once more.

Snow awakened with a start. Her corset cinched her like a vise. She ripped and tore at the laces behind her, gasping for air. Unable to concentrate on the laces, she grabbed the front of the corset and ripped it apart with her bare hands. Her breathing came in large gulps and her head pounded.

My toth! She'd ripped the thing in half. She flung the corset into the corner and looked at her clock; it was 2 a.m. The fever and aches had subsided. *Thank heavens for the tincture.*

A breeze blew in through the window, carrying the scents of the forest to her. She thought about her cabin and her body tingled. *He* was there. A sudden sensation fell over her, and at the very thought of him, her body surged towards the window. She caught herself on the windowsill just as she was about to jump out.

She backed up. What had possessed her to do that? Something inside her was awake. It pulled her toward him. She tried to comprehend what was happening, but she couldn't. All she knew at that moment was, somehow, he was her destiny. It made no sense to think that, but she did. Moving to her closet, she retrieved her practice clothes and tugged them on. She grabbed her rope from under the bed and tied it in place.

When her feet hit the ground, she took off at a run. With a speed she didn't know she possessed, she ran for her cabin. The gentle wind felt wonderful. Her usual thirty minute trek took her only half the time. Her heart beat strong and her breathing was even as the cabin came into view. She smiled at the power surging within her. A sprint of that distance should have at least winded her, but it energized and exhilarated her instead.

She neared the cabin and stopped, about to knock, but the door opened.

"How did you know I was here?" She smiled.

"I smelled you," he said, his voice somber.

The feeling she'd had in her room, to reach him, grew stronger than ever. But now that she was here, it had changed. She still wanted to be in his arms, but more than that, she wanted to hurt him. Snow took a step away from him, confused. She wanted to kill him.

*****

Sage had smelled her a mile from the cabin. The tantalizing scent had awakened him from a deep sleep. Her scent rivaled that of her brothers, but the sweet vanilla had increased, enticing him. It made his veins burn to feel her blood course through them. His throat dried and he swallowed hard, knowing what was happening to her.

He waited. Her soft footsteps rushed through the trees, moving faster than normal. When he opened the door, his heart sank. He could see it on her already. Her face, which hours ago still had a youthful roundness to it, had refined. Where she had been pretty before, she now stole his breath away. Her high cheekbones were matched only by the seduction of her almond-shaped copper colored eyes and supple lips.

It all made sense. This cruel trick of the gods, this temptation beyond comprehension. The answer as to why he'd been so drawn to her from the beginning slapped him in the face. The bloodlust he'd kept down for the past weeks surfaced with a vengeance. His body pulsed with the need to taste her.

Underneath her clothes, her hips curved to support the strong, lean legs toning by the minute. Every part of her was waking up, shifting, strengthening.

She was becoming a Slayer. Taking the place of the brother who'd died.

She came with a smile, but the confusion played in her mind. Her new instincts were taking over.

His body and heart were at war. Despite his rising desire for her, he wanted to drain her, a Slayer. His fangs descended into his mouth.

She took a step back.

"You want to kill me," he said.

"Yes," she whispered.

"It's to be expected."

"No." She shook her head. "Why do I want to kill you? How do you know that I do?"

"Because it is your mantle." Sage stepped out of the shadow.

Her brows furrowed and she retreated again. "What are you talking about?"

"Come." Sage reached out his hand to her. She looked conflicted, but she took it, gripping tightly. He walked her into the bright moonlit glade. Releasing her hand, he faced her.

He removed his leather coat. The cool night air skimmed across his bare chest. "Look at me."

She studied him, but he could tell she didn't see it.

"Look at me, Snow. What do you see?"

"A man."

"Look closer. Feel it inside. What do your instincts tell you?"

He knew she saw it, but wished she hadn't. Wished she couldn't. He moved to her in a single stride and bent close to her, never losing

148

eye contact. His gut clenched at what he knew would follow. He lifted a hand and stroked her cheek. This was the moment. No more games. She had to decide for herself. "Remember," he whispered.

Her pupils constricted and then flooded wide. She blinked rapidly several times and sucked in a breath. Quicker than he could see, she reached out with both hands and shoved him in the chest. He flew ten feet across the glade and landed on all fours. His head whipped up and he bared his fangs instinctively.

"Sage." She grabbed for her sword, but it wasn't there. She advanced on him a step. "You toyed with me, you played with my emotions."

He recovered his composure and stood, wiping the dirt from his hands. "No. I tried to keep you safe."

"You made me think you were my friend. I told you things I've never told anyone and it was all a lie. Were you trying to get to me? To soften me up so you could get to my brothers?"

His chest tightened. He didn't want to lose her. "It wasn't a lie. Yes, I hid who I was from you, but isn't that what you wanted? You didn't tell me who you were. Who your brothers were. I just wanted to protect you."

"From whom?"

"From me." His fangs fully extended. "From your brothers. From yourself. From the vampires that were here last night."

"But *you're* a vampire."

"Yes."

She grabbed her temples. He wanted to hold her, to tell her everything.

"Why did I just do that? Why did I hit you?"

"Because that's what Slayers do."

"I'm not a Slayer. My brothers are Slayers, not me."

Sage shook his head. "One died. Someone must be called to take his place. That someone, it seems, is you."

Snow looked around the glade, emotions playing off her in quick succession. He waited for her to speak.

"I want to believe you."

"Then believe me." He stepped closer.

"How can I? You wiped my memories. How many times have you done that?"

"Once, just that once. I swear."

"I want to believe you, but you're a vampire!"

"What do you know about vampires? I mean really."

"You drink blood."

"I do. But not from humans. From animals."

"But not all vampires do."

"No." He had to admit it. There were very few like him, and the ones he knew did it because he commanded it, not because they chose it. "What else?"

"You're not human."

"I'm not. But I'm not dead either. I'm immortal."

"Like the Fae."

He nodded. Hope lit within him that she would understand. He wasn't the monster of legend. They could work past this.

"No. No." She paced back and forth. "Vampires are murderers of women and children. Slaughterers of the innocent. Why else would my brothers have been called?"

He had no answer for that. Someone or something was ruling Tanah Darah and allowing vampires to run amuck. Whether it was his uncle or someone else, Sage wasn't sure anymore.

"Wait." She stopped moving. "You said vampires were here the other night."

"Yes. That's why I lost you in the woods. They were chasing you."

"You killed them." It wasn't a question.

"To keep you safe, I'd do anything." He let the words hang between them. It was true, he'd do anything to keep her safe. Even from himself.

When she looked at him again, her face was determined. "I don't want to hurt you".

"I don't want to hurt you either." The scent of her blood drifted toward him. His muscles twitched in anticipation of the feed. *No. He couldn't.* Not her. He had to protect her. His heart sank.

She stared at him. "Do you want to bite me?"

"Yes," he whispered.

"Have you been fighting it all along?"

He couldn't answer.

"A vampire," she moaned. "I have feelings for you. I care for you, and now what? I'm supposed to hunt and kill you before you hunt and kill me? Why do you have to be a—No. I can't."

Before he could stop her, she turned and fled.

"Snow!" Sage yelled. She didn't turn. His eyesight sharpened and his predatory instincts took over. Racing at a top speed, he tracked her through the trees. "Snow! Stop, don't run. Please, I can't help it."

His desire to feed burned in his limbs. She smelled so intoxicating. Blood so rich... *It will heal me. No!*

She rounded a bend, and when he reached it, she'd vanished. He scanned the area, but there were no movements. He could still smell her. He wouldn't hurt her. He wouldn't. He could control it. He'd controlled it for decades. He'd never slipped, not once.

Closing his eyes, he listened to his surroundings. The wind rustled through the trees. There was a creak from above and he looked up in time to see her fly at him from a low hanging branch.

"Why?" she screamed, landing on him and knocking him down.

They tumbled to the ground in a heap, rolling in the deep leaves. She ended up on top. Brandishing a knife from her boot, she pressed it to his throat. Her eyes rimmed with tears and her hand shook.

"Why?" she asked again.

"I don't know," he said. Every muscle was attuned to her. The sound of her heartbeat thundered in his ears. The pulsing, throbbing vein at her throat made him yearn to take her. Her breasts heaved up and down as she sucked in a sob.

"Who did this to us? I don't want to be this." Tears dripped onto his bare chest. "You're not supposed to be a vampire."

He lay still beneath her, fighting against the pounding in his ears to control his bloodlust. Her expression changed from anger to confusion to sadness. More teardrops escaped her eyes. Sage raised his hand slowly and wiped them away. Her sadness lingered like a blanket enshrouding her. He slid his hand down her arm and rested it on her slender wrist. The warmth of her skin tingled his fingers.

She'd been through so much, and she was right. He shouldn't have come back to see her. He should have left her alone. If he had, her brother would still be alive, and she would be safe.

He moved the blade from his throat and she dropped it to the ground.

Both of their bodies shook from being so near each other. Just days before it had been so simple. The two of them, in the dark, spending time together. Now, it had all gone wrong. Part of him wanted to drink her dry and leave her for dead, but another part still saw the woman she was. The one he still wanted. Only she could never be his. How could the gods be so cruel? Was it punishment for his past crimes?

She laid her palm on his chest, pulling him from his thoughts. He reveled in the warm feel of her fingertips caressing his skin. His throat burned at the thoughts of drinking from her.

"Kiss me," she said, her breaths coming in shallow, short bursts.

"I don't think–"

"You need to kiss me," she said again. "I can feel it, the part of me that wants to kill you. But there's another part. A part that was there the first time we met. It cares for you. I care for you. If I don't feed that piece of me, the Slayer will take over."

It was a dangerous game they played. But for all of his years of life, he'd never met another that made him feel the way she did. She was refreshing and vibrant. Like a beautiful rainbow in the hurricanes of his life. She stood up to him, unafraid of what he did or said, unaffected by what people thought or what was proper.

He'd been able to show her his true face. The one he'd hidden, after the death of his mother, under a mountain of blood and debauchery. With Snow... He remembered what joy felt like.

If there were even the smallest chance that they could be together...

"You told me before that if I asked you to, you would kiss me. So I'm asking you to, Sage. Kiss me," she whispered.

He ran his tongue over his bottom lip. Once more, he was clay in her hands. What she asked, he was bound to comply. Well, if he was going to die by her hand, he would at least do it with the knowledge that he had felt true joy.

Grabbing her neck, he dragged her down and pressed his lips to hers. She kissed him at first, and then began to fight it. She reached up and raked her nails down his chest, drawing blood. He pinned her hands down and kissed her harder. Her breath was sweet upon his mouth. Her taste danced on his tongue, stirring his excitement.

Sitting up, he pushed his weight into her, flipped her on her back and covered her supple, strong body with his.

An inner battle raged between them, their dual natures fighting for control. She twisted and churned against him, making his arousal spike. She bit him hard on the lip and then probed and licked his fangs with her tongue. He moaned as their blood mingled with their kiss.

He trailed kisses down her neck and bloodlust rose inside him. He licked at the pulsing artery that throbbed beneath his lips. He needed blood, and the blood of a Slayer would heal him completely. His head pounded with the need to taste her.

He grazed his fangs over her skin, playfully nipping at her. She was so close and her skin was so warm. He opened his mouth wider, ready to strike, when she freed her hands from his and dug her nails in his shoulders.

"Sage," she moaned.

The sound of his name on her lips changed his bloodlust into full blown lust.

He pressed his fingers into her hipbone forcing her thighs apart with his own. He moved his mouth to hers. Her scent took on the sweet vanilla aroma; She was his.

Wrapping her legs around his waist, she squeezed and flipped him underneath her. He rolled on his back to find her poised above him. Her eyes flashed as she held a sharp stick above his chest. She breathed hard, her gaze locked onto his. A tear leaked from her eye and her hand shook as she stared at the stick.

"I don't want to hurt you. I don't want to," she chanted over and over.

"You won't hurt me," he whispered, not entirely sure that was the truth.

Her hands shook with great effort. She stared at his chest. Suddenly she screamed into the night and threw the stick to the side. She collapsed onto his chest.

Relief flooded him and he blew out a large breath. He wrapped her in his arms, and reveled in the weight of her body on top of his. She felt so perfect in his arms. Her long walnut-colored hair flowed over him and her slender fingers traced a pattern on his chest. Neither of them spoke. They had barely won this battle, but who knew what would happen next time.

The heat of the change burned off of her skin in waves. She was almost too hot to touch. After several minutes, she turned her face and pressed kisses onto his chest.

"You smell so intoxicating," she whispered. "Everything about you calls to me. It scares me."

She gently licked his skin. His muscles clenched and he arched against her soft tongue. A moan of pleasure escaped his throat and he struggled to hold on to his mounting need. She worked her way across his chest, over his nipples and down his stomach. His mind swam with thoughts of her. It had been so many years since he'd been with a female, touched a female. And now he was with the one female he couldn't deny. Her hold over him grew with each swirl of her tongue. He thought he might die of the ecstasy.

156

"You taste like cinnamon," she said.

"What?" He grabbed her hips, pulling her core closer to his.

"You taste like cinnamon," she said again.

His eyes flew open and he glanced down at her. She'd licked the blood from the scratches she had caused. He'd never let someone taste him before. But he wanted this with her. *Yes, take me in.*

"No! Stop," he said, coming groggily to his senses. He sat up with her still on his lap. The warmth between her thighs melted through his breeches and made him grow harder. His blood had smeared on her face. He wiped it off. "You're a Slayer."

"But not with you." She kissed him. "The Slayer in me wants to get free, but I won't let her. This is what I need from you."

She kissed him again, making his mind fog over. He couldn't think straight with her so near. She rubbed his shoulders and wrapped her feet around his rump. He grabbed her buttocks and kneaded her soft flesh. Her soft breasts smashed into his chest and fear crept over him. He wanted her so much, but what if he lost control? He'd never held back before; he wasn't sure he'd be able to. He had to stop.

He broke free of her kiss and stared at her hard. "You're a Slayer. You'll be a Slayer until you're your calling is fulfilled. Even with me. You're a Slayer with all vampires, but especially with me. You don't know how I used to be. I've never... I can't..."

Her eyes were so soft, so earnest. She trusted him, like no one had before. How could he break that trust by telling her the truth about his murderous ways?

A noise in the trees brought them to their feet in a heartbeat.

"You should go. No one can find out you were here with me." He pressed her behind him, searching for the intruder.

"Why?"

He turned to face her. "Do you think your brothers will approve?"

"I don't care what they think." She touched his face.

He grasped her hands with his own. "You don't understand. There are things–" So many things she didn't know about him. If he told her, he was sure he would lose her. "My uncle wants me dead. If he finds out about you–"

"I'm not afraid of your uncle."

"You should be. He's a powerful man." Sage swallowed. It wasn't the right time, but when would it be? "I am the rightful king of Tanah Darah and my uncle wants to keep the throne for himself."

"The rightful heir," she mused.

She wasn't taking it all in yet. She hadn't figured out the implications of that, combined with her new calling as a Slayer. Her brothers had though, and they wouldn't hesitate to kill him because he was the rightful king.

"Will you be here tomorrow?"

He hesitated. He wanted her more than anything. But this wasn't safe for either of them. Now that she knew the truth, she was in danger from both his uncle's men and her brothers. If they found out the truth—

"No," he lied.

"Be here." She stepped close and kissed him. "We'll work out a plan. Together."

He pulled her to him and kissed her hair. He didn't want her to go, but if someone was out there, she was safest with her brothers.

He grabbed her by the hand and yanked her into action. Together they ran until they reached the edge of the farmlands. When they stopped, he picked leaves from her hair.

"Go." He kissed her and then released her. He glanced at the sky. The sun would soon be up. He needed to get to shelter.

"I'll see you tonight."

He blew out a breath and ran his hands through his hair as she disappeared into the fields below her home. For the first time, the pain of her nail marks on his body burned his chest. The scratches she had caused still stood as open wounds. They oozed blood, where they should have sealed shut. He sighed. This just couldn't get much worse.

CHAPTER FOURTEEN

With every step, Snow fought the urge to run back to Sage. The farther away she got, the more her lusty urges changed back to violence. Confusing and frustrating her. How could she spend her life fighting the desire to kill him? She stopped abruptly.

She wanted to spend her life with him. A vampire whom she barely knew. But she did know him. Deeply, intimately, she knew him, and he was the man she wanted to be with forever. It didn't matter who he used to be. She wasn't naïve. She knew what vampires ate. And killed. A shudder ran through her and she pushed the thought aside. He was a good person, though. He could have killed her half a dozen times, but he hadn't. He'd tried to protect her. Even tonight, at the first sign of discovery, he'd insisted she leave. He was gentle with her and listened. He possessed a wit that she'd come to love and he'd been patient with her while teaching her to fight. The way he understood her, and didn't judge her for who she was or what she wanted out of life, no man had given her that before. No highborn man had accepted her for who she was. Not even her brothers.

Moving forward again, Snow made for the rope at her bedroom window. She climbed it quickly and slid in. She'd just pulled herself through when the lantern to her room illuminated. She gasped. Erik and Flint sat waiting for her.

"What are you— How did you get in?" Her door stood slightly ajar.

Erik produced a key from his pocket and set it on her dresser. Both he and Flint glowered at her, their posture rigid, but didn't speak. They simply looked her up and down.

"You were right," Erik said to Flint.

"She showed all the signs. I'm surprised the others didn't figure it out," replied Flint.

"What?" she demanded, her own anger rising. "What?"

"Did you bother to look in the mirror before your excursion?" Erik asked.

"Why would I have?" She pushed at her hair and picked a stray leaf from it.

"Look." Flint gestured to the mirror.

She sighed and went to the mirror. Her eyes widened. Her face was different. Thinner, more defined. Her lips had deepened a shade, and her shoulders were broader. She stared at herself, barely recognizing her own reflection.

The change had done this to her. It had happened to each of her brothers, and in her rush to be with Sage, she hadn't noticed it until this moment.

"Where were you?" asked Flint.

"I was out." She turned to get a look at her rear. *Not bad.*

"Where did you get those clothes, and why do you smell of blood?" Erik questioned.

Snow noticed the dark stains on her shirt from Sage's blood. She shrugged. "I got in a fight."

"A fight? With whom?" Flint demanded. Erik put his hand on Flint's arm.

"Who did you get in a fight with?" Erik tried to keep his voice level.

She crossed her arms over her chest. If she was one of them now, they needed to stop treating her like a child. "A vampire."

Flint got to his feet and strode across the room, yelling his outrage. Erik wrapped an arm around his brother's chest, to hold him back and calm him. Snow stood tall and raised her chin, refusing to show fear. She shouldn't taunt them. She hadn't really fought with Sage as much as wrestled with him.

The twins pushed into the room, followed by Gerall.

"What's all the ruckus?" asked Ian with a yawn.

"Ask her." Flint jabbed his finger at her.

"What'd you do, Snow?" asked Hass.

"What did I do? I didn't do anything." Her anger spiked.

"She's gotten Kellan's mantle and she went out and fought a vampire. Her first night, with no training, and weaponless, I might add," yelled Flint. "Do you have any idea what that would've done to us if you had died? Did you even think about us at all?"

Her brothers stared at her, taking in her new form.

Guilt ran through her. No, she hadn't thought of that. "I didn't ask for this anymore than you did, Flint," she said.

"You don't even know how to fight." He broke free from Erik's grasp and came at her.

162

As soon as he was within reach, she twisted her body, stomped on his foot and jabbed him in the ribs. Flint doubled over and she grabbed him by the neck, throwing him to the floor. She stood over him in surprised silence. Her brothers stared at her wide eyed.

"I'm sorry." She moved away.

Bleary-eyed, Jamen joined the group.

"I'm sorry, Flint. I didn't mean to... It just happened." She looked at each of her brothers in turn. No, she hadn't meant to do that, but she had. It had been natural. There was no reason for her to apologize. "No matter what you all think, I am capable of taking care of myself. And as for my fight. It was no big deal. Sage—"

"Sage?" The fire in Erik's eyes made her mouth slam shut. "Sage, the vampire?"

"It's not as bad as it seems–"

"Did he hurt you?" Jamen crossed the room and looked her over.

"No. It wasn't like that. He–"

"Where did you see him?" Flint got to his feet.

Snow stopped talking. Something was wrong. All thoughts of what she'd just done were gone. Her conversation with Sage about her brothers' dislike of him flooded back.

They appeared angrier than she had ever seen them.

"What's going on?" she asked.

"Where did you see him?" Erik's intense gaze bore into her.

Snow swallowed. "He was down south by the cow pastures," she lied.

"How far?" asked Flint.

"Are you going to tell me what's going on? He didn't hurt me. He didn't even attack me. I attacked him."

"She has a right to be told," said Gerall.

Erik blew out a long breath. "Let's meet down in the living room after she changes out of those clothes. We'll tell her there."

*****

Dax arrived at the cabin half an hour after Snow had left. "Sorry to have barged in on you two," he said, a grim expression on his face. He dropped the bag of supplies he'd bought on the small table and tossed the bag of remaining coins to Sage.

"I thought it might have been you. It was good you came when you did." Sage weighed the coins in his hand. He was still in a fog from his encounter with Snow. He wanted her more than ever.

Dax opened his pack and took out an apple. "So she's still coming around, then?"

"Yes." Sage sighed. "But not because I haven't told her to keep away. This is bad, Dax. Really bad. I think... I think I love her."

Dax bit into the apple. "And that's bad because her brothers are Slayers?"

Sage hung his head. "That's bad because *she*'s a Slayer."

"What?"

"Her brother died. The mantle has passed to her. And I think it might get her killed, or me, or both."

Dax chuckled. "I don't know what I'd do if my lady wanted to kill me while she kissed me."

Sage looked up and Dax bit into the apple again.

"Because of my feelings for her, it makes her a double target. The vampires will kill her because she's a Slayer. But if they find out about our connection…" He shook his head. Being here was selfish. Forcing her to choose between him and her brothers was reprehensible. "I have to leave. I have to go to the den. No matter the cost, I have to keep her as far from me as possible."

"When should we go?"

He couldn't afford to change his mind. "Now works." Sage stood. "I can't get stuck in here another day. Besides, the curtains here don't keep the sun out fully, and I need to get some real rest."

Dax finished his apple and threw the core out the window as Sage gathered his things. His heart broke, knowing that he'd be gone when she returned. That he wouldn't see her again. But he had no choice. He had to leave. He had to keep her safe.

CHAPTER FIFTEEN

Sage staggered into his room an hour later and threw his coat and sword on the floor. His limbs shook with weakness. The scratches from Snow still oozed. In the past week he had been stabbed twice, scratched, sliced, and almost killed. It was time for him to take a break from his life. He was about to fall into bed when there was a knock on the door.

He groaned. "We'll talk later, Dax."

The door opened and Greeg peered inside. "Sorry to disturb you, Sage, but, we need to talk."

Not now we don't. "Can it wait? I really need some sleep."

"I'm sorry, Your Highness, but it can't."

Sage rubbed his face. Greeg never called him Highness unless it was something that only he could deal with. "All right." Sage let out a weary breath. "Let's go."

In the hallway, Dax opened his door. "You need me?"

"I don't know." He didn't need Dax, but Dax's peaceful presence was nice to have around anyway. The three made their way down to the library. Sage stepped inside to find everyone gathered, waiting for him. In the center, tied to a chair sat a brown haired vampire he didn't recognize. Several bruises already marred the male's face. His large nose sat at crooked angle and blood had dried below it.

A pit grew in Sage's stomach. How had this vampire found them?

The group moved out of the way as he neared.

"Prince Sage," said Greeg. "This is Quintess."

"How did he get here?" Sage demanded.

"We brought him," said Sonya. "While on our hunt yesterday, we came upon him getting out of a pool of water."

"Did the pool of water glow red?"

"Yes," said Sonya.

Oh toth! It was the same pool he and Snow had been at. The one the humans had been sucked into. Sonya was hunting too close to Snow's cabin. Sage frowned. Had he just said *Oh toth*?

The vampire bound to the chair wore a look of annoyance more than anything.

"Quintess, is it?" Sage asked. "What were you doing at the pool?"

He didn't answer.

Sage narrowed his gaze. "Do you know who I am?"

"You're the bastard nephew of the king."

Sage's fangs burst through his gums and he bared them at the vampire. Greeg backhanded Quintess.

Sonya grabbed the vampire by the hair and yanked his head back. "You dare to speak to the rightful King of Tanah Darah with such disrespect?"

Greeg pulled a knife from his boot and pressed it to Quintess' throat. "Say that again and I'll end your existence."

Sage was glad that Greeg and Sonya were on his side. As passive as they may seem, they were actually ferocious fighters and loyal to the death.

A trickle of fear washed over Quintess' face. Sonya let go of him and he stretched his neck.

"I will ask you again. What were you doing at the pool?" said Sage.

Quintess didn't answer.

He clucked his tongue. "I guess we do this the painful way: Greeg, Sonya, take him to the dining room. The rest of you don't need to be part of this. Feel free to retire for the day."

Greeg and Sonya picked Quintess up and carried him from the study. The group moved out and only Omni waited behind.

"He knows where we are," Omni said.

Sage ran his fingers through his hair. "I understand."

Omni didn't have to say the words that everyone, including himself, were thinking: Quintess couldn't be let go. No matter what they got out of him, their prisoner had to die.

Sage tugged a fresh tunic on and grimaced at the still open wounds. Sonya entered his room.

"We've him tied down and—" She stopped short and moved to his side. "What happened?" She touched the scratches on his chest. "Why aren't you healing?"

"I don't know." He dropped the tunic over his body.

She studied his face. "You need to feed."

"I did already." He turned from her.

Sonya reached out and grabbed him by the arm. "What did this to you?"

He turned to her and dropped his gaze to her hand. She removed it.

"Let's deal with one thing at a time. First your guest, then my scratches," he said.

He rubbed his tongue against the roof of his mouth to keep from telling her about Snow and the Slayers. Yes, she needed to know about them, but there was a more immediate situation. Explaining and convincing her of his plan for the Slayers would take more than a few minutes.

Sonya still held a suspicious expression, but she nodded her blonde head and strode out, her boots clicking on the stone floor. She was a formidable ally. As his father's advisor, her favorite thing to do was pry information from enemies with Greeg. And Sonya wasn't just good at interrogations, she'd mastered them.

Sage on the other hand, had never enjoyed torture. He did what was necessary, but he preferred a more diplomatic approach. He doubted the diplomatic approach would work with Quintess.

Dax waited for him in the hall. "I can't go down there with you." He wrung his hands. Sage had never seen him look so pale.

"I didn't expect you to." He laid his hand on Dax's shoulder. "If you need to leave, I understand."

"No. It isn't that. It's just… I have a feeling that I was tortured, sometime in my past."

Sage nodded. It was strange how little Dax remembered about himself. Almost as if magick had been employed. "When this is over and I have my kingdom back, I promise you, Dax. I'll do everything in my power to help you find out who you are."

Dax nodded, but said nothing.

He squeezed Dax's shoulder and then headed off to the dining hall. It was going to be a long day.

CHAPTER SIXTEEN

Snow sat in the solar, holding Sage's note.

"He asked us to meet him and then ambushed us with a group of other vampires," said Flint. "He got Kellan killed."

"But you said they were attacking him too." Sage was a vampire, but her heart told her he wouldn't have done something so low.

"It seemed that way," said Gerall.

"He said one was his brother," Hass retorted.

"He had also said his family was dead, so that was a lie," said Flint.

"It doesn't make sense." Snow frowned. "Why would he send you a note to come all the way to meet him, when he could have just had them attack you here and caught you off guard? I mean, think about it. He had to have known you would be suspicious and arm yourselves out there. Why didn't he just bring all the other vampires and attack us while we slept? That would have made more sense if he were trying to ambush you."

"Who said vampires make sense?" asked Jamen.

"Why are you taking his side? He's the reason Kellan is dead," said Erik.

Snow blew out a breath, trying to calm her unease. Sage hadn't had anything to do with Kellan's death. She'd have known if he did. But convincing her brothers would take brains. "I didn't say I am taking his side. I'm simply saying to look at this logically–"

"I have looked at it logically." Erik rose suddenly from his chair, his eyes piercing Snow. "He called us out. Vampires attacked. Kellan is dead. We are vampire slayers, Snow. It's what we do. We don't discriminate. You'll learn that, now that you're one of us."

Her heart leapt. "So you'll let me fight?"

"No," said Flint, too quickly.

"Yes," Erik countered, meeting Flint's eye.

Flint's body went rigid and the veins in his neck bulged. "No, Erik. Not Snow."

"What would you have me do? She's obviously going to go out there anyway. Look at what she did last night. Do you really want her running around by herself? With no training?"

The arm of the couch creaked under Flint's tight grip. Any minute he would explode. "Not. Snow," he said through clenched teeth.

She rose from her seat and went to Flint. Kneeling in front of him, she took his hand.

"Flint, look at me," she said. "I'm not the same as I was yesterday, or last week. My body is different, my senses are different. You know because it happened to you. I love Kellan as much as you. But I'm a better fighter than he was. I always have been. Father knew it, that's why he taught me to fight alongside the rest of you. I need to be out there. Protecting the humans. Helping those who can't fight back. You're afraid of losing me the way we all lost Kellan, and Mother and Father, but I have to do this. We can do this, all of us. Together."

She waited as Flint searched her face. He was as conflicted about her joining the fight as she was about wanting Sage. His gaze softened and he opened his mouth, but then just as quickly he hardened again and stood.

"If Snow hunts with you, I don't." He strode from the solar, the outside door slamming behind him.

Snow fell to the floor. It wasn't fair, but she knew her brothers wouldn't fight without him. He was the best fighter they had.

"Well that didn't go as planned," said Ian.

"Give him space." All hint of anger drained, Erik squeezed her shoulder. "He'll come around. Let's all get a few hours sleep and then we'll take Snow out with us to the practice grounds and show her what we do."

Her mind was numb. She wanted to fight alongside her brothers. To find the ones really responsible for Kellan's death and to clear Sage's name. But not without Flint. Without him there…

Flint didn't return for the rest of the day. Snow went to the barn with her brothers and down through a trap door into an underground training area.

"Oh, wow." She'd known where they trained, but had never been allowed down before.

"Well, let's get started," said Erik.

Her brothers weren't gentle, like they'd been when their father was alive. Erik was obviously serious about her fighting with them, and equally serious about her learning what she needed to before they let her go out.

To everyone's surprise, she fought with more confidence and agility than even she expected. With her improved reflexes and coordination, what she lacked in strength she made up for in her split second decision making ability. When she fought, somehow she saw attacks before they happened. And that allowed her to attack or defend even better than her brothers.

Her skill with a bow had improved as well. She hit the inner ring or bull's eye on every shot. Her only disadvantage was her lack of strength. Though she was stronger than an average female, she was still smaller than her much larger brothers. In hand-to-hand combat, if they got her on the ground, she was finished. She'd tried the leg maneuver she'd used to throw Sage off her, but it didn't work on her more prepared brothers.

"You have to keep off the ground." Gerall pulled her to her feet.

"Understood." She brushed hay and dirt from her clothes.

After Erik assessed her strengths and weaknesses they moved on to tactics. Everyone had a place and a job within the unit.

"You'll take Kellan—" He stopped and swallowed hard. "You'll use your bow, though you're good with a sword, too. With Jamen's arm out of commission, we'll need another sword."

"Flint won't let her fight that close to him," said Jamen. "If she's standing next to him he's going to get distracted trying to protect her."

"I don't need protecting," she said for the thousandth time.

"We know that, but it won't change how he reacts. Honestly, it won't be that different for any of us," said Jamen. "It's our job to keep you safe."

"It won't be any different," said Erik. "None of us want you out there."

Snow glanced around at her brothers, who all nodded in agreement.

"The only reason I've agreed to let you come is to keep you from going out alone," said Erik.

"Thanks for the vote of confidence," she muttered.

Though she wouldn't admit it, they were right. All of her brothers would try to protect her if she went on a hunt with them. For the first time she thought that it might not be such a great idea. On her own she wouldn't have to worry about getting the rest of them killed because they were distracted. But if she ran into more than a single vampire… She wasn't sure that her skills would be up to the task. Even with Erik's reluctance, at least he was letting her go. And she wouldn't be alone.

"Ranged weapons is where you'll be, until we all get used to you being with us," said Erik.

Snow nodded. She wanted to fight, and they were letting her. Maybe not in the way she wanted – with blood on her sword – but it was a start.

The group broke for dinner and ate leftovers, as she hadn't cooked. It grew dark outside and still Flint didn't turn up.

"He'll come back." Jamen put his arm over her shoulder. "He's probably down at the pub. If he doesn't return in an hour, I'll go look for him."

She nodded. "When you were at the pub the other night, did you happen to see Klaus?"

"Klaus?" Jamen's brows knit together. "I did. Why? What happened?"

"I saw him having a violent conversation with Armie while I was in town the other day."

"Violent how?" His expression became wary.

"When I went to stable my horse, he and a couple other men had Armie up against the stable wall with a knife at his throat. Said something about a business arrangement, but Armie was terrified."

Jamen gave her a tight smile. "Don't worry about it. I'll look into it."

"Thank you." She laid her hand on his arm. "My only worry is for Belle and Chloe."

Jamen nodded. "I understand. Belle's always been a good lass. Sad what she's been through with her father. But don't worry, I'll check in on her. Make sure she's safe."

The group finished their meal without much conversation. With two empty chairs at the table, the mood was tense and somber. Flint came in as the last of the dishes were being put away. He strode in without a word and went straight upstairs. She tried to follow, but Jamen grabbed her arm.

"Let me talk to him."

She sighed. It was probably better that way. He was more like Flint than any of the rest of them.

After cleaning up, everyone headed upstairs to bed. She was slipping into her nightgown when exhaustion overcame her. The day had been both physically and emotionally draining. It was barely 10 p.m. She didn't have to rise before dawn to go train at her cabin, she realized. She could actually get a full eight hours of sleep if she wanted. She remembered Sage and her heartbeat quickened. It was strange that she hadn't thought of him all day.

Looking again at the clock, she decided that six hours of sleep would be plenty. She would wake at four and go to see him.

Her body tingled at the memories of sharing her last evening with Sage. She smiled. Maybe she'd let him get her on the ground again.

*****

Sage dragged himself to his bed, tired to the core. He, Sonya and Greeg had spent the day working on the vampire they'd found, Quintess. They'd gotten very little information from him about Philos, but he was pretty sure at this point it was simply because Quintess knew so very little. He'd been paid by Philos to come to the pool, was given a ring to activate it, and then leave. That had been all. Quintess had no idea what was in the pool, or where it led.

Sage studied the large, currant red stone ring now encasing his middle finger. It appeared to be nothing more than a simple opaque ruby. Dax knocked and entered, as Sage peeled his shirt off.

"Did you find out what you needed to from the prisoner?"

"Not so much. But I got this." He held up the ring.

Dax walked closer and stared at the ring, transfixed.

"Do you recognize it?"

"Not the ring per se, but the stone. I've seen it before," said Dax.

"Do you remember where?"

"A bracelet, I think." After a minute, Dax tore his gaze from the ring. "Sorry, I don't remember anything more."

"It's fine." Sage clapped Dax on the shoulder and reached for a clean shirt.

"You still aren't healed," Dax noted.

"Yes, I noticed that." The scratches festered, and he had no idea why. "I haven't slept in two days. I'm going to get a few hours of sleep and see if that helps. If it doesn't, I'll check the library for answers."

Dax nodded. "I'm going out for a run. I'm not big on being cooped up underground. You need anything?"

"Would you mind running by Snow's cabin? Just to make sure she's all right."

"No problem," said Dax.

He sat on his bed and watched Dax leave. He didn't want Dax to go to her cabin; he wanted to go himself. To see her, taste her, feel her. But he needed to keep his distance, at least until he figured out what to do next. It was for the best. His chest ached from the scratches. He fell asleep, hoping that he would be healed by evening.

CHAPTER SEVENTEEN

Just after four, Snow hit the ground beneath her window and ran across the fields to the trees. A thrill exploded in her stomach and raced through her body. *Sage.* She'd awakened from her six hours of sleep so refreshed it took only minutes to dress in her fighting outfit, grab her sword and get out the window. She hadn't slept for six hours straight in… she didn't remember how long. She dashed past houses and through fields until she reached the woods. Her smile grew wider with every stride she took. The urge to kill him had all but subsided, leaving only the anticipation of seeing him and the desire to feel his skin on hers.

Reaching her small cabin in the glade, she stepped inside and set her sword on the table.

"Sage," she whispered.

There was no answer.

The smile left her face and a knot formed in her stomach. "Sage," she said again, louder. Again, no answer. She walked to the window and threw the curtains open. The moonlight shone in brightly. He wasn't there. Nor were any of his things. Not his coat, his sword, nothing.

Snow ran from the cabin to the clearing behind. Her heart sank. What if something had happened? What if her brothers had found him? Her stomach churned. She had to find him first. She rushed to her cabin and grabbed her sword, sliding it into its scabbard on her belt. She stepped to the doorway and a large figure appeared.

Relief washed over her and she threw herself at the figure. "My toth, are you all right? I was so worried."

The person hugged her stiffly. "I'm fine," he said.

Snow froze. It wasn't Sage. She clung to the familiar frame, her mind working quickly, trying to decide how to cover her mistake.

"You were expecting someone else, perhaps?" His arms loosened and let her go.

"No." She looked up trying to make her voice work. "I'm surprised you're here, but after the way you left the house today and didn't speak to anyone, I'm just glad you're all right, Flint." She turned from him to hide the rushing of her blood and the shake of her hands. "How did you find this place?"

"I'm a Slayer. Tracking is what I do. How did *you* find this place?"

She shrugged and faced him once more, trying to keep her voice light. "On one of my walks, I found it abandoned, so I took it for myself."

Flint crossed his arms over his chest and stared at her. A bead of sweat trickled down her spine. She needed to keep him from thinking she was meeting someone at night and question her.

"I come to practice," she said. "Since you guys won't let me work with you, and Father isn't here anymore to teach me."

"But there's no need. Erik's letting you hunt. So why did you come?"

She needed Flint to leave in case Sage returned. "True, Erik's letting me take Kellan's spot." Her voice cracked at the thought of replacing her brother so easily. She swallowed. "I don't know why I came. I've grown used to coming here at night. I like it here. It's...my own."

At least that part was the truth.

"Look, I know you don't think I should fight. But if you could've seen me today, I'm good. I can do this." She laid her hand on his forearm.

He was quiet for a long time. "Jamen told me how good you are. But–"

"I'll stay in the rear. I'll stay out of your way. You won't have to worry about me."

"No." Flint shook his head and her heart sank. "If you're going to fight, you're going to be right next to me where I can see you. I couldn't save Kellan because I couldn't get to him. I won't make that same mistake with you."

She hugged Flint again. This was what she had always wanted. To be there, in the thick of it, fighting vampires alongside them all. But suddenly standing in her cabin, with memories of Sage surrounding her, she wasn't so sure anymore.

"Don't hug me so fast," he said. "I expect you to be fully trained before you come out with us."

"I will." She let go, her mind conflicted. But if she could perhaps steer her brothers to the vampires that were trying to kill Sage...

"Good. Because the first vampire we're going to track is Sage," Flint said. "And you're going to kill him."

The next morning, Snow came downstairs to find Hass and Ian making eggs and toast, while Gerall set the milk and meat on the table.

"What's going on?" she asked, stunned that Hass and Ian even knew what a pan was.

"Big day." Erik smiled. "Today you train with Flint, and when we're done, you're going to show us on the map the last place you saw Sage. Then tonight we track him."

"I've never tracked before." Her hands grew clammy and a bloom of heat rushed through her.

"You're not going with us." Flint stole a slice of meat from the table as he entered. "When we find out where he's hiding, then we'll take you."

She nodded, but said nothing. Her brothers were determined to kill Sage, and Flint wanted her to do it. Now they wanted her to show them on the map where she'd seen him. Problem was, she'd lied. Flint had seen her cabin. She couldn't tell him she'd seen Sage anywhere near it or he would work out the truth.

She had no clue where Sage was though. He'd said he lived in the Wastelands, but that was obviously a lie. In fact, she knew very little about him. Where he lived, what he did during the daylight, nothing. Surely he wasn't alone in his exile. Aside from the man who'd brought the letter, there had to be others, didn't there? Where could they all hide? The thought of Sage sharing the daylight hours with a woman caused her jealousy to spike. How old was he? He'd probably been with hundreds of women.

"What's wrong with your hand?" asked Ian.

"What?" She blinked hard to clear her thoughts.

"Is your hand all right? You were rubbing it." Ian set a platter of eggs on the table.

She dropped her hand to her side, remembering the feel of Sage's tongue running over her cut. "Just a little sore from yesterday."

"Come on, let's eat," said Erik.

Across the dining table, Flint watched her. She managed to smile at him and take her seat. "I didn't even know you could cook," she said to Ian and Hass. "Smells good."

"Oh, we do," said Ian.

"You just do it better," finished Hass.

Everyone erupted into laughter. She laughed as well, until she spied Kellan's vacant seat. Her heart squeezed. With him gone, her life had become much more complicated than she had ever imagined. She missed him.

The day passed too quickly, and by the end of it, exhaustion overtook her once more. Flint hadn't been kidding about making sure she was ready before she could go out with them. He was a hard training partner, but she hoped she'd at least surprised him a little. He complimented her on her swiftness and agility, and admitted her swordplay was better than he had anticipated.

When they returned to the manor house for supper, she trudged to her room and fell into bed. She didn't even have the energy to take off her boots. She lay there, her thoughts on Sage. She ached to be in his arms. For the taste of his mouth on hers again. Her stomach warmed and her thighs tingled, remembering the feel of her hips astride his in the glade. More than anything, she wished to talk to him, to ask him what she should do, and to find out where he was, so she could protect him.

A knock sounded on her door, and it opened behind her.

"Snow," Gerall called. "We're ready to work on the map."

Her throat went dry. She didn't move. She slowed her breathing, making it rhythmical and soft. She may not be able to save Sage from her brothers forever, but she could save him for tonight.

"What's going on?" asked Jamen.

"Flint wore her out," Gerall whispered.

"Let her sleep. The vampire will still be out there tomorrow. We'll do the map in the morning."

The door closed quietly and her brothers talked quietly outside. She had bought herself and Sage a few hours, but tomorrow she needed a plan, to tell them where to search. She only prayed that the spot wasn't anywhere near his real location.

*****

Sage awoke to the sound of movement in his room.

"Come on, Sage," said Sonya. "Get up. We need to finish with Quintess. It's been two days."

"Two days?" He rolled over and sat up. How was that possible?

"Well, two nights, technically. You've been asleep for eighteen hours. What's wrong with you?"

"Too much fighting, not enough blood," he said. Aches riddled his body. The weakness in his extremities was enough to cause him mild concern.

"Then we should finish up and go hunt," said Sonya.

He rubbed his face. The movement made him look down. His shirt stuck to his chest, his blood seeping through. "Do you really think he has more he's not saying?"

"Yes." Sonya stopped at the foot of the bed. "So let's go."

Sonya had always been more of a sister to Sage than a servant. She'd never coddled him or babied him the way the rest of the castle had. He respected her for that. "You and Greeg can finish without me. I need to talk to Dax."

Sonya crossed her arms. "Why is that Were here, anyway? What do you need him for?"

He stared at Sonya. "Need him for?"

She had been brought up the daughter of a lesser family, but her ruthlessness and cunning had claimed his father's attention. Lothar had personally trained her to be his advisor and chief interrogator. He'd stripped all emotion out of her and left her with only logic and resourcefulness. Only Greeg saw her softer side. Greeg was her only weakness.

"I need him for nothing, Sonya. Dax is a good man, and he's my friend. If he stays for just tonight or a hundred years, it only matters to me because I will be sorry to see him go. I want him to find his place. He's helped me numerous times and so I help him in return. Not out of loyalty or out of obligation, but out of respect and friendship."

185

Sonya studied Sage. He knew she didn't understand. She acted only out of loyalty to him and his father. Loyalty and revenge. Sonya wanted to see Philos dead almost as much as he did.

"I will finish with Quintess without you, then. I can see that you are still in need of more rest." Sonya strode out as Dax walked in.

"Evening," said Dax.

"How did it go last night?" Sage asked. "Sorry I slept so long."

"No bother, you needed it. I went to her cabin. She came looking for you. At least, I assume she would have been looking for you, had her brother not shown up."

"Which brother?"

"The largest. Flint, I think," said Dax.

Sage's anger spiked. He didn't like that her brothers had found out about her special place. *Their place.* Now that her brothers knew of it, she would never feel it was truly just her own anymore. If he brought her here—

He stopped that train of thought. There was no way he could bring her to be with him. Despite the fact that he stayed underground in the Daemon lands, she was a Slayer. Other vampires lived here and they wouldn't understand. They wouldn't see her the way he did, and sooner or later, he would have to fight them all to keep her safe. He'd only kept himself from drinking her by sheer force of will. The others had no reason to show the same restraint.

He cursed Remus and his uncle, Philos, under his breath. This was their fault. If they'd just let him go. Let him live in peace, her brother would still be alive and she wouldn't be a Slayer. Then he

186

could take her as his mate and she would be protected by his blood. No other vampire would dare to trespass against her.

An idea sparked. If she drank from him, Slayer or no Slayer, other vampires would be forced to leave her alone or risk fighting him. She had licked him, but that had been just a taste. She would really have to drink from him for his scent to be upon her. Was it possible? He didn't know. But he needed to find out.

"Sage, you all right?"

"Yes, sorry. I need to go to the library. But first, I need to change my tunic, again."

"You still haven't healed?" Dax's brow knit together. "Is that normal?

"Not at all, I'm afraid. And my excuses about needing to feed aren't going to hold much longer with Sonya and Greeg." He stood from his bed, the movement pulling painfully on the scratches. "Let me wash up, and then you're welcome to join me if you wish."

Dax shrugged. "May as well, maybe there'll be something in those old books that might help to explain me."

Dax and Sage read in the library for two hours before Sonya entered with Greeg.

"He's dead," she said.

Sage looked up from his book. "Did he say anything else?"

"Only that the queen had set up the slave trade system with a man named Klaus. A human who trades with the vampires. Quintess was told to go to the pool and use the ring, wait until the humans entered the pool, and then leave."

"The queen? My uncle isn't mated."

Sonya shrugged. "It's possible he's mated since our departure."

A shiver ran through him. He had a bad feeling about the news.

"What are you looking for?" Greeg motioned to the tomes piled on the table.

"I'm trying to find some information that might help us retake the kingdom. The vampires that attacked us the other night were faster and stronger than they should have been."

"Magick?" asked Greeg.

"Probably." Sage hated not telling them everything, but he needed to settle things with the Slayers before he brought everyone in on it.

"You're bleeding again." Sonya pointed at his chest. "Why *are* you bleeding?"

Blood seeped through his cream tunic. "It's nothing, I just need to feed."

Sonya strode over. "Let me see it."

"I'm fine," he said.

"Sage, you've been bleeding for two days and sleep hasn't helped. Let me see it."

He pierced her with his gaze. "I said I'm fine."

She glanced at the book he read.

He shut it.

The two stared at each other for a long minute. She was stubborn and wasn't about to let this go.

"I'll feed tonight," he said. "If it doesn't help, I'll let you know."

"Do that."

"Come Sonya, let Prince Sage do what he needs to," said Greeg.

After their footsteps faded, Dax said, "You need to tell them about the Slayers before they find out on their own."

"I will, once I figure out how to do it without getting anyone killed. We need the Slayers if I am to regain my kingdom, but do you honestly think that if I introduced them to Sonya and the others now, it would end in anything but a fight?"

"I don't think waiting is going to help on that front and not telling them is more dangerous. What if they run into the Slayers?"

"I'll tell them. I will, but I need the Slayers to trust me first."

Sage met Dax's somber gaze and tried to convince himself that the mission wasn't futile.

He plucked his shirt from his oozing chest. He had yet to find out anything about the Slayers. There were no pictures, descriptions, sightings, nothing. Pushing his current book aside, he reached for an ancient tome that he'd never seen before. He thumbed through the brittle pages, looking for something. *Anything.*

"You find anything that sparks your memory?" he asked Dax without even a sideways glance.

"Sort of, I'm not sure. There was a chapter about the history of dragons that felt familiar."

He laughed. "You went from being a dragon to a bear?"

"I don't think so," said Dax. "But for some reason I feel that dragons are beings I've dealt with before."

"If that's true, the dragons migrated to the southeast about a hundred years ago. Maybe you should look there."

"Maybe. But according to this, dragons don't appreciate people nosing in their business. I'd prefer to get a few memories back before I go trying to find them."

A page caught Sage's eye and he stopped. It was a picture depicting Slayers. Dressed in all black, the figures possessed Cris knives and were surrounded by a golden aura. He scanned the page. There wasn't much. No one knew how the Slayers were picked or who did the picking. All that was known was what the mantle meant. The mantle was bestowed on humans when the vampire nation was ruled by evil. The mantle lasted the span of the Slayers' lives. If the Slayers were unable to eradicate the evil by the end of their lives, the mantle passed on to another, usually a family member.

The usually weapon of a Slayer are: the sword, the bow and the Cris knife. Their inherited speed, agility, and strength are comparable to that of a vampire. A vampire injured by a Slayer's weapon will heal as normal, with the exception of a Cris. However, a wound caused by the hand of a Slayer, has been shown to only heal when the blood of that Slayer is drunk.

Sage sagged in his chair and ran his fingers through his hair. *Oh toth!*

"You find what you were looking for?"

"Yes."

"Is it helpful?" Dax flipped the page in his own book.

"No," said Sage. "I have to drink from Snow."

Dax met Sage's eye. "Why is that a problem? You think she won't let you?"

"It's a problem because I've never drunk from a human that I didn't end up draining, and her blood sings to me in a way none has before. Just a taste almost made me ravish her. If I actually had to drink from her..." The idea swirled in his mind and his gums burned. The mere thought of tasting her again was almost enough to send him out into the night to find her. "I won't be able to stop."

"But you love her," said Dax.

He swallowed hard, his throat dry and painful. "It doesn't matter, Dax. When the thirst takes over...." He turned his gaze to Dax. "You have no idea. It's indescribable. It's a pain that runs through your whole body. A need so intense that you can't focus on anything else. Vampires have been hacked to death in the throws of bloodlust and never stopped drinking. There's a reason I don't feed on humans anymore. I've done things. Terrible things—" He couldn't think about it anymore.

"What if we had her bleed into a goblet? Would that work?"

He thought for a moment. "It might. But just having her in the same room with me... I can't, Dax. I can't take the chance."

Dax stared off into space. "People surprise themselves when it comes to what they can do for the ones they love."

CHAPTER EIGHTEEN

Queen Terona drew the whip back and let it crack against Remus' chest for the tenth time. Blood dripped from his body in rivulets. He shuddered under the lash, making her desire spike.

"No more," he whispered, barely conscious.

She moved in front of him in a stride. Grabbing his sweat soaked face, she jerked it up so his eyes met hers.

"There will be no more when I say there is no more." She pressed her lips to his, biting him hard. He moaned. Sucking his lip into her mouth, she drank the blood. "You disobeyed me, Remus. You allowed your pride to get the better of you. You revealed yourself to Sageren, and then let him escape."

"I told you, he had help."

"I'm aware that he had help. The Weres are always by his side."

"No, not Weres. Humans. Slayers."

Her eyebrows rose. "That's not possible."

"They were. I assure you," Remus said, breathing hard. "And besides, he'll think I'm really dead. That bear almost ripped me to pieces. It was only your magick that saved me."

Her mind raced with the implications. If the Slayers had returned to the lands, it could only mean that someone knew about her. And possibly not just about her, but about her family as well. If the Slayers were helping Sage, it would be harder than ever to kill him. But in order to gain complete control of Tanah Darah, she needed Sage dead. Sage, then Philos and lastly, Remus. Well, maybe not Remus. He was good enough as a toy. Her gaze moved to where he hung naked, chained in the middle of her private rooms.

"Remus," she said with a pout, "you let me down. But possibly you have done me a good turn with this news. If you are right."

"I am, I promise."

"Of course, darling." She trailed a finger down his cheek. "But I need to make sure. I'll have to send out a scout team."

"Let me go," said Remus. "Let me prove myself to you. I can do it."

"No, no, no." She smiled. "You are too valuable to me. I care for you. I can't take the chance of you being injured again. I don't have the magick to save you again. I need what I have left to make a few more Private Guards. No my dear, I have a much better idea for you." Terona kissed Remus again trying hard to keep her fangs at bay. Remus moaned with pleasure. Looking down, she noted that his cuts had already healed. She ran her tongue down his chest, licking the blood off it. She never tired of vampire blood. It was so much better than human.

"Please, Terona," Remus panted. "Please."

"Oh, don't worry, darling," she said, meeting his gaze. "I'll let you down. When I'm good and satisfied. Now, tell me again. Remus, Remus, strong and tall, who is the fairest of them all?"

"You are, my queen. You are the fairest of them all."

"Of course I am." She shed her dress and licked down his stomach, lapping at his blood. Remus moaned.

"Where have you been?" asked Philos, as she slipped into their bedroom.

"I went for a walk," she said with a smile.

Philos was at her side in an instant. "You lie," he spat. "I can smell another's blood on you from all the way over here."

"Oh, Philos." She waved him off. "It was just a little fun, nothing more, my darling."

"Don't toy with me." He flashed his fangs and grabbed her by the arm.

"I'm not." She slapped his hand away. "I sent out a group of my own to find Sageren. Only two returned. But they returned with news and he is now the least of our problems."

"I didn't give you permission to send out a group. I am king here, not you. You don't make the decisions for Tanah Darah."

She stood her ground, curious as to whether he would hit her. His prattle angered her. He thought he was such a big man, being king. Yet it was she who had put him on the throne, her poison that had killed his brother Lothar, her magick that provided the way for the slave trades. It was she who ran Tanah Darah, not their measly king.

"Of course, my darling. I simply wanted to help," she said, pulling him close. "You're busy and that issue of Sage bothers you, so I wanted to try and do something to ease your burden."

"What did they find?" His eyes never left her face as she stroked his hard chest with her fingers.

"There are Slayers in Fairelle."

194

"W-what?" His eye widened. "There haven't been Slayers in thousands of years."

"Even so, they've returned."

Philos stared at her. "I will send out my own group. If there are Slayers, I will know." He grabbed her again by the arm and pulled her close. His hips ground into hers and she had to stifle a groan. His gaze skimmed down to the peaks of her breasts. "You are mine, Terona. Mine. No one else's. You may have your fun, as you call it. But when you come to my bed, you do as I wish." Philos' lips came down in a hard, possessive kiss. She wrapped her arms around his waist and pressed closer. Tonight was going to be painful. Just the way she liked it.

CHAPTER NINETEEN

Snow awoke to find her brothers gathered around the breakfast table with a map spread before them. Her stomach churned as soon as she entered the room.

They pointed at the map and marked off areas they were sure Sage couldn't be. "Ah, there she is. Sleep well?" Erik asked.

"Just great," she mumbled, pulling her robe tighter around her.

"Come," said Flint. "We were just discussing where we should look first. Show us where you spotted him."

"Can't I at least get something to drink first?".

"Of course." Flint's voice followed her into the kitchen. "You said he was south in the grazing field area. But something tells me north might be a better direction to try."

She trudged to the pitcher and poured herself a glass of water. Now what was she to do? Lie? Sooner or later it wouldn't matter. They would track north, regardless. At least if she told them to go north, he wouldn't be there. He was gone. The Daemonlands were suddenly seeming more and more of a likely place for him to be hiding.

"What are you thinking so hard about, little sister?" Flint set his cup in the basin next to her.

"Nothing." She shrugged, sipping her water.

"You know with your becoming a Slayer, I think we might need to get someone in to help out with the day-to-day chores. Keep the house running."

"But we can't take the chance of someone finding out."

"Maybe we can. If we chose someone we trusted."

"You have someone in mind?" asked Snow.

"What about Belle?"

"Yes, but Belle..." Belle, what? Snow didn't know what Belle was anymore. She trusted Belle, but after Snow's encounter with Klaus in the village, she doubted he'd let Belle go all that easily. Maybe this was exactly what Belle needed to finally flee Klaus once and for all. Not that she even wanted to, but if anyone could protect her, Snow's family could.

"I'll ask her the next time I see her," Snow finally said, "But she would have to bring baby Chloe."

"Good," said Flint. "Come on and let's figure out where that vampire is hiding."

Snow set down her cup and watched Flint stride from the kitchen. There was no getting out of this.

An hour later, after the group had mostly bickered and argued, they decided to first check the area Snow told them she'd seen Sage: the cow fields to the south. But Flint was convinced that Sage stayed up north near the wolves, where they'd found him twice already.

To her surprise, he didn't mention Snow's cabin, or finding her there. At least, not yet.

"We'll scour the area to the south tonight. If we find nothing, we go north," he said.

"The wolves warned us about hurting him," said Jamen.

"We can deal with the wolves when the time comes. They're loyal, but they don't want a war with the humans," said Erik. "We find Sage, we kill Sage. He's a vampire, and that's our job."

"What about vampire children?" Snow asked. "I mean, yes, we're vampire slayers, but what does that mean? Why are we doing it? Are we supposed to kill vampire babies in their cribs in hopes that someday they won't kill someone?"

"Vampires can't have children, Snow. They're dead," laughed Hass.

"Well if they're dead, why do they bleed?" she countered.

Hass opened his mouth and closed it several times. He looked to Ian for support. Ian shrugged and shook his head.

"If they can bleed, doesn't that mean they're alive somehow?" She looked from brother to brother, but no one had an answer. They had to have thought about it. Didn't they? She couldn't be the only one who, having seen a vampire close up, questioned what they had been taught.

"The Slayers are called when the vampire nation is ruled by evil," Flint intoned. "That's what we were told. That's what we do."

"All right, so why don't we forget Sage and go for those in power?" asked Snow.

"Sage is in power. He's part of the royal family."

"You said he was exiled and wanted your help to kill his uncle." Her temper rose. She needed to keep in control so they didn't suspect something. Were they really so blinded by anger?

"A lie to ambush us," said Flint.

Snow looked from Flint to Erik. "But you said—"

"Enough." Flint slammed his fist on the table, rattling the dirty plates and glasses. "Enough, Snow. We begin the eradication of the vampire ruling class tonight. Starting with Sage."

Snow narrowed her gaze at him and lifted her chin. "And when you've killed them all, the entire ruling class…then what, Flint? Then whom?"

Flint stared at her, long and hard. "She isn't ready. I won't fight with her until she is." Turning, he walked out of the room.

"So that's your answer for everything, then? When someone doesn't agree with you and things don't go your way, Flint? Shut them out and walk away." Snow crossed her arms over her chest and bit back the harsh names she wanted to call him.

The front door slammed in reply. Every pair of eyes was upon her.

"He's right, Snow," said Erik softly. "You aren't ready. You have the abilities of a Slayer, but not the mindset. You can't think that way and slay. Honestly, I hope you never get it. I hope you stay as optimistic and loving as you are." He looked around at their brothers. "Let's go get some work done around the estate. We leave at nightfall."

Snow's brothers left her standing at the dining table without a word. Picking up the knife Erik used to point at the map, Snow threw it across the room. It lodged in the wall next to a picture of her parents.

Her heart thumped heavily in her chest and her body was awhirl with emotion. She wanted to slay the vampires hunting Sage, to feel them turn to dust on her sword.

Her brothers were wrong about Sage. And if they were wrong about Sage, how many others were they wrong about?

Snow spent the day cooking and cleaning and taking her frustrations out on the house. She beat the carpets and scrubbed the floors until she broke the scrub brush. She crushed potatoes until they were glue and burnt the meat.

She'd stripped the sheets and dusted and done absolutely anything she could to forget about her brothers and Sage. He hadn't been at the cabin when she'd shown up the previous night, and that troubled her. She got the feeling he'd left in an effort to avoid her. She wasn't sure which upset her more, the fact that he wasn't there, or the fact that she'd let him in to begin with.

The heartache at his absence was not something she'd been prepared for. Now she realized how good spending time with him had felt. How for those fleeting hours in the middle of the night, she once again felt normal. Being able to forget the worries and sorrows of her life. He'd been a wondrous escape, or at least, he was supposed to be.

Looking back, her life from a week ago seemed mundane, ordinary even. But now everything was wrong. She wanted a man she couldn't have. She had to kill people that she wasn't all that sure deserved to be killed. And most of all, she had to care for her brothers, who wanted to kill the man she might love.

Snow stopped moving. She might love Sage. Her chest tightened until she thought she might squeeze to death. Oh how she wished she could go back to the nights where she had only dreamed of a man to love, instead of being plagued by heart-wrenching memories of a man she couldn't have.

Pushing a tear from her cheek, Snow chastised herself for her softness. All she seemed to do lately was cry.

Throughout the day, the only respite from her thoughts was the hour she'd spent in her aviary before supper. But the solace had been short lived.

Her brothers returned to the house in time for dinner, telling her that the meat was wonderful. *Liars*. Flint came in last, but didn't sit.

He looked at Erik. "I'll go get ready."

Erik nodded.

When dinner was over, Erik offered to help with the dishes.

Snow's eye twitched and she rubbed at it. Something was up. Erik never helped with the dishes.

"Go on, you guys, get ready," Erik said to the rest of their brothers. One by one, Jamen, Gerall, Ian and Hass glanced at Snow and then headed for the stairs.

"What's going on?" she asked, once they were gone.

Erik picked up three plates and walked them to the kitchen. "We need to cover as much ground as possible tonight, so I want them to hurry."

Snow didn't buy it. Picking up the remaining plates, she carried them to the kitchen. Erik headed out to the table as Snow poured water into the basin. When everything was cleared, Jamen entered. Erik nodded to him and left.

"You going to tell me what's going on?" she asked, placing a hand on her hip.

Jamen shook his head and looked away.

Ten minutes later, Snow and Jamen were finishing up the dishes when Erik called her name. Putting down the rag, she looked to Jamen for support. He chewed the inside of his check. It wasn't a good sign. Lifting her chin, she walked up the stairs and down the landing to her room. Erik stood by the door and Flint waited inside. Snow met him in the middle of the floor, at the foot of her bed.

"We're going now, and you need to stay in tonight and not follow us." Flint gave her a knowing look.

"Don't worry." Snow crossed her arms. "I don't intend to." The last thing she wanted was to be near her brothers.

"We want you to remember," said Erik stepping into the room. "That we all love you. You're the one true light in our dim world, and all we want is to protect you."

"Goodnight, Snow." Flint kissed her cheek and walked out. Erik gave her a tight smile and he followed Flint, closing the door behind him.

Snow stood there for a long minute, trying to figure out what the heck had just happened when a click came from outside her door.

Panic settled in her chest and she ran to the bedroom door and grasped the handle, turning it. It didn't budge. The lock had been changed.

The new one had a large keyhole, and as she grasped the handle again, she realized there must be a keyhole on both sides. She couldn't just lock people out, but they could lock her in. She scanned her room for the key, but there wasn't one.

"Let me out!" Snow shouted, trying the handle again and again. She slammed her palm against the door. "Let me out!"

No answer came.

Snow kicked the door, screaming her brothers' names in turn. She ran to her window and heaved upward, but it wouldn't budge. Running her fingers over the edges of the sill, she found the nails hammered in to keep her window shut tight. Down below, her brothers strode to the barn. She banged on the window, screaming their names.

Gerall turned to look at her. Erik stopped moving and set his hand on Gerall's shoulder, but Gerall shook him off, yelling something incoherent and pointing up at Snow. Erik stood his ground and said something that made Gerall's shoulders slump. Gerall glanced at her one last time and then continued moving forward with the rest.

Anger welled inside her. They couldn't keep her trapped in the house. She wasn't a prisoner. Snow ran to her closet and threw the door wide. She reached for her practice outfit, sword and rope, but they were all gone. She screamed and rushed to the window in time to see her brothers ride off into the fading evening light. Turning away from them, she stormed around her room.

She had to get out.

She bit her thumbnail and glanced around the room. Her gaze lit on her door and she looked at the keyhole again. Marching to her vanity, she pulled a hair comb off of it and then knelt on the floor by the door. Bending the metal she pried a tooth from the beautiful comb and stuck it in the hole. She maneuvered it around for several minutes before giving up. Throwing it to the floor, she screamed in fury and fell on her rear with a thump.

Think, Snow, think. She pounded on her skull with her hands, but it didn't help. When she closed her eyes, all she envisioned was Sage being decapitated by her brothers. A knot formed in her stomach. She had to do something. Her clock struck seven. She stared at the large brass clock for several minutes, watching the hands move. A smile played on her lips as an idea formed.

She pushed to her feet and grabbed the large brass clock. She weighted it in her hands, and with a grunt, she hurled it at her window. The glass shattered, as the clock flew out into the yard. Cheering, she dashed to the window and carefully brushed the remaining pieces of glass to the ground below.

Now, all she needed was a way to get down.

Snow raced into the night, her dress whipping behind her. She bolted for her cabin, where she would have a change of clothes and most importantly, a sword. After she picked them up, she intended to search for Sage herself. To warn him.

A hundred yards from her cabin, voices on the breeze stopped her in her tracks. For a moment, she hoped it was Sage, but it wasn't. It was a man and a woman arguing.

"I'm aware of that, Greeg," the woman said. "But I'm tired of waiting. I want to go home."

"We will, my sweet," the male replied. "Soon. Very soon. Be patient just a little longer."

"We've waited for years. I love Sage as if he were my own brother, but there is no reason to keep waiting. The time has come."

Sage! They knew Sage. Snow surged forward through the trees and then stopped. They knew Sage, which could only mean one thing. *Vampires*. Snow's instincts kicked in full force. Her heartbeat raced and her fingers twitched for her blade. Vampires were in her glade, and vampires were meant to be killed. Her hearing perked up and she peered in the dark for the two people. Leaving her hiding spot behind a tall tree, she inched closer, in an effort to catch a glimpse of them. A twig snapped beneath her foot and her heart caught in her throat.

"Did you hear that?" the man murmured.

"Do you smell that?" asked the woman, breathing deeply. "The scent. It's so… intoxicating."

Snow swallowed hard. Hushed footsteps moved closer.

"Sonya! No!"

She had only moments before she'd be discovered. Her only option was to run for her cabin where her sword and bow awaited. Snow sprinted for the door. Shouts and growls followed close behind.

A tree branch whipped her face, opening a cut on her cheekbone. Someone moaned in delight.

"Greeg, I don't think I can hold back this time," the female said.

Snow made it to the door and ran inside, slamming it behind her and locking it. She reached for the closet when the vampires hit her cabin door.

"Come out, come out," said the female.

"Sonya, remember our promise," said the male.

"I know – but do you smell her? She's intoxicating. I won't drain her, I promise. I just want to taste her. I haven't tasted a human in over a decade."

There was a thump and the female screeched and swore, her voice moving away from the door. Snow reached into the closet and grasped her sword, then unlatched the cabin door and came out swinging.

The tall, dark-haired male grappled with a smaller, but formidable-looking female. His arms were wrapped about her waist. The female clawed at him, desperate to get away.

"Run," the male said, looking Snow straight in the eye.

"Let me have her, Greeg!" screamed the female.

This was it. What her brothers had talked about. The bloodlust of a vampire. Snow's vision sharpened in the moonlight. The male strained to hold on.

"Don't be a fool, girl! Run!" the man yelled.

Snow's gaze raked over the small blond vampire. This monster was what she needed to protect humans from. Whether or not they knew Sage didn't matter. It was Snow's destiny, and the female needed to die.

Snow planted her feet firmly in the dirt and raised her sword. "You want me, vampire? Come get me."

As if a fire lit inside the female, she kicked back with her foot and thrust her elbow into the male's chest. He cried out and let her go.

She was free. The woman charged Snow.

"Sonya, stop!" the male yelled.

Snow prepared for the attack. Her fighting instincts calculated the female's movement patterns. The speed of her gait, the fluidity of her movements. At the last minute, the female sprung forward. Snow slid out of the way and sliced with her sword.

She missed, but so did the vampire. Both turned and the vampire rushed again.

"I love the taste of the blood when they've fought back," the female said, baring her fangs.

"And I love the sound of vampires turning to ash," Snow countered.

The female chuckled and crouched, ready to spring again. "Little girl, you have no idea who I am."

"And you have no idea who I am." Snow swung her sword in a circle and breathed deeply, focusing her energy. Her blood pumped with the need for vengeance. This would be the first vampire to fall by her sword, and with this kill, she would prove to her brothers that she was ready for this calling.

The woman charged again. She slashed her fingernails at Snow's chest. Snow blocked the attack and punched the female in the nose. Pain shot through Snow's knuckles and up her wrist at the contact. Taking advantage of the stunned vampire, Snow crouched and swiped with her leg, knocking the woman off her feet. The vampire fell backward and howled with rage. Kicking out her own legs, she wrapped them around Snow's throat and pulled her to the ground. Snow's sword flew across the ground.

The vampire's legs squeezed tightly around Snow's neck. Panic crept up Snow's spine as she struggled for breath. *Get off the ground, Snow. Get off the ground.*

Flint's words echoed in her mind. She was running out of air. Thinking fast, she turned her face and buried her teeth into the woman's fleshy thigh. The female howled with pain and released Snow from her grasp.

Snow coughed and sputtered as she got up. The female limped to her feet, smiling broadly as blood seeped from the wound.

"That was dirty," the female said.

"Only for me." Snow spat blood onto the ground.

"Sonya, enough," said the male. "Let's go. Leave her be."

"But Greeg, my lover," the female cooed as she and Snow circled each other. "I'm just starting to have fun. And it's been a very long time since I've had any real fun."

"Sage will find out. He won't be happy—"

"I'm not happy." The female rushed Snow again. She made like she was going to punch Snow, and when Snow bent to dodge the punch, the female brought her knee up instead, connecting with Snow's mouth. Pain shot through Snow's face and blood poured from her split lip as she landed on her back. Her head hit the root of a tree with a thwack, and Snow's vision went fuzzy. The trees above her swirled in and out of view. She needed to get up. She sucked in a breath and choked on the blood pouring into her mouth from the wound.

A blurry face floated into view and Snow cried out as a cool body pressed down upon hers, and something sharp pierced her neck. *Oh, dear gods, please don't let this be happening!*

Pain exploded through Snow as the female's fangs ripped and tore at her skin. Snow screamed and clawed helplessly at the vampire. The female sealed the wound with her mouth. A tremendous pressure built as the vampire sucked long and deep.

The tingling started in her fingers and toes, as blood drained from her extremities. Snow bucked and clawed at the vampire, to no avail.

"Get her off or you're dead!" bellowed an eerily familiar voice in Snow's head. She needed to stop panicking and act. She grasped the woman's hair in her fist and pulled her mouth away, ripping the woman's fangs from her neck. Jerking forward, Snow smashed her face into the vampire's. The female fell back, her nose pouring blood. She howled in rage and struck Snow across the face. Snow's mind fuzzed again and all she could see was a face covered in blood.

"Now, I *will* kill you." Baring her fangs, the female poised over Snow, prepared to strike again.

Snow touched the tear in her throat, blood smearing her fingers. But she felt nothing. Everything began to go numb. She was going to die. She thought she was ready to be a Slayer, but Flint had been right all along. And now she would never see her brothers or Sage again.

A roar echoed through the woods. An ivory bear crashed through the trees and knock the female away. The male vampire rushed to the aid of his female companion. Snow lay frozen to the spot as the bear perched over her and roared at the vampires. The two vampires huddled together and backed away.

"I wasn't going to kill her, Dax," said the female. "I wasn't."

The bear shook his heavy head and turned to Snow. An ivory bear had just rescued her. Snow blinked up at him slowly. Her vision blurred and everything went dark.

CHAPTER TWENTY

The doe Sage had taken did nothing to heal his wounds. Again. He'd known they wouldn't, but at least the thirst wasn't killing him anymore. He sat in his room, his thoughts dark. Without Snow's blood, he would never heal.

Hurried footsteps ran down the corridor. Sonya talked to someone very fast.

"I didn't know," she said. "How was I supposed to know?"

"It isn't her fault. I should have stopped her. But we've been down here so long..." came Greeg's voice.

Sage pulled his door open. "What's going on?" It took him several seconds to understand what he was seeing. Dax stood in human form, naked, holding an unconscious woman in his arms. Sonya's face and tunic were smeared with blood and Greeg looked confused and scared. Sage's stomach churned. Dax came to a halt feet from Sage. Sonya stopped talking, her eyes wide with alarm.

"I didn't know, Highness," she whispered, backing into Greeg's protective arms.

A scent hit Sage and his fangs burst from his gums. He looked at the dark-haired woman covered in blood in Dax's arms. *Snow.*

"Oh, my–" Sage grabbed Snow's limp body from Dax. Her head lolled to the side as he rushed her into his room. She bled from a bite wound, a cut to her lip, as well as a cut on her cheekbone. Sage laid her down on his bed gently, paralyzed by fear.

He turned to Dax, his mind racing in a thousand different directions. "She can't be here. There's too many of us," was all he could manage.

"I'm sorry. There was nowhere else to take her without it making things worse."

Panic rippled over Sage. His gaze shifted back to Snow. She wasn't moving, and her coloring was pale. He sat next to her and brushed the hair from her cheek, exposing her neck. The gaping wound still trickled blood. He leaned over and licked her neck shut. His body lurched at the taste and his fangs slammed into his mouth without warning. His blinked several times and held his breath in an effort to subdue his carnal desires. The marks on her neck began to heal.

Finally his mind caught up with him. She'd been bitten. Anger surged inside of him and he leapt off the bed at Sonya, who stood in the doorway. Grabbing her by the throat, he bared his fangs and flung her to the ground.

"You did this," he roared.

Greeg stepped between them. "She didn't know, Sage," he said. "How could any of us have known? She's human."

Sage's anger seethed within him. He clenched his jaw, pressing his fangs into his lower lip. He had to keep it under control. In that moment, he wanted nothing more than to rip out Sonya's throat. Red dots pulsed into view, and his body shook with the need for vengeance.

He kicked at Sonya violently. "Get out," he roared. "Get out, or die." She scrambled to her feet, her eyes tearful. He never let anyone see this side of him.

212

A moan sounded from his bed. Sage turned and Snow's eye's fluttered open.

"Sage," she whispered.

He moved to her side in an instant, kissing her forehead. "I'm here, love. I'm right here."

She reached for him and he wrapped her soft body in his arms, kissing her cheek, her forehead, her nose. He had to protect her. To keep her safe. She was the only thing that mattered anymore. Even regaining his throne was nothing compared to her. The door to his room closed with a click.

Lying next to her was almost unbearable. The scent of her blood and the lingering taste in his mouth caused his mind to swim and his desire to build.

"You left me," she said.

"No, love. No, I'm here."

Her eyes were glassy and unfocused. He pushed the hair from her face.

"My brothers. They're searching for you."

He chuckled. "Of course they are. That's their job."

She looked so vulnerable lying beside him. Her eyes pleaded with him for some reason. She wanted to ask something, he could tell.

"They think you killed Kellan. You didn't though, did you?"

His throat clenched. "No, I didn't kill Kellan. But it is my fault he's dead. Rest. We'll talk about it when you're healed."

She reached up and traced his lips with her finger. "I missed you."

Her lip wept a trickle of blood. He covered her mouth with his own and licked her lip. The cut sealed instantly. Turning her face gently, he licked her cheekbone. Her scent and taste surrounded him and he wanted more. Not just a taste, but to drink from her. To feel her life force bond with his own and mix as he drank from her and they made love. If he drank from her, he'd be healed by the time she woke up.

"What is it?" she asked. Her hand lay flat against his chest.

She was so willing. If he asked it, he was sure she would give herself to him.

"Sleep," he said. "I won't let anything happen to you." He glanced at his door; he needed to lock it.

"I know," she said. "I trust you."

You shouldn't. But he was determined to keep her safe. Even from himself. He would do whatever he had to, including endure the exquisite torture of lying next to her as she slept.

He held her close. Several times in her sleep she called his name and he crushed her closer still. She pressed her body to his and he watched her breasts move up and down as she breathed. She was so beautiful. He ran his hand up her arm and over her throat, feeling where Sonya had bitten her. The tear had healed like he'd known it would. Her cheek was almost healed as well, and her lip sported a small yellowing bruise.

He brushed a dark hair from her forehead and kissed her again on the cheek. She stirred and moaned his name. Sage's arousal grew. He loved nothing more than to hear the sound of his name on her lips.

Hours later, her eyelids opened and she looked up at him groggily. It took a minute and several blinks before they cleared. But suddenly Snow's eyes brightened and she scanned her surroundings.

"Where am I?" she asked in a voice stronger and clearer than he would have thought possible after last night.

"In my room."

"Your room?" she asked, confused.

He laughed. "I told you love, I have a place in the Daemonlands."

So she'd been right to send her brothers south. "How did I get here?"

His smile fell. "You were attacked."

Snow thought for a second, and then her face hardened and she pushed away from his embrace. "A vampire attacked me." She touched her throat, then looked at her hand.

He sat up and ran his fingers through his hair. "Her name is Sonya. She's my friend—"

Snow jumped from the bed, her eyes narrowed and jaw set. "Your friend? She tried to kill me. Where is she?"

Sage could see Snow's new instinct kicking in. "Calm yourself, you're safe."

"Calm myself?" Snow said, whirling to face him. "That stupid vampire tried to kill me."

He was losing her. He couldn't stand for that to happen, not now. He realized how much he had missed her these last few days. Not that he would admit it to a soul, but lying with her for the past hours had been the happiest moments of his long life.

"You have to understand. Sonya isn't like me. She didn't choose to not drink human, I made her. I require it of all those who stay with me, so it's harder for her."

Snow took a step toward him. "Are you defending her?"

"No." He rose from the bed and moved to her side. "I almost killed her myself for what she did to you. I'm just trying to help you understand."

"Oh, I understand. You don't have to explain to me. I saw it first hand. There's a reason I'm a Slayer."

*****

Snow wanted to destroy the vampire Sonya. Her senses were in overdrive, her Slayer instincts firing at a rapid rate. The need to kill almost consumed her.

She and Sage stared at each other for a long, silent moment as the memories of what had happened flooded back.

"Dax is a bear," she blurted out, suddenly remembering.

"A werebear, yes."

"I've never heard of that," she mused. "My brothers said they saw one, but he's so…"

"There's not been one before, I believe. What were you doing in the woods, anyway?" he asked. "I told you not to."

Snow's anger flared and she was nose-to-nose with him in a step. "You left," she said. "I was trying to protect you from my brothers."

"I told you I wouldn't be there. It's best for you if you aren't with me," he said. "It's safer."

"Fine. Then I'll go." Snow unlocked the door and stepped into the hall. Sage grabbed her by the waist and pulled her back to his room, slamming the door and pressing her against it.

He stared at her hard and leaned in closer, setting the palms of his hands onto the wood on either side of her head. His eyes glowed with a beautiful light from somewhere deep within, but they were full of sadness. His arousal pressed into her.

"Don't go."

Warmth rushed through her body, flushing her cheeks and pooling in her belly. The sensation tingled and excited her. His fingers skimmed along her collarbone. He drew her face close and pressed his lips lightly to hers. Fire bloomed inside. Her body betrayed what her mind told her not to want.

Snow's lips parted and she lapped at his mouth with her tongue. He moaned low in his chest making her shiver. Sage wrapped his hands in her hair and crushed her into him.

Breaking his mouth away from hers, he kissed down her neck. She tensed as he reached her torn, but healing throat. His tongue slid tenderly over the still sensitive area. Her breathing hitched. The mixture of pain and pleasure blurred her senses. Her legs trembled and she pressed against the wood for support.

She wanted this. Even after what Sonya had done, somehow she still wanted this. Snow grabbed at his chest and he winced.

"What is it?"

"Nothing." He averted his gaze.

She studied his face. "You're lying." A spot of blood blossomed on his shirt where she had touched him. "Sage, you're bleeding," she said.

"It's nothing." He plucked the tunic from his chest and his face twisted into a brief grimace.

Something pricked in her mind and she ran her fingers under the edge of his tunic, trying to lift it. He planted his hands firmly on her wrists, pulling her fingers free.

"Don't," he said through gritted teeth.

Snow clenched her jaw and narrowed her gaze on him. "Take off your tunic."

"No," he said.

"Let me see." When he didn't move, Snow shook her hands free of his grasp, grabbed the V of his tunic, and ripped it down the middle.

"Snow," he said with an exasperated sigh. "That was a good tunic."

She stared in disbelief. "Those scratches, those are…" She met his eye. "You should be healed. Vampires heal quicker than normal."

He stared at her.

"What's going on? Why aren't you healing?" she asked. "You've fed, haven't you?"

Sage pressed his lips together forcefully and crossed his arms over his chest.

Her mind churned at the possibilities. What could have caused him to not heal properly?

218

"Is it me? Because I'm a Slayer?" Sage turned away, but she grabbed him by the arm. His lips pressed into a grim line and he refused to meet her eye. It was her, or the curse of being a Slayer. "Tell me what to do. Tell me how to heal you."

"You can't." He removed her hand.

"Then why won't you look at me?" she demanded.

Sage stepped up to her and met her eye. His gaze was cold as ice. "You can't help me."

"Why do you keep lying to me?" she yelled. "Why does everyone think they can lie to me and I won't see it?" Snow grabbed his arm, but he yanked free. She gave him a frustrated shove and he flew across the room, slamming into the wall. He bared his fangs and came at her, but she was ready. Grabbing him by what was left of his tunic, she threw him toward a wooden table. He hit it with a smash. Bottles tumbled and hit the floor, shattering. He whipped his gaze toward her and leapt, knocking her to the ground. Pinning her to the floor with his hips, her dress slid up around her thighs and he lowered his weight on top of her.

"Stop," he said. "It's your Slayer instincts trying to fight me, but you need to stop."

She wriggled underneath him trying to get free. Why was she always on the ground? His strong body pressed into hers, heating her blood and quickening her heartbeat.

"Stop moving," he said. "You're making this hard for me to remain calm."

"Tell me what you need!" she demanded.

"I need to drink your blood," he yelled.

Snow stopped struggling. Her breath caught and her gaze locked on his as terror ran through her. Memories of Sonya's mouth on her neck, feeling the life drain out of her. The pain, the helplessness. All of it flooded in.

Sage lowered his head with a heavy, defeated breath. "It's the only way." He rolled off her and crouched on the floor by a curio.

His face darkened and his fangs gleamed in the candlelight. For the first time she saw him clearly for what he was. Sage was kind, and gentle, and strong. But he was also a vampire. He was like Sonya, and the ones her brothers killed. He was a killer, albeit that he no longer fed from humans, he had once.

"How many humans have you killed?" she whispered.

Sage's eyes turned sad and pleaded with her not to ask.

"How many?"

"Many." He hung his head between his knees. "I was spoiled and indulgent. I was given whatever I wanted. I thought for no one but myself."

Snow sat up, her body aching from the stone floor. "A hundred?"

He didn't look up.

"A thousand? Two?" she asked in an almost inaudible voice

He met her gaze, his lips drew into a tight grim line.

Her body shook. She no longer wanted to know. "How long has it been since you've drunk from a human?"

"Over fifty years."

Hope sprung within her. "So you're good now."

"No." He shook his head. "I'm not. I'm a monster and always will be. No matter how many people I don't kill, it doesn't matter. The blood of the ones I have killed, still haunts me."

Snow crawled toward him, but he shied away.

"You should go. Leave this place. Return to your brothers and your home. Find a royal human male. Marry him and have many chubby children. Leave the fate of those in Tanah Darah to me."

"Is that really what you want?" She moved closer still. "Do you really want me to go?"

"There is no hope for us, Snow. No life that we can live in peace. You saw what happened with Sonya. If you stayed here, I would have to fight off all the friends I have left, just to keep you safe."

Snow's heart crumbled at his words. She knew he was right. The game they'd been playing was never to last. She couldn't leave her brothers, and he would never stop trying to regain his kingdom. But it didn't matter. Nothing else mattered. Right now, all she could do was heal him.

"I am sick of the men in my life deciding what is best for me. You, my brothers, all of you. I'm not a fragile doll." Snow straightened her spine and looked Sage dead in the eye. "I'll admit. What happened tonight with Sonya has taught me that I'm not as formidable as I thought, but I'm not a child. I can make decisions for myself. Right or wrong."

Snow moved till she sat directly in front of him. Her heartbeat pounded in her chest. She wasn't invincible, but she knew her heart, and she loved Sage. Fear quavered her voice as she spoke again. "I

221

trust you. You may not trust yourself, but I trust you." Her resolve set, Snow moved ever closer and tugged her dress off of her shoulder. Fear trickled down her spine. She could do this. She could be this for him. Help him. Save him.

He reached out a trembling finger and traced the line of her throat; staring at it for several minutes.

"I can't." He stood and moved away.

Anger rushed through her. Snow leapt to her feet, grabbed his tunic and tore it from him. Sage spun and she pushed him onto the bed. If she didn't act now, her courage would fail her.

"Snow, don't," Sage pleaded as she hitched up her skirt and prowled up the bed toward him.

"Drink from me."

He slid away from her till he hit the headboard. "No. I can't."

"Why? It's what you need and I'm offering it to you." She planted herself in his lap and leaned into him. He pressed his face away from her. "Drink from me."

"I can't. Don't you understand that?" His voice came out strained and painful.

"Why?" she demanded.

"Because I've never drunk from someone without killing them. And I can't risk it." He turned to face her once more. "I can't risk hurting you. Not after what you've been through. Because I..." His eyes were conflicted.

Snow swallowed hard, her shaky hands coming to rest in her lap. She needed to do this. If there was any hope for them, she had to prove

222

to him that he wasn't that monster anymore. Nothing else mattered, nothing but her and Sage and this time they had together. No matter what tomorrow brought, tonight was about them.

Snow bent down and licked her way across his muscular chest. He winced as she licked his scrapes. He grabbed her and tangled his fingers in her braid. She ran her hands down to his waistband, making him groan and grab her tighter.

"You have to stop. I can't...I can't...think...with you..."

She kissed a trail down his stomach and hesitated. Reminding herself that they may only have tonight, she let her hands roam the front of his breeches.

Sage sucked in a sharp breath and bucked his hips toward her. She reached down the side of his muscular legs to the tops of his boots. Running her hands over them, she located what she searched for. Distracting him with her mouth, Snow removed the knife.

She kissed her way up and claimed his mouth with hers, mounting his hips. Heat flushed between her legs as his want grew beneath her. She withdrew from his kiss and raised the knife to her throat.

Sage's eyes widening in terror. "Don't," he begged, digging his fingers into her sides.

"You need this." She tried to concentrate, pushing the memories of Sonya aside once more. "You need me."

"More than you know," he said, his voice strained. "Which is why I can't."

But she did it anyway. Snow pressed the sharp blade into her neck. A trickle of blood dribbled down her throat, between her breasts, staining the bodice.

"Stop." He reached for her hand.

"I'll really cut it if you try to stop me." She winced in pain, pressing the knife in harder.

His hands stopped an inch from hers, his gaze transfixed on the blood flowing from her. His fangs descended once more. Snow reached up with her fingers and trailed the blood over the tops of her breasts. He watched, spellbound. She pressed the blade into her throat deeper and blood flowed freely from her wound. Sage closed his eyelids, his mouth moving in a silent prayer.

"Snow, stop! I can't…" His pleaded with her. "I love you, and if you have any feelings for me, you won't make me do this."

She leveled her gaze at him and lifted his chin. He looked at her again and his feral gaze made her skin prickle. "You'll stop," she said. "I love you, too, and that's how I know you will." Dipping three fingers into her blood, she pressed them to his lips. For a moment, he didn't move. She rubbed the tips of her fingers under his lips. His fangs grew impossibly longer, peeking out from under his lips and stopping almost at his chin, twice the length of Sonya's.

The knife hit the floor with a clatter and he was suddenly on top of her. His soft tongue licked at the tops of her breasts and moved up her neck to the cut. She moaned and raised her hips into his. His hands slid up her skirt and wrapped her leg around him.

Her breath caught and Sage looked at her. He strained to keep control. She could see it on his face.

She pulled his face to her throat and prepared for the pain. A rush of uncertainly washed through her. He licked her neck and lingered above her throat. His cool breath raised the hairs on her arms. She opened her mouth to stop him, but he struck. She squeezed her eyes shut, waiting for the rush of agony, but no pain emerged. Warmth spread through her body and she relaxed, cradling him against her throat. She needed this; they needed this. He pushed up her gown and splayed his cool hand across her bare stomach. Snow gasped his name as his hips pressed on her most sensitive parts, tingling and exciting her. He slid his hand up and cupped her breast making her moan in delight.

She ran her hands up and down his skin, kneading his muscles with her fingers, her mind going to places she'd never been before. She wanted him. Every nerve ending in her body caught fire from his touch. He drank from her over and over until her head lightened.

"Sage, stop," she breathed. "That's enough, Sage."

But he didn't stop. He continued to drink from her, oblivious to her pleas.

"Sage, stop." Snow dug her nails into his back, but he took no notice. She gouged at his muscles with her fingers, but it did no good. Panic crept into her mind.

He released her suddenly and sat up, staring at her with a wildness she had never seen. Her blood dripped from his mouth, and he wiped it away with the back of his hand. Dipping his head again, he licked her neck. The soft, tender sensation shot tendrils of desire down to her core.

His eyes cleared and filled instantly with regret. "I'm sorry," he said. He kissed her face, her cheeks, her chin. "Love, I'm so sorry."

She smiled. "I'm all right." she said.

He scanned her, his face full of doubt. "Are you sure, love?"

The feel of his weight atop her sent every nerve to the brink of exploding. His cool fingers rubbed circles on her stomach causing it to flutter and tingle.

She pulled his lips to hers and murmured, "I'm sure."

He kissed her throat, her mouth, her eyelids. Over and over, he pressed her with soft, gentle kisses. Soon though, his kisses grew heavier and he kissed his way down the front of her bodice making her nubs harden with delight. He slipped her dress from her shoulder and ran his long fingers down her skin. She sighed and arched her body into his, rubbing the hardness of his arousal against her. Lightheadedness gave way to need.

His mouth met hers. Pushing his hands under her gown again, he found the waistband of her pantaloons. His finger skimmed the hem, making her quiver.

"I want you, Snow," he whispered in her ear. "I want you all to myself. Now and forever."

Snow thought she would burst with need. His words swam in her head. He wanted her. And she wanted him too.

"I'm yours," she whispered.

She didn't have to say it twice. He stripped her of her dress and then her underthings. Looming over her, he admired her body with his hands and mouth. She closed her eyes and tangled her fists in his bedcover, reveling in the feel of him. She'd never imagined the touch of a man could feel so good.

Sage kicked off his boots and dropped his breeches to the ground. He pulled down the covers of his bed and they slid between the sheets. The anticipation shook Snow to her toes. He covered her body with his as he slowly entered her. He stopped, allowing her time to adjust. The stretching gave way to a pleasurable feeling of fullness, nearness. Oneness.

She nodded and he moved inside her once more. The sensation sent tingles racing over her skin. He kissed her long and deep as they made love. The smell of his body enveloped her. *Cinnamon.*

His rhythm increased and wisps of sparks of desire shot down to her inner most regions. A thrumming built inside her, coiling tighter and tighter until Snow's mind exploded as her body came to life beneath him. He moaned and his body shook as he strained to hold back. She cried his name, over and over, digging her nails into his flesh. Stars appeared behind her eyelids and her breath caught as her mind emptied of all thought. Moments later, he cried her name, so loud it made the glass in the curio rattle.

Their bodies went limp and he dropped onto her, both of them covered in a slick sheen of sweat. Her limbs hummed in the aftermath. She was floating. None of it seemed real. Had she really just done that? Had she just given herself to him? A moment of apprehension skittered over her and she bit her lip at the tears threatening to spill.

He kissed her softly, running his fingers through her hair. "Be mine," he said thickly from behind his descended fangs. "Let me make you like me so we can be together forever, Snow."

Snow blinked rapidly several times. His glorious naked body poised above her, fangs bared, ready to strike. She wanted to be with him. More than anything she wanted to be with him. Like this, forever. But she was human. She had a family, and responsibilities.

"I want to, Sage," she said, "more than anything, I do. But I...I..." She couldn't find the words.

He covered her mouth with his and kissed her long and hard. Snow clung to him. His hands roamed and explored her body, making her tingle all over. She wanted him again and again.

"It's all right," he said. "I am happy being with you like this. For as long as you want."

Snow swallowed down a lump in her throat. She kissed him hard. All she had dreamed about was a man of her own to love and be loved by; and she had found one. But their time together was already ticking away.

CHAPTER TWENTY ONE

Flint opened the front door and held it ajar as his brothers stepped into their home. All the lanterns and candles had burnt out in their absence.

They'd gone to the place that Snow had shown them on the map. They'd searched the entire area and all surrounding areas and found nothing. Not a trace of vampires. Flint had known they wouldn't, but Erik wanted to check, so they could rule it out. Fairelle was a big place, and just because they didn't find him there tonight, didn't mean it could be ruled out altogether.

"Tomorrow we go north, to the woods." Erik set his sword and sheath on the table.

"Man. Am I itching for a fight," said Hass. He stretched and punched Ian in the arm.

"Maybe we should go north tonight." Ian stepped away from his twin and rubbed his bicep.

"It's late," said Erik. "We need to finish up work here tomorrow. We should get some sleep."

Flint was as pent up as the rest. He yearned to run a Cris blade through Sage's neck and every other vampire in the world. They were vermin that needed to be eradicated. Anger had been a bane Flint had dealt with since his parents had died; made worse by the Slayer calling. The only solace he found was in Snow's sweet, calming spirit, but even that had been tainted.

The Slayer calling was not easy to bear. It changed them all in ways they couldn't describe. But the changes witnessed in Snow were something else altogether. He doubted that her encounter with Sage had been quite as she'd described.

"I'm gonna check on Snow," he said, moving to the stairs. They'd hear about it for locking her in, and he doubted that they'd get her back in her room ever again. But the fear of her running off and possibly getting hurt was all consuming. He had to try to keep her safe. She just didn't understand what dangers were out there in Fairelle. Losing her would be worse than... He didn't even want to think about it.

"Holler if you need any help," Erik said with a wry smile.

Their brothers laughed.

Flint nodded, but said nothing. He took the stairs slowly, knowing he may actually need backup if she decided to attack. He wondered if they'd done the right thing all these years. Hiding the worst of what they saw from her. Maybe if they'd told her everything from the beginning, she wouldn't be so keen to go out and fight.

Reaching the top of the staircase, Flint turned down the landing toward Snow's room. He located a sconce and turned the knob. Soft light illuminated the hallway. He reached her door and turned the knob on another sconce. The light landed on the key that hung on the wall. Flint took a deep breath and then pressed his ear to the door.

Silence. He practiced what he might say to her, knowing nothing would temper her outrage.

He was tempted to just let her sleep and put off the argument until morning, but he had to at least unlock her so she could use the bathing room if needed.

Gripping the key, he pushed it into the lock and twisted as quietly as he could. The lock clicked and he turned the handle. Flint waited for Snow to stomp across the room, throw the door open and yell at him, but there was nothing. No sound at all.

He peeked inside. "Snow?"

The room was dark, but the light from the hallway shone in. Her bed had been stripped. The bedspread lay on the floor, the sheets missing. Flint stepped in the room, his heart pounding. A gentle breeze ruffled his hair.

"Snow!" He scanned the room. A long rope made from sheets was tied to a leg of the bed. He followed the rope to the window. His gut clenched as his boot crunched on something. Broken glass. The braided sheets hung to the ground.

"Dammit!" he roared.

Footsteps pounded up the stairs.

"What's going on?" Erik strode into the room. He scanned the scene with Gerall right behind him. "Where is she?"

"Gone," said Flint through gritted teeth.

"What? Where?" asked Gerall.

Anger seethed from Flint. "I have an idea."

Flint shoved past his brothers, down the stairs, and out the door. The rest of the group followed behind. He headed for the rear of the property and into the woods at a sprint. His mind raged with anger and fear for Snow, his foolish, stubborn little sister. Yes, he decided, they should have told her of the horrors they'd seen. Told her, and then locked her away.

"Where are we going?" Erik matched his stride.

"To the glade," said Flint, refusing to slow.

"The glade? Why would she be in the glade?"

"She's got a cabin there that she visits at night."

"What?" asked Jamen speeding up. "How long has she been doing that?"

"A while." Flint rounded a tree and continued forward.

"How long have you known?" asked Erik.

Flint spared him a single glance. His brother did not look pleased. "I found out last night."

"How could you be so irresponsible and not tell me?" Erik's voice shook with the same fury Flint felt.

Flint stopped abruptly. "Look around you, Erik. Does it look like it would have made a difference?" From the way Erik paced, balling his hands into fists and glaring at Flint, he wasn't sure if Erik would actually take a swing at him.

"Stop," said Jamen. "This isn't helping. We need to just get her home."

Erik turned his gaze on Jamen and finally nodded.

Flint took off again, his brothers at his heels. They came upon the cabin and Flint burst through the door. "Snow!"

The cabin was dark. Cold. There was no one inside. He ran to the clearing behind the cabin, but she wasn't there, either.

"Flint, Erik," called Hass.

Hass and Ian crouched in front of the cabin. In the moonlight, a sword glinted on the ground. Flint recognized it as a practice sword from home. Bile churned in his gut. Reaching down, he scanned the ground. There'd been a struggle. Someone had lain on the ground. He felt around with his fingers and hit something wet. Raising his fingers he smelled it. Blood. *Oh gods, Snow.*

"Where is she?" asked Erik.

A tear leaked from the corner of Flint's eye. "I don't know."

CHAPTER TWENTY TWO

Snow spent the day wrapped in Sage's arms, making love and sleeping. They lay tangled in the sheets and he stroked her arm while she swirled circles on his chest. After drinking from her, his cuts sealed shut almost instantly, and all that remained were frosty scars running down his torso.

Snow scanned his hard muscles. His porcelain skin was marred by many scars. It surprised her that a royal vampire would have so many. "Where did you get all of these?"

"Various places." He caressed down her arm and up again, giving her goosebumps.

"I thought you would heal fully. Without scars."

"Not when injured by a Cris knife, or a Slayer's hand."

Snow rolled onto her stomach and faced him. "What do you know about Slayers?"

He ran a finger down her cheek. "Not much, really. It's been a long time since they were last seen. Well before my time. From what I've found in very few books, Slayers are called upon when evil rules Tanah Darah. They are charged with eradicating that evil."

"So we aren't supposed to just kill all vampires?" Snow said.

"No. Though they do now apparently, and they did then."

"I knew it," Snow said, almost to herself.

His eyes crinkled at the corners when he smiled. "What do you mean, love?"

"My brothers. I tried talking to them about this, but they wouldn't hear it. They said Slayers were supposed to kill vampires. Period. It was their calling."

"Why were you arguing with your brothers?" Sage rolled on his side, pushed her hair from her shoulder and kissed her skin, sending a chill up her neck.

"I tried convincing them that you weren't bad. To get them to see that even as Slayers we have our limits of what we *should* do."

Sage chuckled.

"What's so funny?" she asked.

"You. You're so strong. You have no idea how strong." He slid his hand down her side, making her head swim with thoughts of his body on hers. He had taken her to places she hadn't even dreamed existed. She was sore in ways she'd never experienced, but it was a good sore.

"Sage," she moaned.

"Yes, love?" He kissed his way down her spine.

Snow wanted him. To be with him. Not just for today. But for always. "Tell me what it would mean if you were to turn me."

He stopped moving. His lips lingered above her skin and his cool breath tickled her back.

"The turning process is one of great risk," he said, kissing her in the hollow of her spine. "You have to die, with a vampire's blood in your system. This is usually done by a vampire draining a human, after having the human ingest their blood."

She sucked in a breath. "So that's what you would do to me?"

235

He shifted onto his pillow and pulled her on top of him, her body resting between his legs, her chin on his chest. She stared into his conflicted yet hopeful aquamarine eyes.

*****

Sage held his breath and searched the deep copper eyes that in the last twelve hours, he had come to love more than anything. He'd seen them wide with surprise, hooded with ecstasy and drowsy with fatigue. No matter how he saw them, they were mesmerizing.

And now those eyes were curious, asking how he would turn her. He hadn't allowed himself to hope that she'd want to be with him forever. But looking at her, he knew he couldn't do it. To do so would be purely selfish. She would be his, but it would mean subjecting her to living underground, to being hunted by her own brothers, to fighting the thirst for human blood day and night. That would be no life for her. It wasn't a life for anyone.

"No." Sage traced a line down her throat and then hugged her. "No, love. I wouldn't do that to you."

She pushed on his chest and sat up. Her brow furrowed. "But you said–"

His ribcage tightened. Why was he doing this? Why was he denying her? He'd wanted this from the beginning, and she was willing. "I know what I said, but I wouldn't wish this on you. To become like me, to live this life. It isn't fair to you."

Snow got off the bed so quickly it startled him. She pulled the sheet with her as she went. "I see." Her voice had a hard edge.

What did he say? "You see what?"

"Nothing," she said. She bent down and reached for her dress.

"Wait, Snow, what's wrong?" He stood. What had he done? Just moments before, everything had been perfect.

Snow moved around the room, collecting her garments. She refused to look at him. With rigid movements, she yanked on her clothing.

"What did I say?" He tried to grab her arm. Snow shot him an icy glare and he stopped.

"Nothing, Sage. I understand. I do. The bloodlust got the better of you. Made you say things you didn't mean."

"Say things I didn't mean?" He'd meant everything he'd said.

"Me!" she yelled, pulling her dress on. "You asked me to stay with you. To let you turn me. I get it, though. It was just a moment of passion." Snow found her shoes under the bed and slipped them on.

Sage stood, speechless. She didn't believe him. "Snow, I did mean it."

She whipped around to face him. "Then why did you just say no?"

"I did mean it." He ran his hands through his hair. How had this gone so bad so quickly? Didn't she understand that she deserved so much more than to be hunted like he was? Didn't she understand her worth? "I do mean it. I mean, I do want you with me. I just—"

"Want to protect me?" she spat.

"No. Yes. I want to protect you, but not in the way you think. You say you want this, after we've spent a night and day together, but in a week, a month, a year, you would change your mind. You'd see that

I'm not worth all this." He gestured around himself. "And your brothers—"

"They can take care of themselves. They don't need me."

Sage shook his head. "Don't lie. You don't mean that. You love your brothers and they love you. They need you and you need them. You told me once that family was the most important thing." He tried to take her hand, but she jerked away. "Snow, don't do this. Don't be like this."

"Be like what? Like me? Don't be myself?"

They stared at each other. He wanted to say something to make it better, to make her understand.

"Snow, I—"

She held up her hand. "Don't. Don't tell me you love me. Don't tell me you want what's best for me. Just... don't."

She was out in the hall in a wink. Dax opened his door and peered out.

"You know the way out of here?" she asked.

Dax nodded.

"Let's go." Snow marched down the hall. Dax glanced at Sage and then followed, showing her the direction of the exit.

Sage swore loudly, grabbed the discarded sheet from his floor and wrapped it around his waist.

"Snow," he called, running after her. Sonya and Greeg appeared cautiously from the lower hallway. Sage gave Sonya a hard look, his anger flaring, but he said nothing and trailed after Snow. He caught up just as Dax arrived at the entrance. He pushed Dax to the side and grabbed Snow around the waist.

"Snow, wait. Let me explain."

She shoved at his hands. "Let me go."

"No," Sage said, trying to hang onto her. "I am Prince Sageren of Tanah Darah and I command you to stop and listen to me!"

Snow twisted in his grasp and punched Sage in the jaw.

"Hey!" Sonya ran up the hall, but Dax stepped in her way.

Snow's eyes widened and she took a step back. "I'm sorry," she said, "Sage, I'm so sorry. I didn't mean to–"

"No." His fangs descended and his anger bubbled inside of him. Stripping off the sheet, he held it to his split lip. A droplet of blood dripped onto his chest and then staunched. His heart ached beneath the anger, but his head told him this was the right thing to do. He'd said all along this was no place for her. As much as it killed him, he had to let her go. Sage removed the sheet and lifted his chin. "You're right. You should go."

Snow's face was conflicted, the way he was used to seeing her. *Let her be angry.* Her anger would keep her safe. Sage refused to let the gathered group see how much pain the decision brought him.

"Dax. Let her out," said Sage. He turned and headed to his room. This was for the best. "Make sure she gets home safely," he called over his shoulder. She needed to be as far away from him as possible.

His heart broke with every step. He passed Sonya and Greeg without a word.

*****

Dax pushed the boulder open and Snow stepped out. She coughed and sucked air into her lungs several times before she acclimated to the sulfurous, burnt smell. Disbelief struck her. There was no mistaking the scorched, dead wasteland that lay before her and beneath her feet. Blackness and gray ash blanketed everything, as far as she could see. Every rock stood blacker than the next in the moonlight. Nothing lived, nothing moved, not even a breeze brushed her skin. Silence emanated from every direction.

Sage had been telling her the truth the whole time. Her gut clenched and she turned in time to see Dax closing the passage where Sonya and Greeg still stood staring at her. It amazed her how natural the entrance appeared. If she hadn't just come through it, she never would have believed that it was a door.

She bit her lip as agony filled her. She should go to Sage. Apologize again.

No, she wouldn't beg. He'd told her to go, and so she would. Though how she was going to explain to her brothers where she'd been was a whole big problem she didn't want to think about.

Dax walked over to her; his large, solid frame caused the rocks to crunch under his feet. He was a hair taller and broader than Flint, but his eyes were gentle.

"Come on," said Dax with a tight smile. "Let's get you home."

He took her by the hand and led her forward. She slipped on the rocks and cursed herself for not having grabbed some boots before she'd left home, instead of her silly flat slippers. But how was she to have known where she would end up?

Her time with Sage had left her body sore. Memories of their lovemaking floated back to her. The feel of his touch, the sensation of his tongue, the feel of his–

Her palms became slick with sweat at the barrage of images that accosted her. Snow slid her hand from Dax's. Her throat tightened. Dax stopped.

"How did you come to be friends with Sage?" she asked, trying to distract herself.

"He helped Prince Adrian find the missing Sisters of Red a few years ago. He'd been helping keep the vampires at bay for a long time before that. Over the past few years, we have formed a bit of a kinship, seeing as how we are both misfits. We began patrolling together a few months ago."

A few years ago had been when her brothers were called. "Where are you from, Dax?"

Dax helped her over a rock. "No idea," he said. "Ten years ago or so, I found myself in the woods of Wolvenglen, naked and alone. I hadn't gone far before being attacked by vampires. I shifted into bear form – which I can tell you was quite confusing to both myself and the vampires. I ran and ended up on Adrian's doorstep. He took me in and made me a part of his pack. I had been there ever since until a few weeks ago."

How strange that he didn't know how he'd become a werebear. "And you have no memory at all from before that?"

Dax shrugged. "Every once and again I'll see something, or hear something or smell something and it triggers images. Half-formed memories. But for the most part, no."

Snow thought how that would be. No ties to anyone. No obligations. Answering to no one, and doing as she pleased. Dax trudged ahead of her and she quickly realized the loneliness he must feel. She would miss so much. Her brothers. Their home. Sage.

"I'm sorry," she finally said.

They reached the tree line and the familiar scents of the woods soothed her a bit. Her feet were sore from the trek across the sharp pebbles and stones that covered the Wastelands. Snow collapsed onto a boulder and massaged her feet.

Dax watched her, as if he might speak.

She cocked an eyebrow. "You have something you want to say to me?"

"It's not my place," he replied, looking away.

Snow sighed. "Say it. Everyone else does lately."

"It's just–" Dax stopped and looked over the Daemonlands, as if trying to figure out how to phrase what he wanted to say. "I understand why your brothers are angry. But Sage had nothing to do with your brother's death. I was there. Those vampires ambushed us all. Sage is a good man. He isn't a saint, that's for sure. But he is a decent being. And he loves you. He's trying to protect you. He just doesn't know how."

Snow stopped rubbing her foot and slipped her shoe on. "So you think he's right? That sending me away is for the best?"

242

"I didn't say that," Dax said. "But to him, I think it is. Your brothers are stronger as a unit than he is. They can protect you better than he ever could. They're Slayers. As a group, there are few things more formidable."

"Well, well, well. What have we here?" a deep voice spoke from behind a tree.

Snow scrambled off her rock, closer to Dax as six vampires moved out of the trees. She swallowed hard and reached for her sword, but it wasn't there. She was weaponless.

"Run," Dax whispered.

"Yes, run. Please do," said the leader. "I love a good chase."

When the lead vampire stepped into the moonlight, the blood drained from Snow's face and her heart constricted.

Sage?

Snow blinked twice. No. It wasn't Sage, but the vampire was almost a mirror image of the man she loved. A few inches shorter, he had the same hair and build. His face was hard, though, and his eyes cold.

"You're dead," Dax said. "I killed you."

The vampire laughed. "Oh, you tried, werebear, but there are forces stronger than you that still want me here." The vampire stepped forward and then stopped short, sniffing the air. "Mmm... What is that? That has to be the most tempting scent I have ever smelled."

Snow's fingers twitched, aching to grip her sword. Her blood pumped quicker, anticipating a fight. "Who are you?"

"You do not want to hurt this woman, Remus," Dax warned, pushing Snow behind him.

"Hurt her? Of course not, bear. I have no interest in harming her." A wide, icy grin crossed the vampire's face, his fangs long and sharp like Sage's. "Come out, female, and let me have a look at you."

Snow took a step to Dax's right, but he threw out his arm, moving her behind him.

"It's all right." She looked up at him. "I'm not afraid of them." She gave him a confident smile, but her gut clenched tight at her lie.

Dax's limbs twitched and spasmed. His joints cracked and a rumble escaped his chest. She laid her hand on his forearm, took a deep breath, and moved to stand in front of him. Head raised, she turned and stared into the vampire's face, so much like Sage's, but not Sage.

His gaze skimmed over her with great appreciation. She glanced at the vampires behind him. Each leered at her with lusty eyes, making her blood chill.

"Come here," he commanded.

"No," she said.

"No?" A smile played on Remus' lips. "I love a girl with spirit." His pupils contracted and then expanded. "I said, come here." His voice became hard and reverberated around her in an echo, but Snow felt none of the effects that she had originally with Sage. Now a full Slayer, his tricks didn't work on her.

"No," she said again.

His eyes widened in surprise and then narrowed. "You're a Slayer," he said.

She didn't answer.

"You are." He smiled. "Wonderful. Bring her to me." The other vampires moved quick as lightning. Quicker than Sage had ever moved. Four of them were on Dax before he could shift, pinning him to the ground, a knife to his throat. Two others grabbed Snow, pushing her toward their leader. Snow kicked out and connected at the knee with one assailant. His step faltered and he loosened his grip as he snarled and reached for his leg. Snow jabbed the other in the ribs and stomped on his foot, but he barely noticed. Grabbing both of her arms from behind, he pinned them together and lifted her off the ground, carrying her to Remus. Behind her, a bear roared.

Remus grabbed Snow and yanked her toward him. Bending, he sniffed her neck.

"Amazing," he whispered. His tongue snaked out and he licked her collarbone. He shuddered and his breath caught.

Memories of Lord Balken and Sonya overwhelmed Snow's senses. She screamed in panic. Sage, she wanted Sage.

Remus sniffed her once more, inhaled deeply and then chuckled.

"Oh, this really is lovely," he said. "You've been spoiled by my brother, Sageren."

Sage's brother? Did Sage know he was still alive?

"He always did get all the good ones. But don't worry, love, I'm not picky. I'll happily take his leftovers."

"I wouldn't, if I were you," Snow warned. "And don't call me, 'love'."

He laughed again. "I love the spirit. Probably the first thing Sage saw, too. That and of course your beauty. You really are quite exquisite."

Snow spit in Remus' face. He blinked once and then ran his finger over the spittle and pulled it into his mouth. His eyes closed a fraction and then he clamped his mouth down on hers, hard. She was too stunned to move as he kissed her with a fervor she had never felt. His kiss was fierce and possessive. The image of Lord Balken sprung to her mind once more. His tongue probed and claimed her mouth. She ripped herself from his kiss and slapped him in the face so hard that his face rocked to the side. A vampire grabbed her roughly from behind.

Dax roared with rage and swore up a storm as he fought the vampires that held him.

Remus locked eyes with her and Snow's throat went dry. The smile on his face told her that he'd enjoyed the slap. Pulling her hard into his body, Remus whipped her head sideways, exposing her neck.

"Stop, or I'll drain her dry, bear."

Sweat trailed down Snow's neck as Remus pressed his fangs at her throat. Bile rose in her throat. She wouldn't be a toy again.

Snow wrenched from his grasp and locked gazes with Remus. "Sage will kill you for this."

He smiled broadly. "Oh, love. I'm sure hoping he'll try again." Remus ran a finger down her throat to the tops of her breasts. "You really are quite perfect," he mused. "I may just turn you and keep you for myself. You even put the queen to shame with your beauty."

Snow's blood ran cold at the thought, but her mind started to churn. Her options were severely limited. She was weaponless and miles from home. Even if she ran, she would never make it. She stared at Remus, whose leering gaze scoured her the way Balken's had when he'd burst into her room on that terrible night. If she could manage to keep herself alive long enough, Sage would come for her. She knew he would.

Snow looked over her shoulder at Dax. Still pinned to the ground, his hands had become enormous paws, and his teeth and nose had lengthened beyond belief. She owed him. He'd saved her from Sonya, and now it was her chance to return the favor. Reaching up, she laid her hand on Remus' chest.

"Let Dax go, and I'll come with you." She let her fingers stroke his sinewy muscles through his shirt.

His gaze narrowed and his smile fell. A look of unease overcame his features. "Why?"

"Because." Snow smiled and allowed her body to rub up against his. "I want to become one of you."

CHAPTER TWENTY THREE

"She's a Slayer?" Greeg said.

Sage nodded grimly. "Yes."

"How long have you known that Slayers have returned?" asked Sonya.

"Since I brought Dax back with me. I tried to form an alliance with them, but we were ambushed. By Remus."

"Remus?" Sonya yelled, springing to her feet. "Remus is dead."

"He wasn't. But he is now."

"No, he's not." Dax entered the library.

Sage looked at Dax's grim face. "Where's Snow? Did you get her home safely?" He paused as Dax's words sank in. "What do you mean he's not dead?"

"Remus took her." Dax crossed to where the group gathered.

Sage jumped from his chair. It wasn't possible. This couldn't be happening. He was supposed to keep her safe.

"We were at the border and she stopped to take off her shoes. Remus came out of the woods with a group of vampires."

Remus has Snow. My Snow.

"She told him she would go with him if he spared me. He seemed enthralled by her. He–" Dax broke eye contact and Sage moved to him in an instant, his grip tight upon Dax's arm.

"He what?" Sage demanded. He was being too forceful, but the gnawing in his gut was too much to bear.

"He kissed her and said he wanted to turn her and keep her for himself. He didn't care that she'd been with you."

Sage howled in rage.

"We should go after them. It's time to regain what is yours. Your kingdom and your female," said Sonya.

"We aren't strong enough," said Omni. "There are barely a dozen of us here, and only you and Greeg and Sonya have ever fought in combat. Besides, how would we get in? We can't very well walk up to the front of the palace. We'd never make it past the outer walls."

"No," said Sage, looking down at the red ring on his finger. "We wouldn't."

Birds from a small aviary cooed and an owl hooted in the late night hour. The smell of farmland and animals filled his nostrils.

"Are you sure about this?" asked Dax, standing beside Sage.

"No." Sage stared up at the large house. Several lights glowed from inside. The men within the large stone structure held either his saving grace, or his ultimate demise. "What choice do I have?"

"This could be over before it begins."

"It could."

Sage took a deep, calming breath. He needed to make them understand. If he didn't, Snow was as good as gone. Walking up the steps, he reached the front door and knocked. Several sets of heavy-booted feet ran to the door. Two identical brothers yanked it open and peered out at the porch.

"Snow!" they said together.

Sage backed up as they looked him over. Recognition dawned on their faces. Flint shoved the twins aside.

"You," he said. He didn't wait for words. He lumbered out onto the porch, his fists already clenched.

Sage backed up further, and Dax moved to his side.

"Get my sword," Flint yelled.

All the brothers piled out, every one with rage on his faces.

"Wait," said Sage. "I must speak to you."

"There's nothing to talk about, vampire. You killed Kellan. Now you die."

"You need to listen to him," Dax said.

"No," said Erik, storming forward. "We listened once before and our brother died."

"Your sister will too, if you don't stop," said Dax.

The six Slayers surrounded them in an instant, forming a circle. Things were not going according to plan, but they were going as expected.

"You side with a vampire, kill our brother and then you threaten our sister, bear?"

Dax's skin rippled. "I did nothing. So don't accuse me of murder."

"Wait," shouted Sage, stepping between them. "We're trying to save her."

"Save her from what?" asked Jamen.

Jamen's voice was level, so Sage decided to address him. "From the vampires who killed Kellan," Sage bellowed.

The brothers stopped moving. Sage took a deep breath. "The vampires who killed Kellan, the ones who tried to kill me, they took Snow."

"Why?" asked Flint.

"Because he wants to hurt me. His name is Remus; he's my brother. I thought he was dead."

"What do you mean, hurt you?" asked Jamen.

"Wait," said Erik. "How did you know our brother's name was Kellan?"

Sage wasn't sure how to answer. If he told them the truth about him and Snow, they would probably kill him just because they were her brothers.

"Snow told me," he said.

Erik took several steps forward. He clenched and unclenched his fists several times before he spoke again. "When?"

"Last night."

Flint moved so fast it took all of his brothers to hold him back. He bellowed in anger, cursing and reaching for Sage.

"She came looking for me. I told her to stay away. I told her it was too dangerous–"

"You watch your tongue, vampire! Are you calling my sister a harlot?" yelled Flint, struggling with all five of his brothers.

"No," said Sage. "I told her to stay away because I love her."

Flint stopped moving.

"I love Snow. I loved her before she became a Slayer. And my love put her in danger. Look, we don't have much time. My brother,

Remus, has taken her to Tanah Darah. He intends on making her a vampire. I don't want that for her."

The brothers struggled with the news. He knew they wanted to hate him, but they wanted their sister back.

"Our sister would never be caught with a bloodsucking murderer like you." Flint spat on the ground.

Sage opened his mouth to speak.

"Does she love you?" Gerall asked softly.

All gazes moved to Gerall. Sage swallowed. This was the moment of truth. Not his truth, but hers. It pained him that she wasn't here to tell her brothers herself. It wasn't his place. "I believe she might," said Sage.

"Liar!" Flint yelled.

Erik blew out a heavy breath. "You say you love her—"

"No!" yelled Flint. "He's lying. It's a trap. Just like with Kellan. He wants us dead!"

Sage's anger took over. He moved in a flash till he was mere inches from Flint. "I am Prince Sageren of Tanah Darah. My father was King Lothar, I am the rightful heir to the throne, and I will not stand here to be called a liar and a murderer any longer." Flint's eyes held the same rage that Sage felt. "I did not kill your Kellan and I do love your sister, whether or not you agree. I have come here in an effort to save her life at the risk of my own. I do not now, nor do I ever, expect us to be friends, Flint Gwyn. But I do expect you to love your sister enough to fight at my side and save her life."

Silence fell thickly over the group.

"Are you willing to risk everything you have to save her?" asked Erik.

"Yes," Sage said without hesitation.

"Then we'll follow you," said Erik.

"No," said Flint.

"Yes." Erik met his brother's eye. "Do you want her back or not? This is the only way."

Flint stared at Erik for a moment, and then his body relaxed and everyone let go of him. His gaze traveled to Sage. "I do not trust you, blood sucker. And you are still my enemy. But if it will save Snow, I'll go with you."

Sage smiled tightly. "Finally we understand one another."

"Where do we start?" asked Jamen.

"I have a plan," replied Sage.

Dax went on ahead to the woods beyond Snow's cabin. By the time Sage and the Slayers joined him at the pond, Adrian, Redlynn, a pack of wolves and their mates waited on one side and the band of Sage's dozen vampires waited on the other, each group eyeing the other. Between the two groups, Dax stood as peacekeeper.

Sage arrived, and Adrian shifted to human form to greet him.

"Thank you for this, Adrian," Sage said, clasping his hand.

"We're pleased to help." Adrian's gaze strayed to the vampires grouped together.

Sage looked over the wolves. "Are you sure? About bringing the females, I mean."

"We can look after ourselves," said Redlynn. She stepped forward, her bow secured on her back, her sword hanging loosely at her side.

"Besides," said Yanti, now a young woman with flowing blond hair. "We owe you for saving us." The last time Sage had seen her, she'd been no more than a girl, trembling and chained to the wall of the ruins, being fed upon by his cousin Garot and Garot's men.

"And I wouldn't mind getting a little payback, either," said Sasha, with a grin. Sasha too had grown into a full woman. She stood with her hand on a large protective looking chestnut wolf.

Sage nodded. "All right then. Let's see if this works." He stepped to the muddy water at the edge of the pond. Reaching down, he touched the currant colored ring to the surface. A bright red light burst from the bottom and then dimmed a little.

"What is that?" asked Adrian.

"A portal," said Sage. "It leads to Tanah Darah. It's how we'll get in without being seen."

"A portal in this pool? All this time?" Erik mused.

"I don't know," said Sage.

"Let me take a look." Dax waded into the water before taking a deep breath and diving under.

Everyone watched Dax swim down to the light, his shadowy form illuminated in the dark water by the murky crimson glow at the bottom. After a minute, he reappeared on the surface and sucked in several deep breaths.

"It's a mirror. I can see the frame of it. I've seen one before."

"Where?" asked Sage.

"No idea," said Dax, shaking his head. "Come on. You have to touch it to go through."

"Where in Tanah Darah will it lead?" asked Sonya. "I've never heard of a portal in the castle before."

Sage was unsure where they would come out on the other side. From the little he had heard of mirror travel, you needed to have clear knowledge of where you were headed, otherwise you could end up anywhere. And if you didn't have an open mirror to connect to, there was no telling what could happen. His only assurance was the ring he wore from Quintess, and the fact that the Slaver had used this pool to send slaves to Tanah Darah.

"What are we standing around for?" asked Flint. "Snow is in there. Let's move."

"Everyone in," said Erik.

"No, wait," said Sage. But it was too late. The brothers jumped in and dove to the bottom of the pool before anyone could stop them. There was a flash of light and they disappeared. "Dammit!"

The wolves shifted to human form and jumped in next. Finally, the vampires submerged, followed by Sage.

This had to work. It just had to.

CHAPTER TWENTY FOUR

Terona sat in the great hall and tapped her sharp fingernails on the arm of her throne. She grew weary of her life in Tanah Darah. Nothing seemed to be going her way. She needed a plan to get rid of Sage and Philos so she could take the kingdom for herself. Her magick-imbued vampires had been killed, save one, and Philos had insisted she use the last of her magick to imbue his own men. Even Philos' affections had begun to wane. The night before, she had anticipated a glorious and painful romp with Philos, but he had barely even waited for her to achieve climax before leaving their bed.

She glanced over at him and snarled, but he took no notice. He busied himself with a young female that had recently been sent over by Klaus. Philos kissed her wrist. The girl turned her red rimmed eyes pleadingly at her, but Terona simply looked away in disgust. A dozen or so noble vampires milled about, talking and sharing glasses of wine. Terona stroked her werewolf's fur as he crouched beside her in chains. She no longer even derived pleasure from taunting the beast.

If she took Tanah Darah, it would be the first in uniting the lands under her family's banner, and from there, they would take control of all of Fairelle as had been prophesied. One kingdom at a time. Humans, Fae, dragons, Nereids. All of them would fall, and when they had, they'd journey into Wolvenglen Forest and crush the Werewolves into submission once and for all.

Dragos was counting on her. If she failed, his and Morgana's displeasure could mean her exile, or worse, her death.

The entrance to the throne room pushed open and Remus strode in, a human female on his arm. At the sight of her, Terona noticed Philos stop toying with his plaything and look over. He dropped the human slave girl to the floor and stood as Remus and the woman drew nearer. Terona arose and placed her hand on Philos' arm. He shook her off and took several strides forward. Her blood rose in anger.

The girl was lovely, with creamy skin and sparkling brown eyes. Her hair hung thick and shiny to her waist. She marched next to Remus with the air of royalty.

"What have we here?" asked Philos, his eyes never leaving the girl's face.

"A Slayer, your Highness," said Remus.

"A Slayer?" Philos said. The glee in his voice apparent. "Is she really? I've never seen a female Slayer before." Philos almost purred as he smelled her. "She's weaponless too, and alone. What's your name, girl?"

"Snow Gwyn," she said.

Philos continued to look her over. "You are quite spectacular, my dear. Are you sure she's a Slayer?"

Terona's eye twitched watching Philos and Remus pandering over the girl, Snow. It was enough to make her scream. "Shall we feast on her blood?" She smiled up at her husband.

"Oh, most definitely," said Philos. "But she's too lovely to kill." Philos cupped Snow's face in his hands. Slowly he bent forward and kissed her forehead. Snow's eyes drifted to Terona for the first time. The girl said nothing, but her eyes spoke volumes. She was playing nice, but the act wouldn't last forever. Her skin prickled for the first time in a long time.

Remus had brought a predator into their den. A predator that had been sent to kill Terona herself.

She needed to get her husband's attention away from Snow. "Darling, think of all the fun we could have together. You and me, bathing in her blood." She ran her hands up Philos' chest and locked her arms around his neck, giving him her most seductive look.

"I want to become a vampire," Snow said.

Philos' attention whipped back to Snow in an instant. He disengaged Terona's hold and pushed her aside. Rage rolled through her and her temperature rose. The slight was almost enough to make her break. No one had ever pushed her aside before. *No one.*

"Do you really, my dear?" asked Philos with a new found interest. "A Slayer wishes to be a vampire?"

"I do," Snow said, raising her chin an inch.

"I want her, Uncle," said Remus. For the first time, Terona saw sincerity in Remus' eyes. "Please."

Her mind was awhirl. She was losing them. Losing them both to a mere human. This couldn't be happening. Not to her.

Philos eyed the girl closely and then stared at Remus. He was about to speak when his gaze shifted to Terona. Philos' lust hung heavily in the air. Both men wanted Snow. Philos had killed his own brother to sit on the throne. What would he do to all of them to have Snow? Terona swallowed hard. Her position was more tenuous than ever. Not only was her life in danger from Snow the Vampire Slayer, but from her own husband, as well.

"Then you shall have her, Remus," said Philos with a gracious smile. "You have been a loyal nephew, despite your indiscretions with my wife. You've stayed true to me all these long years, and for that, you shall have Snow Gwyn."

Remus smiled and bowed to one knee before Philos. "Thank you, your Highness. You are most gracious."

Philos held up a hand. "But I shall be there to help you turn her."

Remus' gaze shot up and met his uncle's. It was unheard of for two vampires to turn someone together. The wheels churned in Terona's mind and she tried not to smile. This actually couldn't have played out better if she had planned it. Perhaps the gods were on her side after all.

"I think that's a fair request," she said. Both men looked at her. "You are the king, after all. You should be allowed to sample all the goods in your own house. But first, let me take the girl. Let me clothe her properly; a gown befitting our soon to be princess. Then I will bring her to you."

The men watched her suspiciously. She made her face passive, continuing to stand and smile at them.

Terona sniffed the air. "At least let me cleanse her while you bathe, Remus. You reek of sweat and soot."

"We're fine the way we are." Remus took Snow's hand in his.

"Yes, I quite agree," said Philos.

"Oh, come now." Terona threaded her arm through Snow's. "I'm sure the girl would appreciate a bath and having a few moments to herself. Her journey has been long and tiring. Besides, her blood will taste all the sweeter if she's eaten first."

"Yes." Snow looked up at Remus. "If you don't mind."

Remus eyed Terona uncertainly, then Snow, and back again.

"All right." Remus kissed the back of Snow's hand and then let go. His eyes ever on the girl. "If you wish it."

"Wonderful," said Terona. She yanked Snow across the room and toward the hall leading to her private quarters.

"You have one hour," Philos called.

"Of course, darling." Her smile disappeared the instant she stepped into the hall. She dragged Snow along next to her at a rushed pace. Passing door after door, she finally made it to her sitting room. She threw Snow inside and shut the door behind them, locking it.

Snow fell into a table from the force and then turned to face her.

"Now." Terona tapped her fingers on her hips. "What to do with you?"

*****

Snow hadn't thought past the part where she saved Dax. Remus had taken her to a cottage north of Westfall and just south of Volkzene. He'd marched her up to a mirror, pushed a red stone on the top and then pulled her through. She'd screamed as her body was gripped by a large fist and jerked through space. Moments later, she landed on her knees on a stone floor, the wind knocked out of her, her stomach heaving.

Kneeling down, Remus had rubbed the small of her back. "Sorry about that, love. The first time is always a bit jarring. I would have warned you what we were going to do, but I feared you'd change your mind."

"What was that?" she managed through gulps of air.

"Mirror travel. It's much faster than walking, I assure you."

Snow balled her hands into fists and swallowed her fear. He helped her to her feet as the other vampires hit the ground behind her. She turned to find an old mirror covered in vines and dead flowers set against a large stone wall.

Snow got her first look at Tanah Darah. They were in a garden of sorts, though everything was dead. The castle, an imposing onyx structure had loomed above her.

Now, Snow stood totally at a loss, looking around the queen's chamber. Somehow she was more afraid alone with this woman than she had been with both Philos and Remus fawning over her. The men wanted her, desired her. Terona wanted her dead. Snow's Slayer instincts made her blood pound in her ears. Just being close to the queen lit her with a need to run Terona through with a sword. Where her desire to kill Remus, or even the King had been strong, in the presence of this woman, the need to slay was almost all consuming.

"Well," said the queen with a smile, "why don't you eat, and then we'll get you bathed." The regal woman removed a bowl of apples from a shelf above her alchemy supplies, her long blond plait swinging behind her. She set them on the table in front of Snow.

Snow's stomach grumbled as she looked at the multicolored varieties. There were large, pinkish-buttercup ones and blood-red ones, lime shiny ones and deep plum colored ones. It had been almost a day since she'd last eaten, but there was no way she could trust anything the queen gave her.

Snow scanned for a weapon. "Are you going to poison me?"

"Poison you? Of course not, you silly girl." The queen laughed. "I'm going to let them drink you dry. Have an apple. They are quite spectacular, I promise."

Snow's hunger gnawed at her.

"Here, I'll share one with you," said the queen. She plucked a deep purple one from the bowl.

Snow snatched up the pinkish-yellow one and bit into it. It was crisp and tart and the taste was amazing.

"See," said the queen. "They were a present, from my sister. She lives in Ville Defree and the Fae really do have the best produce. She sends me a bushel every month."

The queen licked her lips and watched Snow devour the apple. Before Snow knew it, she had eaten down to the core. The flavor still lingered in her mouth. She eyed the apples, pondering which she would choose next.

"You may have this one as well," The queen handed over the purple apple and then pulled the basket away and returned it to the shelf. "No more than two, though. Wouldn't want you to get ill."

Snow took in the room as she bit into the second apple. There was a couch, lounge, and settee. A table with alchemical items stood in the corner. There were shelves and shelves of bottles and potions Snow had never seen before. Her curiosity piqued as the queen grabbed several bottles and walked into an adjoining room. Terona poured pails of water into a tub and then a drop from each bottle. Snow's gaze traveled to the basket of apples on the shelf.

"Why don't you just let them have me then?" Snow asked.

The queen strode into the room and took a dress the color of sapphires from her closet. She held it up, inspecting it. "Because I want to know about the Slayers and who called you to it." Terona hung the dress on a hook and moved into the bathroom. "So who was it? Who called you to be a Slayer?"

"I wasn't called. My brothers were called. Kellan died, so…"

"But who called them?" The queen returned and stopped to look at Snow.

Snow bit into her apple and shrugged.

"Oh, I'm sure you know. Don't be shy."

"All I know is she wore a jewel like the one at your throat." And similar to the one in the ring Sage now wore.

The queen's eyes widened. Her fingers traveled to her red stone necklace. She fumbled with it for several moments. "That is interesting. What did she look like?"

"She came at night, right as we were heading to bed. She wore a cloak and never showed her face." Why was she saying all this? Better yet, why did Terona care so much?

"And what did she say to your brothers?"

"That there was a calling. One that hadn't been used for hundreds of years. But that it was necessary when evil sat on the throne of Tanah Darah. She said, 'The years of uniting are coming. If we do not stop the evil now, Fairelle will be lost forever.'" Snow remembered the rich pewter of the woman's cloak. The fierceness of her voice as she spoke of the evil that must be eradicated. The ancient words she'd chanted had filled the air with pearly mist and settled on her brothers in turn.

When Snow looked up, her sight blurred. She blinked rapidly trying to clear her vision.

"Let's get you bathed." Terona marched toward Snow, plucked the almost finished apple from her hands and set it on the table. She then ushered Snow to the bathing room.

Snow stared at the water. Colors of coral, blush and gold swirled inside the tub. She swayed slightly and gripped the sides, steadying herself. Her gaze traveled over to the apple sitting on the table. Something was wrong.

The queen chuckled. "Don't worry dear, the apple won't harm you, it was only to help you relax a bit and not put up a fight. I would hate for Remus to be injured while draining you." The queen stepped forward and stripped off Snow's dress before she could protest.

"Oh!" Terona stared in surprise at Snow's ripped underthings. "Well, you have been naughty, haven't you? Not a woman of virtue, I see."

Snow covered her breasts in an attempt at modesty and swallowed hard, trying to force her fuzzy brain to think. She tried to remember her training sessions with her brothers, but nothing had prepared her for this.

Visions of Sage filled her head and she reminded herself why she was doing this. If she was a vampire, they could be together. Dax had gotten away and would run straight to Sage and tell him what had happened. They would come for her. They would save her from Remus and Philos. She had to believe that; it was all that mattered.

The queen moved close and breathed in her scent. Her eyes flew open and for a moment they flashed silver.

"You've Sageren's scent on you." The queen's pupils contracted until they were cat-like slits. Her fangs descended. Unlike Sage's or Remus', or even Sonya's, the queen had a full row of razor-sharp teeth. Snow took a step away and bumped into the edge of the bathing tub. She lost her footing and fell in with a splash. The queen leaned over Snow as she struggled to find her footing in the slippery, warm water. Snow cried out for help and the queen clamped a long clawed hand over Snow's mouth.

"Now, now then deary, no need to scream. I'm not going to kill you."

Snow's heart pounded in her chest. The queen's face shifted, she wasn't a vampire at all. She was something worse, much worse. She was the evil that sat upon the throne in Tanah Darah. She was the evil the Slayers had been called to kill.

*****

The group heaved themselves out of the water on the other side of the portal and collapsed upon the ground. Sage sucked in air, trying to calm his churning stomach. He felt like spiders crawled inside him. Groans and whimpers sounded all around.

"What…the hell…was that?" asked Jamen.

"Oh man, I never want to do that–"

"Again," said Hass and Ian. Then they simultaneously vomited into the grassy area.

"Where are we?" Flint peered around, then his eyes went wide and he heaved before belching.

"In the garden." Sage breathed in and out rapidly, then stood on wobbly legs.

"Queen Helena's garden?" asked Greeg.

"Yes," said Sage. His body trembled at the familiar scents of verbena and lemon balm. It only grew in one place in Tanah Darah: his mother's private garden. He hadn't been here in so many years. He looked around and his heart sank. The garden was overgrown and choked with weeds. Apparently no one else had been here in a long time, either.

"Let's go," said Sage.

"How do we get in?" asked Erik, coming to his side.

"There's a door over to the right that leads into my parents' bedroom. We can get through there." Sage took off, followed closely behind by the Slayer, vampire and werewolf warriors.

"How many are inside?" Redlynn asked.

"I don't know. We've killed so many guards over the years. There can't be more than a few dozen left, unless they've been turning hordes of humans."

266

"What a dismal place," one of the wolves said.

It wasn't always. Sage made his way to the door and tried the handle. Surprisingly, it turned. He opened it slowly and peered inside. The interior was pitch black, but it didn't matter. Sage knew every inch of the room by heart. He'd spent hundreds of hours in it, both in the weeks preceding his mother's death and in the months after. His step faltered as he took in the stale air. The smell of his mother's perfume still lingered on every surface.

"What's wrong?" someone whispered.

"Nothing," said Sage, making his way to the inner door. He was about to turn the knob when a clatter came from behind him and then a crash. Sage lit the lantern he knew would be on the wall. A large, ornate mirror with four red stones lay smashed on the floor. It was the twin of the one he had seen on the bottom of the pond. He'd never seen it in the room before.

"Sorry," said Omni.

Heavy footsteps rushed down the hall outside. They all froze. Sage blew out the lantern and pressed against the wall. The Sisters knocked arrows in their bows as a key sounded in the lock. Light poured in from the hall and five guards stood in the doorway. Sage grabbed the first, and ripped out his throat; the guard disintegrated into dust. The Sisters loosed their arrows, taking down two more. The remaining two guards ran out of the room and down the hall to sound the alarm. Adrian and Sage charged after them, with Dax close behind.

"Don't let them get away," Sage yelled.

Adrian pounced on a vampire, knocking him to the ground as Sage grabbed the second and pushed him to the floor. Retrieving the knife from his boot, Sage took the vampire's head while Adrian ripped out the throat of the other.

The rest of the group moved out into the hall with Snow's brothers leading the way. Flint's eyes were full of anger.

"We're the Slayers here. We go first," he growled.

"You may be the Slayers, but this is my house. I know it best, so unless you want to get yourself killed, you follow my direction," Sage countered.

"Come on, Flint," said Erik. "There's enough for all of us. Let Sage get us in there."

Sage nodded and then continued down the corridor. Flint's loathing gaze burned into his back.

Sage entered the front hall and stopped. Standing in the middle of the foyer was Terona. He sneered at the beautiful woman who'd tried to seduce him for years.

"Sageren!" she yelled running and throwing her arms around him "Sageren you have to help me."

He tried to disengage her from his chest.

"Thank the gods you are here. Your Uncle Philos forced me to become his wife after he murdered your father. He's with Remus, draining a poor Slayer girl."

A chill oozed down Sage's spine. He pushed her away. "Where?" he demanded. "Where is she? Where's Snow?"

"In Remus' room, with Philos." Tears fell from her eyes.

"This way." Sage ran across the foyer. "Keep her safe," he yelled to Sonya.

Sage and the brothers were almost across the entrance hall when two dozen red-eyed vampires rushed in.

"Sageren," said the vampire in the front. "Been a long time. Remus said you would come for the girl."

"Jonas," said Sage. "Let me pass and I'll let you live."

Jonas laughed. "Can't I'm afraid. The girl is Remus', and you have a death sentence."

Sage held out his hand. "You were my friend once, Jonas."

"Times change. I'm Captain of the Guard now."

From behind Jonas a lone wolf emerged with a collar embedded deep in his neck. Its dark brown fur was dirty and matted. Redlynn stepped up next to Sage.

"I've waited a long time to see you again," she said to Jale." Redlynn spat at the wolf. "But where's your brother? Is he too cowardly to face us now?"

The wolf growled and his ears flattened to his skull, but didn't retreat.

"Don't worry, we'll find him sooner or later, right now, I'll just take this one. Time for some revenge mongrel." Yanti pulled her bow, her eyes trained on the wolf.

Sasha joined her fellow Sisters. "You helped the vampires capture us and chain us up to die. Your turn."

Sage rushed Jonas as Slayers, wolves and vampires collided. Redlynn brought the dirty wolf to the ground as Sisters let their arrows fly and Sage's vampires attacked without mercy. Sage swung at Jonas. Jonas dodged and slipped behind him. He needed to get out of here and find Snow. Jonas pulled a dagger from his belt and sliced Sage across the back, splitting his coat. Sage whirled in time to catch Jonas' dagger in its downward arc for his throat. Kicking hard, he propelled Jonas backward.

"That was my favorite coat you bastard!" Sage yelled.

"You always were predictable in your fighting technique, Sage," said Jonas.

"What about me?" asked Sonya, coming up from behind Jonas and opening his throat. Jonas' eyes widened and then he turned to mist. Sonya looked at Sage. "Go. Get your female."

Sage nodded and surged toward the end of the hall as Sonya attacked another vampire. Dax's roar made Sage pause and look over his shoulder. Flint swung wildly as three vampires took him to the ground. With the swipe of a massive paw, Dax knocked one away before ripping his head off. Flint gave Dax a respectful nod and together they took care of the other two. Redlynn had Terona's pet wolf on his back, her blade protruding from his chest. The younger sisters looked on as Adrian ripped out his throat, finishing him off.

Sage turned a corner and headed for the other end of the castle. The sounds of the fight dwindled with each step. He passed portraits and decorations, his heart squeezing to finally be home after so many years. The familiar scent of the castle permeated his nose. The whiff of obsidian and oil, of blood and death.

He dodged around a corner, reached Remus' door and threw it wide. The scene before him almost caused his knees to buckle. It was true: Remus was still alive. But Snow very nearly wasn't.

She lay on the bed, her skin pale as ash against a royal blue silk dress. Her eyes lit on him, but she wasn't moving.

Remus, a bloodied mess, leaned over her, his teeth sunk deep into her neck. Philos lay mangled on the floor, his eyes wide and staring lifelessly at the ceiling, a discarded Cris knife by his body. He had been slashed to ribbons. Parts and pieces of him were everywhere.

Above it all, the smell of Snow's blood grabbed Sage with force, and his fangs burst through his gums. It was on everything in the room. But it was more than that, stronger, more pungent, as if she had bathed in her own scent.

Coming to his senses Sage leapt onto Remus, tore him from Snow's throat and threw him across the room. Sage gently picked her up from the mattress and cradled her to his chest. He felt for a pulse; it was there, but faint. He was losing her. He licked at her wound in an effort to seal it shut.

"I'm here, love. I'm here," he said over and over. "Stay with me, Snow. I was a fool. Stay with me." She'd be all right now. She'd heal. She was a Slayer.

"Get away from her," Remus yelled. "She's mine!"

He searched her face. Her mouth opened and closed several times and a horrible gurgling sound rose from her throat. Sage's gaze burned into his brother. "How could you Remus?"

"Sa—" Her voice was hoarse and barely a whisper.

"Get away from her!" Remus yelled.

Rage overpowered Sage's senses.

He set her down and the two brothers met in the middle of the room. Sage fought with a ferocity he didn't know he had. He slashed and tore at Remus, tearing his clothes, neck and throat with his razor-sharp nails. Remus fought with equal intensity. He landed a slash to Sage's cheek that split it wide. Sage punched Remus in the gut and then his nose. Remus gushed blood onto the floor. Snow's brothers rushed into the room.

Flint cried out and ran to the bed, lifting Snow's limp body. "Snow! Snow!"

She didn't move.

Remus stopped, watching the brothers gather around her. Sage bent to the floor and swept up the Cris knife. Tackling Remus, he poised the knife above Remus' throat. His hand shook. All those years of grieving for Remus. The years of pain, of guilt. Wishing he could go back and change things. And now he was about to kill his brother with his own hand.

"I can save her," Remus said. "She isn't quite all gone yet. Let me give her my blood, Sage. Make her one of us."

Sage's gaze shot to the bed, but he couldn't see Snow for her brothers surrounded her in a protective shield.

He set his jaw and glared at Remus. "No."

"But she wants to be a vampire," said Remus, confused. "She told me so. Let me make her like us, brother. We can have her together.

You and I, like we used to have females, we can have her forever, and the three of us can rule Tanah Darah."

Sage shook his head. "What happened to you? How did you become this person, Remus?" Sage asked, bewildered. "How did you become so low?"

Remus' face hardened. "Terona. It was her, Sage. She put the idea in Philos' head to kill Father, after she killed Mother."

"You lie." Sage gripped the knife tighter.

"Why would I? She wants the throne to herself. She tried to seduce you, but you turned her away. Philos and I were not so strong willed. You don't know the truth. You don't know what she is."

"Sage!" Erik called from the bed.

Dropping the Cris, Sage rushed to the bed. The brothers moved aside so he could see Snow. Her eyes were open, but she was barely there. She still bled from her neck wound which wasn't healing.

"Sage," Snow whispered. She tried to lift her hand but it fell onto her lap.

"I'm here, love." He moved to her side and entangled her fingers in his. Her hand was cold. Much too cold.

"Terona...she isn't...vampire...something else..."

"I know, love, I know," said Sage. He needed to heal her. He had to do something.

"Evil...behind...the throne," Snow breathed. Flint held Snow's head in his lap, his face a mask of anguish. "I came...to be with you...forever..."

"No, Snow," Sage said. "That's not what I wanted for you."

"It's what I want."

Confusion plagued him. Why would she be willing to give up everything for him?

"Do it," said Erik.

Flint's gaze shot up. "No."

"Do it, Sage," encouraged Erik. "Save her, make her like you."

"No!" Flint bellowed, pulling her away.

Erik stared at Flint and then looked at each of his brothers in turn. All eyes rested on Sage. "It is better than not having her at all, Flint," said Gerall.

"To make her a monster that we'll have to hunt down?" Flint yelled. "Better she were dead than we be forced to kill her."

"We aren't the evil behind the throne," said Sage. "When will you realize that?"

"If you don't try, she'll die," said Jamen. "Please Sage. Save her."

Sage looked at Snow again.

Sage's heart and mind battled. He wanted her, he loved her. To lose her would be worse than death.

"It might not work," Sage said. "She's a Slayer."

"We have no other choice," said Jamen.

"All right. Give her to me."

Flint pulled Snow tight and refused to let go. Tears streamed down his cheeks as he kissed her forehead. Snow lifted her hand and laid it on his cheek.

"It's all right, Flint," she whispered. "It's what I want."

Erik reached out and took Snow from Flint's arms and laid her in Sage's lap. Sage stroked her face. Her eyelids opened and closed very slowly, her breathing shallow. He lifted her up to his chest and bit into his wrist. He moved it to Snow's awaiting mouth when a sharp pain shot through him.

"If you won't let me have her, you can't have her either," Remus wailed.

Sage cried out and Remus shoved the Cris blade deeper into his back. Sage groped for the knife as the poison ebbed up his spine to his neck. Flint sprung from the bed, yanked the knife from Sage's back in one fluid movement and cut off Remus' head. Remus' body fell to the floor.

Flint spit on the lifeless body. "For my brother and my sister you bastard."

Sage sucked in a ragged breath as the white hot Cris poison coursed into his body.

"Do it," said Erik. "Sage, do it, she's fading."

"I can't," he said. "My blood is poisoned by the knife. If I feed it to her, she'll die."

Erik glanced around wildly. "Get someone else," he told Jamen. "Go find someone else!"

Jamen raced from the chamber. Snow's eyelids fluttered, barely open.

"Stay with me," said Sage. "Stay awake. Stay with me, Snow. Don't leave me." Sage looked up and locked eyes on Snow's brothers. The pain in their eyes matched his own. "Stay with us," he whispered.

"Stay with all of us." His shoulder spasmed and contracted, forcing him to let go of her. He needed blood.

Jamen rushed in, followed closely by Sonya and Greeg. Sonya already had her sleeve rolled up. She bit into her wrist and crossed the floor dripping blood along the way. Climbing onto the bed, she took Snow from Sage and pressed her wrist to Snow's mouth. Snow didn't move.

"Come on," said Sonya, "swallow, dammit."

"Come on love, swallow, just once," said Sage. "That's all. Just one swallow."

Snow's head lolled to the side and the blood dribbled out. She didn't respond.

Greeg moved to the bed and picked up Snow's wrist. Somberly his gaze met Sage's. "I'm so sorry. She's gone, Highness."

Sage's head spun, the pain that wracked his spine was nothing compared to the pain in his chest. He grabbed Snow from Sonya's arms and held her close. This couldn't be happening. She couldn't be dead. He'd just found her, just held her, just made love to her. Blood red tears streamed from his eyes as he buried his face in her fragrant hair. How had this happened? All he'd wanted was to protect her, and she was dead. Bile rose in his throat. There was only one person responsible.

Laying Snow in Erik's arms, Sage ran from the room.

"Sage!" Erik called after him. "Come back!"

Sage raced to the entrance hall. Ashes were strewn throughout. Blood smeared every surface. The wolves and Sisters stood watch over the thing he was looking for. *Terona.*

"You did this," Sage spat picking up a discarded blade as he advanced. "This is your fault."

"Darling, what has happened?" Terona asked. "What's wrong?"

"You did this. You killed her. My one love." Sage backed her against the wall, the blade pressed to her throat.

Her eyes were wide with fear. "No Sageren, I didn't, I swear. I didn't."

"Don't lie to me. Remus told me how you seduced him and my uncle. How you killed my mother and tried to seduce me to get on the throne. To get to Tanah Darah."

"No, Sage, I–" Terona stopped talking and her façade fell. She rolled her eyes and heaved a sigh. Gone was the terrified woman. What appeared in front of him was the truth underneath, who had deceived them all. "I knew I should have magicked you instead. So many times you rebuffed me. It's amazing how strong and smart you've become, Sageren, considering how simple and arrogant you were when you lived here. If I'd known you would someday become this man, so commanding and sure of yourself, I would have magicked you into my bed long ago. But unfortunately, I too was arrogant, and didn't want to have to use trickery to get you."

Sage lowered his blade, sickened by her words.

"Oh Sage, Sage, Sage. You have no idea the hardships, the tedium I've endured to get the throne. And I almost had it, too." She moved around him. "It was all falling into place. Remus was going to kill you, and then Philos and then I was going to kill Remus.

"But then he came back with *her*, and I saw it all unraveling, slipping away. With one look at her, both Remus and Philos were ready to tear each other apart like dogs. To think, they thought *she* was more beautiful than I. I am the fairest of them all, not *her*. So that's when I decided to kill two vampires with one enchanted apple." She sniffed the air. "It did a wonderful job, didn't it? The spell enhanced her scent; I can even smell her from here. And once she was in the room with them, I only had to wait for their bloodlust to take over. I assume it worked since you're standing here, instead of your brother or uncle. Now the only one left standing between me and the throne is you."

"In case you haven't noticed, you're surrounded." Dax motioned to the wolves and Sisters that filled the hall.

"Oh, silly bear, still don't remember what happened to you? Trying to remember how you ended up in Wolvenglen chased by vampires? It really would be so much fun to tell you the truth. But I promised I wouldn't."

Terona produced a vial from her dress and threw it to the floor. A cloud of smoke filled the hall and everyone gasped and coughed, choking on the fumes. One by one, the wolves fell to the floor, with the Sisters and Dax following suit. Sage covered his nose and mouth, holding his breath. He squinted through the smoke and found Terona running down the hall though which they'd entered the castle. He raced after her. Terona dashed into his parents' old bedroom, and Sage

278

kicked the door open before she could lock it, but she didn't seem to care.

"Nooooooo," she screamed, running to the mirror Omni had smashed. She bent over the shards of glass and red stones, picking them up, trying to piece them back together.

Sage pounded over to her, grabbed her by the arm and yanked her to her feet. The stone on the mirror began to glow.

The jewel in Terona's necklace mimicked the one on the mirror. Reaching out, he grabbed the necklace and ripped it from her. She screamed and clutched at her throat.

"Give it back," she screeched, clawing at Sage.

He pushed her away and she fell to the ground. Her shrieks started out as human and slowly changed. The pitch became so high that Sage had to cover his ears.

He watched in horror as Terona's form morphed. Her legs fused and became a long, snakelike tail. Her fingers lengthened and ebony talons grew in place of her nails. Eggplant colored scales appeared all over her body. Her eyes glowed silver and the pupils changed to slits. Horns sprouted from her skull and rows of sharp teeth descended in her mouth. It wasn't possible. Her kind hadn't been seen in Fairelle for a thousand years.

"Look what you've done to me, Sssssssssageren," she hissed.

She flopped on the floor like a fish out of water until dark, veiny wings protruded and stretched from her back and carried her into the air. She flew straight at him. He hefted the sword and swung it at her, but his back spasmed and he swung low, his arms weak from the Cris poison. His blow glanced off her side. She howled and slashed at him with her talons. She connected with his shoulder before he spun out of her reach. She flew at him again, her wings knocking perfume bottles and other items off his mother's vanity, sending them crashing to the floor. She advanced on him tossing an end table and chair out of her way.

"What the hell?" Erik asked from the doorway.

Terona stopped and bared her teeth at Erik. He grabbed a sword from the hands of a dead vampire and advanced into the room.

Terona reached out with a leathery wing and sent Erik sailing back toward the door. Her tail whipped back and forth and caught Sage's leg, spilling him onto the ground. Sage flipped over as she came at him. Erik rushed in at the same time and sliced at her wing. She cried out as Sage thrust his sword up and caught her in the chest, slicing her wide. Ebony blood spurted from her. She gasped for air as she hit the floor and slid across the room, slamming into the foot of his parent's bed. Sage got to his feet shakily brandishing the sword. Terona flopped and writhed on the ground.

She smiled up at him in a gruesome grimace. "You may have killed me. But you haven't sssstopped us. There are others, and we will take Fairelle. It will be oursssssssss."

"Not as long as I breathe, daemon." Erik plunged his sword into her neck, severing her head.

Terona's mouth gaped open and closed several times before she stopped moving. Both Erik and Sage gulped for air. Sage blew out a heavy breath and stumbled to the floor. The poison burned through him and tears streamed from his eyes as his mind caught up with what had just happened. Snow was dead. Remus was dead. Philos was dead. And he was king. He'd gotten everything he'd been dreaming of for the last half century, and he didn't want any of it without Snow by his side. He hung his head between his knees. Minutes passed with him sucking in labored breaths.

"What the hell is that?" Erik asked.

Sage raised his gaze. In the remaining shards in the mirror, half the face of a woman reflected on the other side. She stared at him through one bright silver eye. Then the mirror went dark.

"Terona's kin," Sage replied.

CHAPTER TWENTY FIVE

Sage lay on the bed in his room in Tanah Darah. His torso was bound with gauze, so he sprawled on his stomach. A mostly empty bottle of human blood sat on his nightstand. He stared at the fireplace, watching the flames flicker. He hadn't been in the room in so long, yet the space was as familiar as his own voice. Only his bed remained, everything else he had smuggled out years before.

The fire crackled, but it gave no warmth. His mind played and replayed his moments with Snow. Their first touch, first kiss, the first taste of her hand. Her laugh, her stare, the feel of her skin. The way they'd made love, with her inexperienced and him showing her the way. All so glorious, but all so painful, now that she was gone.

Dax entered the room and sat on the edge of the bed. "It's time."

Sage didn't move. He was too tired to even lift himself up. Two days had passed since Snow died, yet it felt like she'd been gone for a lifetime already.

"Her brothers are waiting," Dax said. "They're ready to leave."

Sage rolled painfully toward the wall. He didn't want to see her carried from his home in the glass coffin reserved for vampire royalty. Taken back to Gwyn Manor for her funeral rites never to be gazed upon again. To see her dead body and know that he would never hold her again.

"You need this, Sage. You need to say goodbye."

So much pain. When he'd lost his mother, and later his father— then thought he had lost Remus, more than once— those moments seemed merely sad compared to this heartbroken agony.

Her loss buried deep in his bones. Into his soul. His reason for living had been ripped away. He wasn't sure his legs could even carry him forward anymore.

There was a knock. "We're going. Did you want to say goodbye?" asked Erik. His voice cracked and he cleared his throat.

"No," said Sage, his back to the door.

"You should."

"I can't." A red tear streaked from his eye. "If I say it, it means she is really gone." He felt weak, crying like a babe in front of Dax and Snow's eldest brother. He stared into the flames, praying to be left in his misery to die.

"Then I shall say goodbye for you," said Erik.

Erik's footsteps receded down the hall. A weight lifted from the bed and Dax's footsteps soon followed.

Left alone with his thoughts, Sage closed his eyes. All he saw were hers, large and copper colored, sparkling with spirit. Her hair as it flowed to her waist in a long walnut cascade. Her slender wrists and lean, strong arms.

In his mind, she appeared out of the mist, her eyes flashing with fire. She pushed him to the ground, straddled him, and kissed him on the lips. *"Will you not even tell me goodbye?"* she whispered in his ear.

Sage's eyes flew open. She was right. Leaping from his bed, he ran down the hall for the entrance. Her brothers lifted the glass coffin off the floor, preparing to leave with Adrian and the wolves.

"Stop!" They paused and looked at him. He reached them just as they sat the coffin on the stone floor again. Sage knelt beside it and lifted the lid gently. His gaze swept over her. She'd changed. Her skin was alabaster, her hair dark as night, her lips the color of blood.

The deep indigo dress fit her frame perfectly. Her hands were clasped over her breast, and a small ring of sungolds crowned her hair. She looked beautiful, so peaceful in her eternal slumber.

Reaching over to brush a lock of hair from her forehead, a tear fell from Sage's eye and dropped onto her lips. He watched her for several minutes. Waiting, willing her to life. But she didn't move. Minutes passed with his tears raining down on her.

"Please love," he whispered. "Come back."

Again he waited, but she didn't stir. Grief grabbed him afresh. He bent and kissed Snow softly on the mouth. The tears smeared on her lips, staining them.

"Goodbye, my love," he whispered. "Wait for me. I will join you soon as I'm able. It won't take long, I fear."

After a moment, he closed the lid and collapsed to the floor his head in his hands. Dax sat down next to him as the brothers picked up the coffin and moved toward the exit.

Redlynn knelt in front of him. "My dearest Sage, words cannot express the sorrow we share over your pain."

Sage said nothing, watching his tears drip onto the stone beneath him.

"We would give anything to take this torment from you, my friend," said Adrian.

284

Redlynn wrapped her arms around Sage and held him close, smothering him in her warmth. "I'll return in a few days to check on you." Then she stood and followed the coffin from the building with Adrian.

Sage sucked in a ragged breath. The emptiness in his chest was like a stone dragging him down to the bottom of the Fairelle Sea.

A moan sounded and Sage's head whipped up. No one else seemed to have heard. Had he imagined it? A second breathy moan escaped from somewhere, and the hairs stood up on his neck. He knew that sound.

"Stop! Put her down."

"Sage, I don't think–" said Dax.

"Put her down!" He demanded, pushing Hass and Ian away and taking the coffin into his own arms. Setting it on the floor, he threw the lid wide.

"Erik, this is too much. I want to get her home," said Flint

"Come on, love," said Sage. He ran a hand down her cheek. "Come back to me." Minutes ticked by.

"Enough," said Flint. "Isn't it bad enough she's dead? Do we have to stay here and endure this, as well?"

"Snow," Sage begged, smoothing her hair. "I know you're in there."

Snow's body lurched upward as she sucked an enormous breath into her lungs. Her eyelids flew open and she grasped the edges of the coffin. She gulped in air, staring wide-eyed at everyone surrounding her.

Finally her gaze settled on him. "Sage," she whispered.

"I'm here, love," he cried. His heart beat so hard and loudly he thought it might explode. He couldn't help but continue to weep.

She reached out and touched his face. "Your eyes are bleeding."

"They're tears, love." He helped her from the coffin. She clung to him as he pulled her close and kissed her hair. "You returned to me," he said.

"Did you expect me not to?"

Sage laughed and then kissed her forehead, her cheek, her nose, and finally her mouth. Her tongue mixed with his and fire shot through him at the feel of her. She was really alive and she was his.

A cough sounded nearby, and then a throat cleared.

Finally Hass said, "All right, already. We don't want to kiss her like *that*, but at least let us hug her."

Sage and Snow laughed as he set her on the ground and she ran to her brothers, hugging them. Only Flint hung back. The group parted and Snow moved to Flint. He took a step away from her.

"Flint?" she asked in confusion.

He shook his head, his gaze roaming the other faces in the room.

"Flint, it's me."

"No." He moved away again. "It isn't... I can't–"

Sage stepped forward and put his hands on Snow's shoulders.

"We're the same as you Flint, we're just not mortal. This is still your sister. Your Snow. She's still the same person inside, only now she is my kind. She is vampire."

"Flint." Snow stepped cautiously toward him again. This time he didn't move. She closed the distance between them and wrapped her arms around his waist. He stiffened and then relaxed, hugging her tightly. His eyes misted and then he locked gazes with Sage.

A chill ran down Sage's spine; he knew what was coming before it happened. Flint pushed Snow away. Sage caught her in his arms and bared his teeth.

"Flint," she cried, reaching for her brother.

"We aren't the evil on the throne, you know that now," said Sage.

"I can't – you're not my sister, you're a monster. This isn't right." Without another word, he fled into the night.

"Flint," Erik called. "Flint, come back!"

But he didn't.

"I'll go with him," said Dax. "I'll make sure he's safe."

Sage nodded and Dax ran out.

Snow leaned her forehead against Sage's chest and wept. He held her close and her remaining brothers gathered around them in support. It was a sight Sage was sure he would not see again in his lifetime. Slayers hugging vampires.

*****

Sage looked gorgeous as he stood at the altar in the moonlight. His hair was tied in a strap at the base of his neck and he wore a coat of plum. His eyes sparkled in the candlelight as he stared at her in a way that she had always dreamed a man would. At that moment, all of her dreams had come true.

"I pronounce you mated under the moon. Kept in blood and tied forever," said Omni. "You may bite the bride."

Snow's heart soared. Sage leaned in close and kissed her on the mouth. The scent of cinnamon mixed with her own vanilla scent, making her gums ache. Sage dipped down and bit into her wrist. Snow's fangs burst into her mouth. A sensation she still wasn't used to. She leaned over and bit Sage on his wrist. The taste of his blood sang to her. Then they kissed once more and the crowd erupted.

All of Tanah Darah had come to see them mated, the noble families as well as the lower castes. Those who had turned on Sage's father, as well as those who had remained loyal and joined Sage in exile. Since he'd been made king, there were apologies and groveling from those who'd betrayed him.

The sheer number of vampires in Tanah Darah surprised Snow, though Sage told her there were not half as many as there had been before the war with the wolves.

In the weeks since Sage's return to the realm, his kingdom had been in a state of upheaval. Sage and those who had gone into hiding with him spent day and night setting things right. First and foremost had been dealing with the human slaves. He had seen to it that those who didn't wish to stay were allowed to return to their homes. Surprisingly, several of them stayed.

Before the bonding ceremony, Snow had gone home with her brothers to set her affairs in order. She'd helped them search for Flint and Dax, to no avail. Two days ago, Sage had received word from Dax that he and Flint were on the move, but safe. He'd sent word to Gwyn manor and she'd returned to Tanah Darah almost immediately.

Upon her return, Snow's brothers had insisted that she and Sage not share a bed until they were properly wed, as was only right. So the announcement of their mating had been made imminent.

Erik clapped Sage on the shoulder. "I never thought I would see the day when my sister wed a vampire."

"I never thought I would see the day when I would have six brothers to compete with for my wife's affection." Sage replied. "And Slayers, at that."

Snow leapt up and hugged the twins.

Erik laughed heartily.

She squeezed her brothers even more tightly. "All right, all right, Snow," said Hass.

"We can't breathe, Sis," said Ian.

Erik and Sage laughed together and she let go.

"Sorry," she said.

"Man, maybe I should become a vampire too. You have the strength of both a vampire and a Slayer," said Ian.

"A vampire Slayer," laughed Hass.

"As long as she isn't a Slayer vampire," said Jamen.

It was still unclear whose blood had changed Snow from human to vampire. Had it been Sage's blood that she'd licked from him? Or had Sonya's blood somehow made it into her just before her heart stopped beating? No one could say for sure, but Snow wasn't about to look a gift horse in the mouth.

Sage reached for her and she pressed herself to his side. She was so happy she thought she might burst. Only the absence of her Flint and dear Kellan dampened her spirit.

The night drew on and the group danced and laughed and drank. It was all so very normal. Like the days before the deaths and callings. Two young female vampires eyed Hass and Ian for attention. The twins grinned, but were obviously out of their depths.

She watched her brothers get sufficiently drunk. Only Jamen, surprisingly, did no more than sip his wine. She began to worry where they would end up for the night.

"Don't worry," said Sage, sliding up behind her and wrapping his arms around her waist. "Sonya and Greeg will make sure they get to their rooms. *Alone.*"

Snow leaned back on his shoulder and relaxed her body into his. She listened to the music from the orchestra and swayed her hips to the rhythm. Sage purred as he bent down and kissed her neck.

"I like how that feels, love." He pressed his arousal against her.

"I see that you do, *husband.*"

"Come, let us turn in for the night." He pulled her into the shadows and slipped his hand down the front of her gown cupping her breast with his hand and running the pad of his thumb her sensitive nub.

Snow gasped in delight the sensation exploding down to her core. Sage kissed her neck and caressed her skin till she thought she might reach climax right there.

"Sage," she moaned, throwing her arms around his neck behind her. "You rake."

Turning her head, her lips met his and he spun her to face him. His tongue shot into her mouth in a fiery passion. Her knees went weak. "Sage, take me to bed," she whispered.

He scooped her up into his arms and, keeping to the shadows, left the grand hall and strode to their bedroom. His lips never left hers as he carried her. She assumed that living for hundreds of years in the same place made it possible for him not to look where he was going. He had barely gotten the door closed before they ripped their wedding clothes off each other.

His hands roamed her body, making her reach new heights of excitement. Lifting her, he carried her to the bed and laid her down on soft sheets. His large body loomed over her. She reached up and released his hair from its leather strap. It cascaded down over his shoulders. Leaning in, he kissed her full on the mouth. Her fingers scratched and dug into his skin, making him quake. He arced and stared at her intently.

"When vampires mate, I've heard that drinking from each other while making love is the height of all ecstasy," he said.

"Well," said Snow, her fangs descending. "I say we find out."

He kissed her again and his fangs bit into her lip. She shuddered with pleasure. She needed more. Pulling away she licked Sage's neck and then pierced him hard. His muscles shook as she drew from him. She clung on to him as their bodies became one.

He bit down on her neck, making her core explode with waves of pleasure. Her fangs disengaged from him as she called his name over and over. Moments later his fangs left her neck as he too, gasped her name.

When they were both spent, their lips met again. He gazed at her with shining eyes.

"Snow. I love you."

"You too, love," she replied.

Zelle and The Tower

Fairelle Book Three

REBEKAH R. GANIERE
Coming Early 2015

Ville DeFee, Fairelle
Autumn, 1210 A.D. (After Daemons)
CHAPTER ONE

Flint pushed through the crowed street with precision and speed. He shivered and scowled at the feel of magick in the air. Pulling his cloak tighter around him, he kept his head down. The footsteps of the King's Guard could be heard a block behind.

"Find them!" the captain shouted.

It had been a mistake to stop and ask for directions, but Flint only been to Ville DeFee once and with all the blasted brightly colored structures and smells, he'd gotten turned around. Standing out amongst the slender, graceful Fae, he lumbered through the streets unable to blend in.

"Check every shop," a guard called.

A shrill call from a blushing pink bird pierced Flint's ears, making him wince. He thanked the gods he hadn't been born in Ville DeFee. He wasn't accustomed to such brightness and merriment.

Dax shoved Flint sideways into a darkened alcove, away from an oncoming merchant carrying a basket full of fruit he didn't recognize. Dax squeezed in next to him as the fragrances of the fruit wafted from the basket, making his stomach growl. How long had it been since he'd eaten?

The merchant passed without a glance in their direction. Flint stuck his head out and scanned the area. The guards were still several shops away.

"We have to keep moving." He darted back out onto the street.

"Do you really think this is a good idea?"

"No." He kept moving.

Flint was on a mission, and only the king himself would be able to stop him. He rounded a periwinkle colored building and headed toward the end of the row. A Fae youngling stopped skipping to stare at Flint. He dropped his head again. His boots looked even filthier against the immaculate stone road. When was the last time he had washed them? Or taken a shower? Again, he didn't know.

All of the days since leaving Tanah Darah, and then Wolvenglen seemed to blend together into one horrible nightmare that he lived and relived. Only his hours in a drunken stupor and a couple of hazy memories with several tavern wenches broke up his personal hell. His gut clenched at the thought of seeing Snow as a vampire. Her skin, her eyes, her hair; it was all different. She was different. Gone was the sweet younger sister that he'd tried to teach to dance. What she was now... was a creature he was bound to kill.

A screech and a crash pulled him from his thoughts.

"Excuse me," Dax said. "I'm so sorry."

Flint stopped and turned.

Dax threw apples into an overturned barrel as the shopkeeper looked on wide-eyed, mouth open.

"Leave it," Flint growled, scanning the street for the guard. All around people had stopped to stare at Dax. Hood off, his shaggy blond head and tan skin screamed human.

Flint's skin itched and he clenched and unclenched his fists to keep from scratching his arms. The magick of the Fae permeated

295

everything. From the large, juicy, unnaturally grown foods to the highly polished never dirty streets. It wasn't natural, it wasn't right.

Dax righted the barrel and stood.

Flint glanced skyward past the twinkling lanterns floating above. The moon had barely made an appearance, yet but already the streets were crowding. They needed to get out of sight before night fell. Then the streets would be packed with Fae, singing, dancing and making merry on this All Hallows Eve.

"End of the street," Flint pointed. "Move it."

Dax nodded.

He hadn't wanted Dax to come along, but somehow the giant werebear had gotten the notion that he was responsible for Flint. After one fight together and Dax saving his neck from being chewed on, and suddenly they were best of buddies.

In the past months though, Flint had come to appreciate Dax's company. Having lived with six brothers and Snow so long, the loneliness of being parted from them was not something Flint had expected when he'd stormed out of the castle at Tanah Darah. And despite what he said, Flint liked Dax. He didn't talk too much, and he didn't pry. He kept his head straight and Flint's neck out of a noose.

Flint moved at a quickened pace till he reached the end of the street. He rounded a corner and found a smaller street, darker than the one before. The shops had already begun to close down for the night.

A bright peach building with iris colored awnings sported clusters of people coming and going. Loud talking, laughing, and glasses clinking could be heard floating out the open windows of the pub.

Flint's eye twitched and he licked his lips at the thought of getting a drink. The sounds of a flute lulled him closer. He stopped momentarily.

"Not here." Dax's large hand fell heavily on Flint's shoulder.

He shook it off and continued on.

Drinking was not something he'd done regularly before. Now it seemed more like a daily routine. What would Father have thought? Flint pushed the pain aside and stomped down to a seafoam green building. The old apothecary sign swung lightly in the breeze. A giant bluish tree wrapped around the building in a hug. Vines in every color and variety snaked up the sides like a protective cocoon.

Flint looked through the entrance, but could see nothing except bottles and herbs. He pushed open the door and two birds chimed a tune in unison. The scent of nature filled his nostrils. Roots and plants, herbs and flowers. It reminded him of Snow's cabinet where she kept her healing supplies. Again he was hit with a pang of guilt for how he'd left things with her. But it didn't matter; all that separated them would be gone soon.

Every surface of the shop was covered in jars, bags, and containers of various sundries. A beautiful woman of about forty with light tawny hair arranged shelves with various items. She turned at the sound of the birds. Flint removed his hood, as did Dax, and the woman started, dropping a bottle. The contents splashed on the floor, the glass shattering everywhere. A silent scream played on her berry colored lips.

Flint threw up his hands. "I'm sorry to frighten you. I just need to speak to Lord Rondell, and then I'll go."

The woman's mint green eyes lit on Dax. Horror remained solidly planted on her features. She stared at Dax without blinking.

Flint turned and gave Dax a questioning look. He shook his head and shrugged. Voices floated in from the street and alarm bells went off in Flint's mind. If the woman screamed, the guards would be alerted.

He turned back to the woman. "Madame, I know we should not be here, but—"

An even more beautiful young woman with bright lapis colored eyes and rosy cheeks appeared from the back of the store. "Stepmother, is there a prob—"

Her eyes scanned from Flint to Dax. Swiftly she stepped around the counter and approached the woman, grabbing her by the arm.

"It's alright, stepmother. I'll take care of this. You go home. I'll clean up and close the shop."

The woman finally tore her gaze from Dax. She stared at the girl for a moment before yanking her arm away and composing herself. With a sideways glance in Dax's direction, the woman nodded.

"Yes, of course you will. That's your job." She straightened her dress and hefted the hem so as not to step in the mess she'd made. "And if these two get caught in here, I'll not take the blame for it."

The girl nodded. "I understand."

The woman looked at Dax one last time and then strode into the back room.

298

The trio watched her go. When the back door slammed shut, everyone sighed.

"Flint Gwyn. You sure do know how to make an entrance, don't you? Do you know what will happen if you're caught here?" Quick as light, the girl rushed to the front door, magicked down the shades and dimmed the lights.

"I'll be thrown in prison."

"*I'll* be thrown in prison." The girl waved her hand and mumbled a word he couldn't hear. The smashed bottle reformed, in her hand and the liquid on the floor disappeared. She turned and put it on the shelf, then faced him again, a smile on her lips.

Flint relaxed at the sight. *Coy girl.* "Cinder. You're looking well. Last time I saw you, you appeared no more than a teen and I was no more than eight or nine."

"Good to know that I have aged well," she laughed. "I'm old enough to be your mother. However, I'll settle for being considered your older sister."

The mention of 'sister' made Flint's heart squeeze. Snow was the only reason he was here. Her well being was worth risking his freedom and his life.

Taking several strides forward she reached out and embraced him, then pushed him to arm's length and looked up at him. "You used to pull my braid and hide my favorite doll when we would come visit."

"And you would magick my pants so they wouldn't allow me to wear them."

They laughed in unison and hugged again.

He pulled her hair. "Last time I saw you, you were pining over that Prince Charming of yours...what was his name? The one you were always talking about and comparing my brothers and I to? I'm surprised to see you haven't married him yet."

Cinder blushed and smacked him. "His name is Rome and he is just fine and we are just friends."

Flint nodded. "Of course you are. The color of your cheeks tells me as much."

Her blush of her cheeks deepened, proving his point that she still held a flame for Prince Rome. He wondered why she had never done anything about her feelings for Rome, they had to both be close to fifty now.

"Don't misunderstand me," she finally said. "I am happy to see you, but what in Fairelle are you doing here? You could have been seen."

"I'm looking for your father."

Cinder let go of him and glanced down. Her eyes misted. "He is no longer with us, I'm afraid."

Flint's heart sunk. Lord Rondell had been his last hope.

"I'm sorry," he said. "I had not heard of his passing."

"It was quite sudden. We aren't exactly sure what happened. But he is in the Fade now, with Mamette. And I know they are happy together."

"Of course." Flint blew out a heavy sigh. He had come all this way. "Well then, it seems I have traveled for nothing. It was good to see you Cinder. We should go before the soldiers come."

"Wait." She grabbed his cloak. "You came such a long way, what is it you need?"

"I doubt you can help, but thank you." He patted her hand and nodded to Dax. They replaced their hoods and turned to go.

Cinder harrumphed behind him. Arms crossed over her chest, she slid between Flint and the door.

"Now you listen to me, Flint Gwyn. I am my father's daughter. And anything he could do, I can do. You look as though you haven't eaten in weeks, and your scent says you've bathed even less. Just the mere sight of your shabby unclean appearance was enough to scare my stepmother away.

"Now you and your friend will sit at my counter, eat my food, use my wash basin and tell me why you came. For if you do not, I shall spell you and force you to. And I know you don't want that." With a wave of Cinder's hand, two chairs pulled themselves up to the shop counter and the front door locked.

She flashed him a brilliant, pearly smile and pointed to the chairs. He glanced at Dax who shrugged and headed for the counter. *Traitor.* Flint wasn't sure whether she was lying or not about the spell, but he was sure about one thing. She was definitely her father's daughter. And if that's what he could get, he'd take it; because only a spell from the Rondell family would be able to break Snow's curse of Vamperism.

THANK YOU FOR TAKING THE TIME TO READ

Snow the Vampire Slayer

IF YOU ENJOYED THE BOOK, PLEASE TAKE A MOMENT TO LEAVE A REVIEW ON YOUR FAVORITE RETAILER.

TO FIND OUT MORE ABOUT REBEKAH R. GANIERE AND *The Fairelle Series*, OR HER OTHER UPCOMING RELEASES, OR TO JOIN HER NEWSLETTER FOR SWAG AND FREEBIES, PLEASE CONNECT WITH HER IN THE FOLLOWING PLACES:

BOOKS WITH A BITE

NEWSLETTER: WWW.REBEKAHGANIERE.COM/NEWSLETTER

GOODREADS: WWW.GOODREADS.COM/VAMPWEREZOMBIE

TWITTER: WWW.TWITTER.COM/VAMPWEREZOMBIE

FACEBOOK:

WWW.FACEBOOK.COM/VAMPIRESWEREWOLVESZOMBIES

Made in the USA
San Bernardino, CA
20 September 2014